P9-BZD-662

THE DODECAHEDRON

OR A FRAME FOR FRAMES

THE DODECAHEDRON
or A Frame for Frames

Paul Glennon

The Porcupine's Quill

Library and Archives Canada Cataloguing in Publication

Glennon, Paul, 1968–
The dodecahedron, or a frame for frames / Paul Glennon.

ISBN-13: 978-0-88984-275-5.--
ISBN-10: 0-88984-275-2

I. Title.

PS8563.L46D64 2005 C813'.6 C2005-901472-5

1 2 3 4 • 07 06 05

Published by The Porcupine's Quill, 68 Main Street, Erin, Ontario NOB 1TO.
http://www.sentex.net/~pql

Readied for the press by John Metcalf.
Copy edited by Doris Cowan.

Represented in Canada by the Literary Press Group.
Trade orders are available from University of Toronto Press.

We acknowledge the support of the Ontario Arts Council and the Canada Council for the Arts for our publishing program. The financial support of the Government of Canada through the Book Publishing Industry Development Program is also gratefully acknowledged. Thanks, also, to the Government of Ontario through the Ontario Media Development Corporation's Ontario Book Initiative.

Canada Council for the Arts   Conseil des Arts du Canada

Canada

For my parents

CONTENTS

IN MY FATHER'S LIBRARY

Some books are to be tasted, others to be swallowed,
and some few to be chewed and digested.

– Francis Bacon, *On Studies*

My father wrapped his cloak around his shoulders as he left last night, but the rain had not started yet. I heard the first sounds of the drops on the roof of the library hours after he left. They were big hard raindrops at first, like pebbles hitting tin, and then a quick hurrying sound like someone saying hush. It was still raining when the strangers – the investigators – came to see us this morning.

The ringing of the little bell beside the front door made me jump. I am not supposed to be in the library without father. Father wouldn't ring the bell before coming in, of course, but it's hard to tell your bones that.

I hid behind the newel post at the top of the stairs while my mother spoke with the investigators. There were three of them, but only one asked questions. He was tall and young-looking and he talked like a schoolmaster, making the sound of all the words carefully, as though he thought my mother wouldn't understand. My mother stammered and answered confusedly. I was ashamed that she did not have better answers. The tall investigator didn't speak the language of the house – the language of fine song notes that father speaks. He spoke to my mother in her own language, a noise like angry dogs and bad coughing, so she should have done better. She had no excuse.

While the tall man asked questions, the other two stood behind him and tried to stay still. They didn't look as if they liked it. They were not as tall as the other man, but they were wider and had stupid-looking eyes and flat noses. They kept looking around and touching things, but the man asking about my father stood between them and the house and there is not much to see in the foyer. One man looked very closely at the barometer on the wall, narrowing his little eyes as if he thought it very suspicious. The other jiggled the handle of the front door until the man asking the questions turned around and looked at him angrily. The tall young one must be their captain.

When the captain had finished asking questions he tipped his black hat to my mother and looked up the stairs towards me, as if he had always known I was there. I took a look at his face and then hid again. He had a handsome face, like the face of Galahad in my *Tales of the Round Table.* He looked too young to be the captain of the other two.

When they were gone mother went to the parlour and undid the needlepoint she had done that morning. I came here to the library 'to work and think' as father does. Mother thinks I am in my own room, but she never comes up the stairs to check. I do not know exactly what the three strangers want, but I don't like the look of them. The two silent ones were strange and rough. They looked like soldiers, and the captain asked peculiar questions. Sometimes it sounded as if he knew where my father was. Sometimes it sounded as if he was trying to find him. He said that he wanted to help my father, but he did not sound helpful. He used that tricky voice that schoolteachers have when they are trying to trip you up on an oral examination. This captain and his thugs must work for my father's enemies. I knew they would come some day. I have always known that father had enemies. Why else would he have so many secrets?

I have never known my father to have friends, only visitors. His visitors arrive every few months. They never stay for dinner, but spend most of their time behind the closed door of the library with father. Father's visitors dress differently from the people you see on the streets and sometimes they speak strangely, in the languages of the library.

I don't know what it is my father does in his room with his books and his strange visitors, but I've always known it was important and secret. He will tell me about it one day, but for now he is protecting me, so I can not be tortured or tricked into revealing his secrets. He plans to tell me when I come of age, as they say in books, but that may be too late now. Now his enemies have come, and I must figure out his secrets for myself.

Now my father's enemies have revealed themselves. This should tell me something. All three of the visitors wore long black coats with belts and red emblems on their shoulders. The man asking questions had a little gold pin on his hat. They must be uniforms, but I don't recognize the insignias or the marks of ranks. The visitors may be inquisitors or gendarmes or carabinieri. I can't remember what they have here. Sometimes I forget which things are only in books. Father took me to the zoological gardens once and we saw an elephant. I was surprised. I thought they were made up, I mean mythological. I asked father if dragons were real too. He just laughed. I think that means no.

I didn't think it was so strange that father did not come home last night. Father often goes away for days at a time. I can never tell when he is going to leave or come back. He never says to me, 'Son, I will be gone for three days, but I will be home to have dinner with you on Friday. You are the master of the house until I return. Look after your mother.' That would be a fine thing to say, but he never says anything like this.

When father takes his bag I know that he will be gone for a night or more. I wish I could remember if father took his bag last night. I can see him with it in his hands, but that might just be my imagination. I don't know for sure that he had it when he left, but I didn't see it in the hallway this morning either. It is a very large black leather bag with handles, and silver buckles to fasten it. When I was much smaller I used to think that I could fit in the bag myself so father would carry me away with him on his voyages. I no longer think such foolish things. All that I have ever seen go in or come out of this bag are books.

Last night, long after I was supposed to be in bed I heard the little bell beside the door ring again. I crept to the top of the stairs to see who it was. Perhaps someone had come with news of my father. I was surprised to see the captain of the investigators at the door. He was alone and he took his hat off and ran his fingers through his thin blond hair while he talked to my mother. I was careful to take a better look at him and to listen to his questions, so that I can make a proper report to my father. I noticed his long nose and his grey eyes, but I was still too far away to see the emblem on his cap.

'Madame,' he said, 'I did promise to keep you informed of the progress of our investigations, but I must caution you that I have not come with any significant news.'

I couldn't see the look on my mother's face and she did not say anything. I waited for another trick from the captain.

'But there is something you might be able to do to help us.'

My mother said that she was sure that father would be back soon, 'Maybe he has already sent a letter explaining why he is late. Perhaps the letter is lost in the post. Letters are often lost in the post.'

'That very well may be, Madame. Letters do get lost.' I could tell by the sound of his voice that he was really laughing at mother. I was angry with her for saying such foolish things. 'Even so, we should perhaps not count on the letter and make some effort to find him ourselves?'

My mother only repeated that she was sure he would be back soon.

'Your husband is a careful man, Madame. I am sure no harm has come to him, but we would all rest more comfortably if he were safe at home.'

Mother must have nodded.

'Your husband is a renowned scholar. Most likely he is travelling on some scholarly pursuit.' The way he said 'scholarly' made it sound like another trick question. He dragged the word out as if it were a new one to him. 'I am sure that if we took a look at his books, it would become clear where he has gone. Perhaps it is some footnote he needed to research at a nearby institute. Perhaps it is some new translations he has gone to pick up on the coast.'

'It must be something like that,' my mother mumbled. When my mother spoke I realized how loudly the captain had been speaking. I would have heard him even if I was still in the library. Though my mother was not being helpful, the captain did not sound angry. He just spoke very loudly, as if she might be deaf. After a short silence he said good-bye to my mother. I heard the door open. Then he said, just as loudly as before, 'If your husband has not turned up tomorrow, I shall come back and have a look at the books,' even though my mother had not invited him to.

I must do everything I can to stop the captain from reading my father's books. He cannot be allowed to learn their secrets. Though he speaks to my mother in the language of the shopkeepers and the servants, the language that my mother speaks when she talks to herself doing needlework, I can't risk that he knows other languages. He looks clever and asks sly questions. It is possible that he knows the secret languages.

For a long time I didn't understand about languages. Some words and ways of putting them together I only saw in books. I thought maybe there were no sounds for them or maybe it was against the law to say these words. I used to imagine a lot of things when I was little. Then I started to listen to my father's visitors. They didn't use the same words my father and I use. It sounded funny, as if they were making up sounds. My father once scolded me for laughing at the way a visitor spoke, and I have never done it since, and as I listened more I began to think I understood them somehow anyway. One day I realized they were speaking the words in the books.

That's how I learned about languages, from my father's books and his conversations with his visitors. It was easy, once I listened to a visitor speaking for a while, to see the words from the books I had read. I still practise making the sounds every night. It is not difficult. Sometimes you can guess what sounds you should make just by looking at the words in the book, but I think I sometimes mix them up and I am too afraid of making a mistake to speak in front of my father. I don't know if my father knows that I understand. Still, it was good to learn. Now I understand that there are ways of speaking that are only meant for secrets and books. Those are the languages in my father's most precious books and the languages of his visitors. My mother and all the people outside the house only know ordinary language. My father knows the secret languages, and I, because I've been reading his books, am learning them too.

If they are interrogating my father, they won't get answers easily. My father doesn't answer questions. One of my father's guests told me once that I was a strange little boy, because I didn't ask questions.

'Eyes so full of curiosity and yet a mouth that does not know the shape of a question!' he said. I did not know how to answer this. I never knew that you could ask a grown-up questions and expect to get an answer. In my head I began to make a list all the questions I wanted to ask. I wanted to know so much. What colour is God? Why are there countries? What is the use of writing? I took too long to pick my first question. My father sent me out of the room before I could say anything. If they are interrogating my father he won't be able to send them out of the room, but he still won't give them answers. He might ask them more questions than they ask him. Still, I hope they are not torturing him. It won't be the young captain who is torturing him. It will be the short fat ones with the pig eyes. The captain will probably leave the room while that is being done.

There is another reason why I do not ask questions. My father doesn't answer questions, this is true – but also my mother just tells lies. This is another thing that the captain and his two men do not know that works in our favour. My mother is a Romantic. A Romantic is a very special kind of liar, the best kind of liar, my father says. A Romantic is someone who thinks what she feels is true and right. A Romantic would rather tell you a pretty story than give you the correct answer to any question. Whatever my mother tells the captain it will only be pretty stories. She has probably told him that my father is the Cardinal's special envoy delivering a message to the Great Khan, or that he has sailed on a voyage of exploration to the Northern Ocean, or that father has gone to the Levant to retrieve the stele that will help him decipher the texts in his library, or she may be telling him that I don't have a father, that she was widowed during the war and that I never knew my father.

She should not mention the library if she can help it. The library holds all my father's secrets. That is why the captain is so interested in it. I am not even allowed in the library by myself and father always scolds mother if she tries to dust or rearrange things. Once a week father invites me into the library to choose a book for myself. I may only choose one book a week and if I choose badly I have to put up with it until the next time. There is only one wall of books that I am allowed to choose from. Father says I am not old enough for the others, though sometimes he will let me stand beside him while he reads at his desk. I hardly ever understand what is in these books, but sometimes it is nice to stand beside my father while he reads.

There is one cabinet, though, that I have never seen inside. Father hasn't ever told me I mustn't, but that makes it worse. He always tells me not to go into the library and not to read past my bedtime, but he always makes me feel that he is really saying the opposite. He expects me to do these things because he did them when he was a boy. If I want to be like him, I should sneak into the library and read secretly in my room past bedtime. But he has never told me not to touch the books in the glass cabinet. It's because a good son shouldn't need to be told not to spy on his father when he is hiding the keys under the desk drawer, and not to take out the library stool and slip the big knobbly key into the brass lock of the cabinet. I know that I am not supposed to do this, but I think that this time it is an emergency.

There is something special about these books. I've always known that. I knew that when the tall captain wanted to see father's books, it was these books he meant. There must be something in them that explains where father has gone or who has taken him.

I took the first book down from the shelf very carefully and carried it to the desk. None of the books in father's locked cabinet have titles on their spines. This one just had silver swirls and patterns in the red leather. My fingers itched when I opened the cover. I licked my lips as I read the title. It was a good title – *The Land Beyond the Western Sea.* Even though I was very eager to read it and find out about my father's secret, I remembered to be careful. I turned the pages with the blunt side of the paper knife, the way I've seen father do it, so that he doesn't get the pages greasy or dirty. I found the book a little hard to follow at first. The language was very old-fashioned and there were some words I didn't recognize, but I stayed up all night reading it.

When I was done, I ate all the pages. I tore the paper into inch-wide strips, stuffed them into my mouth and chewed them until they were tight balls, easy to swallow. The paper tasted sweet and was pleasant to chew, but after a while my jaw ached. It took me four nights to read the book and eat all its pages. I would fall asleep with the book in my bed and dream about my father's voyages. I decided that my father had sailed to the land described in the book. This land is a great secret. Not even the king knows that it is there. Only certain people in the church know about it and they did not want anyone to go there. I don't really understand why people aren't supposed to go there. *The Land Beyond the Western Sea* makes the people in the church sound evil and corrupt, like the cardinal in *The Three Musketeers*. It's the bishops and cardinal who keep people from going to this land across the sea. The cardinal must have sent three inquisitors to stop my father from reaching it. The book said that the land was very far away and that it would take a sea voyage of many weeks to reach. Father hasn't been gone a week yet, so he must still be at sea. My father's enemies must hope to catch him before he arrives. I suppose that they have faster ships, but I don't know how much faster they might be. Even so, they don't need to catch him before he arrives. If they know where he has landed, they can chase him there, and capture him before he returns. The cardinal must silence my father before the secret gets out.

The inquisitors must want the maps from the book. There are three charts that fold out three times, so that they are the size of six pages. I ate them last, because I wanted to remember them properly. I might have to follow my father's route one day. To punish him the church might destroy his ship and leave him shipwrecked there. In case I have to rescue him, I memorized the maps and ate them last. The maps worry me. They are crammed with pictures of terrible perils. There are huge water creatures in every part of the sea, kraken with broken ships in their tentacles, whales with sleepy eyes and gaping mouths and maelstroms filled with bits of wood and ship's masts. This western land doesn't look very habitable either. Big areas of white space are marked with bones. The north is a vast sea covered with ice and broken ships. Most little islands seemed only to have cannibals, horrible man-eating tigers, or serpents covered with feathers. Still, there were some of spots where my father might safely go. Some of the small islands had giant trees with strange prickly fruit and one large city of paper houses.

I believe my father is heading for the middle of one of the white deserts to a circle of seven cities around a jewelled chalice. At night I dream of my father's ship being eaten by the kraken and of him being caught by the cardinal and sent to the island of the cannibals. If I can help it, this will never happen. *The Land Beyond the Western Sea* won't fall into the wrong hands.

When I had chewed and swallowed all the pages I put the empty cover back next to the other books in father's special cabinet and hid the key again. I have made sure that *The Land Beyond the Western Sea* is safe, but there are still four more books in the cabinet.

I was very surprised when my mother spoke to me today. Since the inquisitors first came she has hardly said a word to me. She wanders around the house as if she has lost something. I suppose she is worried. But at breakfast this morning she said that I looked pale, and that she should take me to see a doctor or maybe to the country for a rest and some sunshine. I was worried that she might take me away from the library, so I said that I just hadn't slept well, because of nightmares. She said it must be something I ate. Later I thought of asking if she would take me to the seaside instead, so I could investigate the harbours, but when I suggested it she didn't seem to remember anything about going away. I don't know why I bother talking to mother. It serves no possible purpose.

Mother made me come out with her, because I looked pale and tired. I don't see how that should help. The sun was not shining and if I am tired, it doesn't seem to make sense to go stomping around the streets holding her hand. I would have rather had a rest on the couch in the library. While we were out we saw a horrid parade. It was led by a military band with two kinds of drums, big ones that make the bottom of your stomach quake and high quick ones that make your teeth hurt. They were followed by a stream of soldiers who carried their hats on the tips of their weapons and their weapons over their shoulders. Everyone else on the street had stopped and we couldn't get through the crowd, so we had to stop and watch the parade too. I tried to close my eyes for most of it and if it were possible to fall asleep standing up, I would have. When the soldiers had passed, my mother squeezed my hand to tell me to come, and we walked away quickly. Lots of other boys chased after the parade, imitating the soldiers' march and screaming awful noises. I hadn't known that so many people here spoke that awful language.

The inquisitors came again today. I was afraid that they might be coming for the books, and I am only halfway through the second one. They asked about the books once more, but my mother was at least not stupid enough to invite them into the library. The captain said that they had heard some rumours about my father, nothing definite. They needed just one piece of evidence and he would be in their grasp. I didn't think this sounded nice. One of the rough men behind the captain made an ugly face at me, while the captain spoke, and smiled wickedly when I jumped. It almost made me glad that the captain was there, to keep the big men away from us.

I chose the second book, because it looked difficult and father always told me to never put off doing what's difficult. Its cover is soft brown suede and it doesn't have a title anywhere. It is not a regular book, set and printed with even letters. It looks hand-written, but very neatly with thick black ink, and there were lots of drawings. The author doesn't even write out his whole name, just his initials, A.T. and the words *vere adeptus* which I know means 'very clever'. I suppose A.T. *is* very clever because I don't really understand anything in his book. Sometimes I think that it is about the planets, because it talks about Mercury and Venus and Mars and Jupiter, but these are also the names of the old gods and sometimes it does sound like the book is talking about people. The pictures don't even help. There are just lots of circles with arrows and lines. Sometimes I skip ahead to other sections. There are four sections, and they are called 'Panacea', 'The Philosopher's Stone', 'Alkahest' and 'The Elixir of Life'. These don't make me think of planets or old mythology. I must work harder at understanding this tonight.

It has taken many hours in the library with the funny brown book, but I think I understand something about it now, not all of it, just a little bit. I stayed up late in the library and reread the sections that were especially mysterious. It came to me in my sleep. I dreamed that all the little diagrams in the book came to life. Rows of circles moved across the page towards other circles, or triangles or whatever other shapes, and then they fought. When one side won, they swallowed up the other shapes and changed their own shape just a little, like when a king conquers a country and adds that country's coat of arms to his own. When I woke up I knew that the diagrams were battle maps, and then I looked through for the names of generals and kings. I found lots of people called Magus, which means great, which is a thing a lot of kings have after their names, and there is somebody called Bombastus, who seems to be a great general, so that must be it. It is a book about a great war.

The brown book gave me a new idea about my father's mission. I don't know if these generals are from the countries here in the known world or from the land beyond the western sea. Maybe there is going to be a war about this land. Maybe we are going to be invaded. I don't know who is fighting whom, but I know that my father is on the good side. Maybe he is a spy working for the good army and we live in a country ruled by an evil tyrant or usurper. This wouldn't surprise me at all, now that I have seen the captain and his two guards.

I didn't eat this book right away. There is something about it that makes me not want to destroy it. Maybe it is because it is written by hand. It might be the only copy of the book in the world. I can imagine a person writing it out. It must have taken a very long time to do. I feel awful about destroying it, even though I know that it isn't truly gone as long as I eat the words rather than burning them, but it is still all very mysterious, these symbols and kings' names. You shouldn't eat a book until you really understand it. I have put this book back in the locked cabinet. If I have to, I will eat it last.

The third book is the strangest yet, but at least it has a title and tastes better than the first. It is called *The Volume of Itself,* which I didn't really understand until I had read many pages. On the cover in letters much larger than the title were two sets of Roman numerals XII and *xii.* I figured this out too by the time I had read most of the book. It is a volume of an encyclopaedia and it comes from a place called Cathay. Cathay, I know, is far away and to the east, so it is hard to see that this book has anything to do with the land beyond the western sea and their wars. I like this encyclopaedia though. It has lots of little pictures of mechanical birds and machines of all kinds for making paper and printing books. The first part of the book is like this:

And the Emperor commanded that this book be written to catalogue the glories of his empire, so that all the world might know the vastness of the empire he ruled. All the scholars and all the scribes and all the book makers of his great and unsurpassed empire were brought to the capital to make his book. First they catalogued the wars, the victories, the peoples and the kings he had conquered, a volume for each. Next they catalogued the lands, the rivers, the cities and strongholds that were his, a volume for each. Next they catalogued the generals he had glorified, the generals he had beheaded, the horses that he had tamed and the horses that had died beneath him in battle, his wives and his concubines, a volume for each. Then they catalogued his great thoughts, his aphorisms, his philosophies, his inventions, his laws and his religious meditations, a volume for each.

See how perfectly I remember it. That's what eating a book does.

The Volume of Itself keeps on like this, describing all the things that were in the Emperor's great encyclopaedia. I skipped over lots of this, because I didn't think it was important to know that there was a volume for flying insects and a volume for insects that burrowed in the ground, or that there was a fat volume for the Emperor's injuries and for the Emperor's assassins, for all his dreams and for all his jokes, for all the fish in his empire and all the ways he had invented to catch fish. I thought it was enough to say that everything in the world was in the Emperor's book. I couldn't understand what my father wanted with this book, but at least the pages tasted good. The paper was very thin. The leaves melted on my tongue and made it tingle. I didn't have to chew at all, just swallow my flavoured spit. Most of the pages were sweet, but some pieces were horribly sour. They made the sides of my tongue curl and I would giggle at the unexpected taste.

After the part that described all the different things that are in the Emperor's book, I could not think of anything that was missed, but the Emperor did.

When the book was done the scholars presented the book to the Emperor and said, 'Now the whole world will understand the vastness of your empire, the immensity of your conquest and the magnitude of that you rule.'

'Have you truly put everything that is in my Empire in that book?' asked the Emperor.

'We truly have,' the scholars answered.

'You have not,' replied the Emperor, 'because you have not written of my great book which catalogues the vastness of my empire, the immensity of my conquest and the magnitude of that I rule.' So he sent the scholars away to write a volume for the book itself. This is that volume.

And then the book tells everything about the encyclopaedia. It tells how many scholars and scribes worked on it, for how many years. It describes how many pages of paper it contains and how many vats of ink were made for it. It tells how many lashes were given to each scribe for errors or for falling asleep at his work. It describes the colour of the cover and the names of the horses whose hides were used to make them. It made me sad to read that there were one hundred and forty-four books, because I had only one. I thought it would be nice to have them all.

When the scribes had described the whole encyclopaedia, there was still one page left in the book, and this page described this volume itself. It described how many pages it had, how many stitches were in the binding and how heavy it was. I had eaten most of the pages already, so I couldn't count the pages or the stitches and I didn't have a scale to weigh it, but I will take the scribes' word for it. On the back cover in very small writing was a sentence that described the last page of the book. Though I used a magnifying glass I couldn't find anything that described this sentence. It may have been in one of the pages that I had already eaten.

I couldn't guess what this book meant to my father, but I was glad that I had read it and eaten it. I knew that if I ever needed to know these things, I had the knowledge inside me. Someday they will make sense to me and I will understand what they meant to my father.

By the time I had finished with *The Volume of Itself* the inquisitors were coming every night to bring news of my father. One night the captain brought my father's bag with him, the black one that father takes on his trips.

My mother cried when she saw it. I was angry with her for being so weak; I rushed down the stairs and snatched the handles of the big leather bag. One of the quiet, ugly inquisitors put his big hand on my shoulders and held me down on the floor and the tall captain lifted the bag out of my reach.

'Now, now, little scholar,' he said. 'I know you are anxious for news of your father, but you don't think he is in this bag, do you?'

Then he handed the bag to me and tried to pat me on the head. I ducked away, taking the bag to the bottom of the stairs to look inside it. I knew it would be empty, but I had to look. The captain spoke to my mother.

'Perhaps you will allow us to examine the library. We may find something there that will help us bring your husband home to us.'

My mother was still crying, but she shook her head. I was very proud of her then, but the next day the captain came by himself and she let him into the library anyway.

I had been playing out in the big walled garden behind the house. I had made twelve paper boats, and I was pretending they were sailing across the pond to the land beyond the western sea, so that they could relieve the siege of my father's stronghold there, but the goldfish in the pond thought they were being fed. They rose to the surface and sank the boats with their noses.

When I stepped into the library I was remembering that according to *The Volume of Itself*, the goldfish in the twelve ponds of each of the Emperor's twelve cities are described in Book VII, Volume xi, of the Emperor's encyclopaedia. I had expected the library to be empty and I took a quick deep breath when I opened the door to see the captain and my mother. My mother was seated carefully in my father's reading chair. The captain was standing in front of the glass cabinet with his hands behind his back. I was glad that I had put the empty covers of the eaten books back.

'Ah, little scholar. Did you find your father in the bag?'

I didn't like the way he tried to sound kind, even though he was teasing me.

'No, eh? Well, perhaps you know where we might find the key to this little cabinet then?'

I shook my head and closed the door without entering the library. I didn't want him to trick me into revealing the location of the key. But as I closed the door I heard him say, 'No great matter. We could always break the glass if it came to that, couldn't we, Madame?'

There was a smile in his voice that disappeared suddenly and he said, 'Please remember that holding back any information only delays our investigation. Nobody wants that. Nothing is accomplished by this.' Like the time before the captain spoke very loudly, so I could hear.

That night I knew I must hurry with the last two books. The captain was getting impatient. Whatever had stopped him from ransacking our house so far, it would not stop him much longer.

I have just finished the fourth of my father's secret books and have only just understood something I should have thought of much sooner – four of these books are false. They must be. The books I've read so far aren't about the same things at all. They can't all be about my father's secret. It must be a trick. Father put four of these books in the cabinet to confuse his enemies. I wish I knew which were the false books and which were the true. I would rather not eat the false ones. It doesn't seem right. But I can't guess which one is the important one. That was my father's ingenious plan, of course, but I think that I, as his son, should be able to tell. It's hard not to think that I am failing my father by not knowing.

The fourth book is called *The Eurypyliad.* Eurypylus was one of the companions of Achilles and brave Odysseus whom I have read of in other books, but this story is not so great an adventure as those, as the hero is only a poet and not a great warrior. *The Eurypyliad* begins when Eurypylus leaves Troy with his war trophies, but instead of jewels and armour he takes the scrolls of the Trojan poets. Just like in Odysseus's story, Eurypylus's journey is delayed by monsters, foul magicians and the evil schemes of the gods. Mercury does not want the Greeks to have the gift of writing he gave to the Trojans. He sends an acidic rain to melt the ink into puddles on the page, but Eurypylus protects the scrolls by placing them in barrels sealed with tar. Mercury then persuades the winds to capsize old Eurypylus's ship. Eurypylus and his crew have to climb on top of the floating barrels to save themselves. The barrels carry the sailors to the isle of the Papyrophagites, a race of monsters that eat books. The Papyrophagites devour many of Eurypylus's scrolls, but he manages to steal a boat from their harbour and escape with some of his treasure.

This adventure amongst the Papyrophagites reminded me of own mission to destroy these dangerous books, but there is a part of *The Eurypyliad* that is even more important. After Eurypylus escapes the scroll eaters, Mercury disguises the stars so that the ship sails off course into a region of ice and cold. Mercury expected the sailors to burn the papyruses to keep themselves warm. Instead, Eurypylus tells his crew to wrap the scrolls around themselves like cloaks. Many papyruses are destroyed this way, but still Eurypylus keeps a few and passes eventually through the region of ice to an undiscovered land. I stood up and walked around the library when I read this part. I was already thinking that this must be the land beyond the western sea.

Eurypylus drops the last of his scrolls in this unknown land beyond the region of ice. When the scrolls hit the ground, they start to grow like plants. The paper takes root, forms foundations and begins to spiral up like towers. Even the fragments of damaged scrolls are piled by the winds like stacks of cards until they take the shape of walls and battlements. A towering city of paper shoots up above the rocks and pines of this wilderness. It is the first city in this unknown land. Eurypylus lives in this city for twelve years before he finally sails home to Greece. Half of his crew remains in the city of paper. The other half returns home safely but without any treasure or a single scroll.

I read the book in my bed until late at night. I ate it with jam I stole from the pantry. I spread a thin layer of jam over each page, rolled it up like a proper jam roll, then took bites out of it. I didn't even have to look at what I was doing. I just kept spreading and rolling and biting while I ate. That night I dreamt that I was looking for my father in the city of paper. The city was on fire and I had to rescue him. I ran around the paper streets trying to find him, but I could not find him anywhere. Smoke and bits of burnt paper swirled around me and made my eyes sting. I lay down to cry. As I lay there I found a single piece of scroll that wasn't burnt. The page said that it was my fault my father had been sent away and that it was me who burnt down his magnificent paper city. I screamed out loud that it was not true and woke myself up. Thankfully, no one seemed to hear my cry.

This evening the captain of the inquisitors came again to the house alone. I was in the library about to start the final book when he arrived. I had to put it back quickly and hide the key in my pocket. It was lucky I did, because the captain came right up the stairs, with my mother following him. I was still in the room when he arrived.

'Ah, hello, little scholar,' he said. 'In your father's library again, I see. I wonder what your father would say, if he found you here.'

He was making fun of me, but my mother looked at me fiercely as if he was right.

'Perhaps you can help us, little scholar,' the captain said. 'We have a very interesting piece of paper here.' He held out a small piece of paper. I picked it carefully out of his long fingers. It was curled at the edges like it had been rolled like a small scroll, and I had to hold it with two hands to keep it straight. It looked exactly like the piece of paper I had seen in my dream, except I couldn't read it. I saw right away that the writing was my father's, but I didn't understand any of the words on the page.

'It is a very strange little message, isn't it?' the captain said. 'I'm not sure I've ever seen such a language, have you?'

I shook my head, still wondering whether this had anything to do with my dream. There was something familiar about the shapes. The captain sat down in my father's chair and stroked his chin like he was pretending to think hard. I looked at my mother, but she said nothing.

'And if our little scholar has never seen this language, perhaps we should conclude that this isn't in any language at all,' the captain said.

The captain seemed to think he was making a clever joke. I wanted to give him back the paper. I felt that by holding the paper I was helping him to find my father or to prosecute him, whatever awful thing he was doing.

'Perhaps the scroll isn't a strange language at all though,' the captain mused. 'Perhaps it is a code, a cipher perhaps. What kind of cipher would a scholar like your father employ? Can you help us solve this mystery?' The captain looked at my mother only for a few seconds and focused his bright blue eyes back on me.

'You don't have to say it. I can see what you are thinking. I don't know why I didn't think of it myself. A book cipher of course. A scholar like your father would use a book cipher naturally, but it poses another dilemma. Which book is the key to the code. Your father has so many in his library. Have you an idea?'

He stood up then and took the little scroll out of my open hand. I shook my head and tried not to look towards the locked cabinet. I put my hand in my pocket and fastened my fingers around the key.

'Ah, well, maybe with a little thought. I am sure that it will come to you,' he said.

My mother was following him out of the library and down the stairs, and he told her again that he was doing everything in his power to help my father. Before his head disappeared below the level of the stairs, he turned and looked at me, but it wasn't an angry look that he gave me. He suddenly looked very kind and I thought for a moment that he might actually be trying to help. Only for a moment though. As soon as I heard the door close and my mother start to sob again loudly, I remembered that he was my father's enemy.

I don't know what to think about the cipher. I hadn't thought of this before. Maybe the books are the keys to a secret code. If they are, I have made a horrible mistake. To decipher a book code you need to know exactly the letters on each page. I have a good memory and I know eating a book helps you to remember it, but I can't remember that well. What if the key to rescuing my father is in a code that I now won't be able to decipher? It makes me think twice about eating the remaining books.

The last book is called *The Calligrapher and the Genie*. It is the smallest of them, so I am glad it is the last, and it is the best story. It is set in the East and it is like some of the tales father used to read to me when I was much smaller. I love all the beautiful shapes of these letters. They are long and graceful like swishes of paint on the page, and the colours of the illustrations are beautiful. I think that the light blue and the dark red might be poison though, because they taste very bitter and make me gag when I swallow them. I have to be very careful to take them with lots of water. I brought a pot up from the kitchen and used it to boil water in the library fireplace. When I finished each chapter of *The Calligrapher and the Genie* I ripped its pages into strips and placed them in the boiling water. I stirred the pot until it was a pulpy mush that I can eat with a spoon. I made five pots in all of this book porridge.

In *The Calligrapher and the Genie* a genie is imprisoned in a sacred book. A boy finds the book, reads its words aloud and releases the genie. Because the boy has released him, the genie must be his servant, but the genie is a sullen genie and he doesn't want a master. He has to grant the boy his wishes, but he always tries to make the boy suffer for them. When the boy wishes for a princess to fall in love with him, the genie chooses a princess who is already married to a great warrior. To escape the jealous husband, the boy has to leave the school where he was studying to be a calligrapher. In the desert outside the city that he has fled, the boy then wishes for a great fortune. The genie leads him to a cave that conceals a great treasure. The boy takes the finest of jewels from this treasure and travels on to a neighbouring kingdom. He does not know the treasure was stolen from the sultan of this kingdom. The boy rides into the capital city wearing the sultan's greatest jewel in his turban and he is immediately thrown in jail and sentenced to death. Though he escapes again, the boy has learned to be careful what he wishes for.

The boy now wishes to be the world's greatest calligrapher. This is what he was studying when he was forced to run away from his school.

The genie grants him this wish and accompanies the boy to the court of the Sultan of Cordoba. The Sultan recognizes the boy's talent immediately and makes him the court's chief calligrapher. The calligrapher's wealth and power grows during his many years in Cordoba, where he becomes the Sultan's chief advisor. The calligrapher never calls on the genie again, because he knows that the genie is still plotting against him. When the calligrapher has grown old and wants to retire, he decides it is time to trap the genie again, so that he can do no more mischief. The calligrapher writes the story of the genie on a long scroll of rice parchment, brought by the caravans from the kingdom of Cathay. The final embellishment of the text draws the genie into the paper like a stream of water being poured out into the dry desert sand. Then, to ensure that the genie can never escape again, the calligrapher eats the scroll for supper. The next morning his talent for calligraphy is gone, but he is already old and rich. The Sultan allows him to retire and he spends the rest of his days reading books and eating dates from his own magnificent garden.

When I read what the calligrapher had done, I was very pleased with myself. I had eaten five pots of book porridge and felt completely full and tired. I felt like the mush had lined my stomach walls and was protecting me. Surely this means that I have done the right thing and I have saved my father. The captain can bring his louts again and smash the cabinet to get to my father's books. They will only find the covers. In fact, they needn't smash the cabinet. If they try to open it, I will give them the key. I wonder if he will know that it was me who defeated him, that it was me who destroyed the evidence against my father. They will have to release him now. They have nothing to bring against him, and it is all because I knew to eat my father's books. I knew that I was right. I just knew deep down like a rumbling in my belly that it was what I should do.

There was only one book left to eat. I had second thoughts about eating the handwritten book, the book of strange symbols and battle plans. I had set it aside to save for last. I kept thinking about what the captain of the inquisitors said about book ciphers. If ever there was a book that looked like it had been written in a cipher, it was this one. I looked at it again for a very long time, and made sure I had memorized it before deciding to complete the job. Its pages tasted worse than all the others. I couldn't chew it by itself. No matter how much I chewed the pages they stuck in my throat and made me gag. The pages didn't seem to dissolve in water. I tried to make a pot of book porridge again, but the pages didn't come apart in the boiling water. The water just became brown and thick. Finally I just poured the brown liquid out of the pot into a large mug. It tasted awful at first, but I added some milk and sugar and I began to like it a little as I drank more.

I tried to eat what remained in the pot after I strained it. I wolfed it down without chewing it, but my stomach started to heave. I vomited the whole thing out of the library window into the pond below. The sun was just coming up, and I could see the goldfish flashing about, gulping at what I had not been able to keep down.

Mother made me play outside the next day. It was cold and the fish were lazy. I threw leaves into the pond, but the fish would not come up to the surface, so I piled more and more into the water, until the pond was covered. I was stirring the pond up with a long stick when I saw a light in the library window. I dropped the stick. How had I left the library? Had I left the cabinet open? Where had I put the key? I put my hand in my pocket and felt the key there and my heart steadied a bit, but I still didn't like seeing mother in the library. I knew I'd done the right thing, but I didn't want mother to know just yet. I knew she wouldn't understand. She has probably never eaten a book in her life. Just then two large silhouettes covered the window. The inquisitors were in the library.

The thugs were bringing down the first crates of books as I rushed up the stairs. When I got to the library the locked case was already empty. Somehow they had opened it and the empty covers were gone, probably in the crates that I'd just seen carried downstairs. The captain and my mother ignored me. She just stood and watched him take the books down from the shelf. The thugs returned with more crates and continued to empty the shelves. I could not watch it. I slipped out of the library and climbed the stairs to the next landing, where I could watch the thugs trudge up and down the stairs, carting away my father's books, emptying his library while my mother and I watched. I tried to imagine where my father was now and what he was thinking. Was he still at sea, reading his charts and guiding the ship towards the mysterious western lands? Was he riding quickly across the continent, pursued by his enemies, a secret message sewn somewhere into his clothes? Or was he already in the inquisitors' dungeons? Would he know that I had hidden the evidence against him and that he would be safe?

My mother had been crying. The captain pretended to be

sympathetic as he himself carried the last crate out of the library. His face showed no strain. His cheeks were still smooth and relaxed.

'I am sure the clue we need is in here somewhere, Madame,' he said. 'Rest assured we will leave no page unturned.'

I wanted to rush him. I wanted to fling myself against him and knock him down the stairs, but I knew that I was too small, and that it would be a sort of victory for him. I must not let him think he has won. He looked up at me as he descended the stairs. 'It must be very hard on the boy,' he said to my mother. How could she let herself be fooled so?

The night after the captain and his thugs pillaged the library, I fell asleep on the floor of the empty room. I didn't hear the bell the next morning. The sound of the two thugs kicking the mud off their boots woke me. I heard myself make a funny squeak like a mouse as I woke, and I looked around to see if anyone had heard. The sound of the inquisitors' boots was already coming up the stairs when I got up off the floor. They would catch me there for sure. I looked around for somewhere to hide. Then I remembered what they had done. The books were gone and there was no reason to hide, so I stood up and waited for them. The sound on the stairs had stopped by then. I heard the captain of the inquisitors say something in a quiet voice. It was a voice that reminded me of my father. The boots of the other two banged back down the stairs again.

'Who is this? Is it the little scholar or the dog with eyes as big as saucers guarding his treasure?' I cursed myself for thinking that this man ever sounded like my father. 'Your father would be proud of you, saucer dog, but there's no use standing guard any longer. There's no treasure left in there. It's safe with us.'

'Don't worry about the books. Your father is not lost in the books. You won't find him there. That thing we imagine is out there cannot be captured on paper.'

I thought I could knock him down, if I charged him and hit him in the belly with my head like a ram, but I just stared at him.

'Come along, saucer dog. Your mother is packing for you.'

I ran up to my room. My mother had already half filled my father's big black bag. I watched her fold and put the last of my clothes into it and fasten the silver buckles. The captain had followed me to my room. It was he who picked up the bag and carried it downstairs. The two thugs were waiting in the foyer with my mother's baggage. My mother pulled my coat on to me roughly. She gave me no time to hold my shirt cuffs and the shirt bunched up beneath my coat sleeves. The captain locked the front door behind us. I felt that if I asked where we were going the inquisitors would have won. The captain helped my mother into the cab and the thugs loaded the bags. I don't know why, but the sight of my father's bag with my clothes in it made me saddest. Father had never carried anything but books in that bag. My eyes and face stung as if I was being stabbed by hundreds of falling needles. I saw that the captain's cloak was wet. It must be raining, but it was such a fine rain, I could not see it. Behind me the sun shone through a lighter cloud and made my back feel hot and my neck sticky. One of the thugs held a door for me. I did not feel like entering any door that he held, but I had no choice. I tried not to look at him as I climbed up. As I passed him he whispered something in my ear.

'Had a little bonfire, did we?' His voice was ugly, like collecting snot, for a bad spit. 'Maybe you don't want papa to come back, eh! Maybe the little boy likes having his mama to himself.'

I turned around to look at his fat sneering face. I was about to utter the worst insult I knew, in a language the fat idiot would not understand, but when I opened my mouth, the voice came out like a squeak, as if I was about to cry. The fat thug's face sputtered into a cruel laugh. I sat down and looked out the window at the house. The captain himself climbed into the cab. He made a hand signal to his thugs and they nodded as we moved away. Inside the cab, he sat next to my mother, across from me. I could feel him looking at me, but I kept my face pressed against the cold glass of the window and watched the house roll away. My father's books were inside me. I am sure I don't understand them completely yet. What is there is just semblance, a faded cipher of what was meant. But I will understand it all one day and I will have my revenge.

THE PLOT TO HIDE AMERICA

In 1982, during the closing days of the Argentine Junta's power, thirty-two labourers on a Rio de la Plata archaeological dig are 'disappeared'. In 1971 a popular Massachusetts parish priest, Father Martin Malone, leaves his parish for a California retreat; he is found six months later in a San Francisco flophouse, dead from a heroin overdose. In 1998 Jojo Villeneuve, a St Petersburg, Florida, trailer park resident, uses the advance on her first novel, *1001 American Nights*, to purchase a monumental concrete-and-glass summer house overlooking Acapulco Bay. Three widely disparate events, all were news stories of some sort. All three have turned up on my desk as story leads. One, the story of Father Malone, I knew very well, having interviewed him for my exposé of sexual abuse in the clergy, but I never put the three events together. I never would have if a fourth apparently unconnected story hadn't crossed my desk last year.

Connecting the four stories was a small miracle, but nothing about it is reassuring. The sheer luck of it makes me doubt my own profession. I'm reminded of how many stories are out there undiscovered. Even when the characters and events are known to everyone, luck has to intervene to assemble the story. It convinces me that for every story we chance to piece together, thousands of others remain disassembled and lost. For every person like myself with an interest in reintegrating distant facts into a coherent story, there are many others who would prefer to keep those facts scattered and confused. It reminds me that there are people working to assure that the thing we imagine is out there cannot be captured on paper.

The fourth lead, the one that connected the other three, was an investigative piece on forged art and antiques. My piece, finally broadcast as 'The Book of Lies', focused on the market for early printed books or incunabula. The trade in incunabula, as in most art objects, is shrouded in a secrecy and exclusivity that encourages fraud. The market for the very rarest of early printed books consists of a few dozen highly competitive individuals, so envious of each other's collections that who exactly owns what isn't always known. Book dealers use these rivalries to drive up the price of pieces. For many pieces there are more buyers than product and the most unscrupulous dealers find it too tempting to sell the book to all of them. This is why forgery is such a problem. A market exists, so supply expands to meet demand.

Some experts have suggested that 60 percent of the incunabula sold to collectors in the last ten years were forged or misattributed. This second category is the great 'out' of all fine art dealers. Very few dealers knowingly pass off forged work, but they depend on the knowledge that the identification of these books is not an exact science, and there is always room for doubt about the authenticity. They rely on their suppliers, the bookfinders, to provide a provenance, a frame story that the dealer might plausibly believe and pass on to collectors. No self-respecting dealer in incunabula will guarantee the authenticity of a piece. They will only suggest that certain works are supported by a believable story.

During my investigation, I went undercover amongst these bookfinders, posing as an art historian, the type of character who helps concoct these believable stories. My recommendation came from a respected professor of Renaissance history, Dr Sengeon, who set me up as a tenureless professor looking to supplement my university income. My contacts correctly interpreted this to mean that my opinion could be bought.

One of the first works that I was asked to assess was a volume of a Chinese encyclopaedia, translated into Italian. The bookfinder suggested it might be a translation of an encyclopaedia brought from the east by Marco Polo and printed in a very limited edition by Manatuas Aldus in 1490. In book dealing circles the name Aldus has an almost alchemical power. It can transmute the most mundane book into gold. The dealer expected me to assemble a précis that justified this attribution.

My research assistants here at the network worked diligently to come up with these justifications. We found evidence that certain of Aldus's patrons were dedicated sinophiles. We uncovered lists of objects that Polo brought back from China that included encyclopaedias. We even found a 1494 letter from a Vatican librarian requesting that a certain set of books about China be spared from burning. The librarian admitted that they were sacrilegious and would mislead the faithful, but since they would provide a valuable resource to the inquisition, they should be preserved, protected and restricted, but preserved. There's no evidence that anybody paid any attention to the librarian and preserved the Chinese books. There is lots of evidence that people paid attention to our own hasty amateur scholarship.

On the authority of a précis written by a journalist and signed with the name of a non-existent historian, the volume was sold to a very highly regarded New York book dealer and then on to one of his clients for a sum in multiple millions. The book dealer had no way of knowing that the book was authentic other than my statement. I had no way of knowing that it was a fake, but the eagerness of the middlemen to solicit and accept my opinion wasn't reassuring. The Chinese encyclopaedia made my reputation in the industry and I was asked to evaluate several more clearly dubious books. My précis always backed up the story that the seller suggested. I was very co-operative and when I expressed an interest to get into other parts of this business, no one suspected my motives. Over three months working with the dealers I learned how collectors' wish lists are assembled and how long chains of suppliers and dealers work to bring the items on these wish lists to the top of the collecting food chain. This is the substance of my documentary 'The Book of Lies'.

Most of the frauds foisted on gullible collectors are not out and out fakes. It is almost not worth the effort of acquiring the right paper, a believable press, the right ink, the right binding, never mind a plausible text. Most of these frauds are old books. They are just not as old, as rare or printed by the same printer that the collector is led to believe.

My Chinese encyclopaedia turned out to be one of these frauds. Towards the end of my investigation I received a second volume from that same set of encyclopaedia. I never intended to concoct the fake history for this second volume. My investigation was wrapping up and it wasn't required, but I did do something that people rarely do with these old books – I started to read it. I had been with the Associated Press in Rome during the late eighties and had picked up enough Italian to read the daily newspapers. Renaissance Venetian dialect was a bit of a stretch, but during the few weeks that I had the book I fell into the habit of opening it at random and struggling through a few paragraphs before falling asleep.

The article on the continent of America didn't put me to sleep. It kept me up all night with rewrites. This was too good, the perfect kicker for my exposé. At the time of the supposed publication of this book in Italy, Amerigo Vespucci had yet to sail for America. The Chinese original upon which the Renaissance translation was based was supposed to be even centuries older. The forgers had missed this detail. Clearly this was a much later work that they were trying to pass off. In their arrogance and sheer carelessness they faked the provenance for a book without even scanning it for such damning contradictory internal evidence.

When my 'Book of Lies' story broke, the volume passed from my hands to the police. During the criminal investigation, it was given to Dr Sengeon, the same professor of art history who had set me up with the bookfinders. Surprisingly, the Chinese encyclopaedia was never brought as evidence. I thought that it would have been an obvious choice. I asked the professor about it a year later when we met again at a documentary awards gala. His assessment of the encyclopaedia was startling. Of the books he examined on behalf of the prosecutors, the Chinese encyclopaedia was, on the face of it, the most authentic. Tests done on the ink, the paper, the binding, even the binding glue, placed it around the right date and an analysis of the type forms concluded that it had indeed come from Aldus's press. I was astonished. I asked him if he had *read* the book. He laughed so heartily that we were shushed by the tables around us. Under my breath, I suggested he might find something interesting if he did.

About a month later Sengeon left a message on my answering machine. He had found the American article. He was absolutely flabbergasted, he said. It was a glaring anachronism, totally out of place. But, he continued, he had gone back over the earlier evidence and still found it convincing. Something was clearly wrong here. He had sent new ink and paper samples from the America article to the lab. If I called next week, he would have the results.

Until that evening I hadn't even thought of Martin Malone. As I sat going over my notes on the Chinese encyclopaedia that night, I remembered something he had said during my single interview with him. Malone had been in a bad state when I met him. It had been eighteen months since the scandal broke back in his Massachusetts parish. He'd been accused of making sexual advances to an altar boy. I'd already tried to talk to the altar boy and his parents in Massachusetts but they refused to speak to me, presumably as a result of some gag order as a condition of the settlement they'd received from the diocese.

In the midst of the furore, the Church had whisked Malone away to a California retreat. When I met him in San Francisco he had been out of the sanctuary for three months. He looked as if he'd lost about thirty pounds and was rubbing his forearms in a distinctly strung-out way. His time in the retreat had not helped him come to terms with his crimes. He was deep in denial and now also very paranoid. He kept insisting that the

Church was out to get him, first to discredit him, now to kill him. The Pope himself had signed his death warrant, he claimed. He compared himself to Salman Rushdie. When I asked him why the Church would possibly do such things he leaned close and whispered, 'Because of what I know. Because I know that they tried to hide America.'

I should have stopped the interview there, but Malone went on. He told me that he had evidence that the Church had known about America for years before its supposed discovery by Columbus. It was the Pope's private empire, he said. Its gold had financed the Crusades and all the glories of the Renaissance. As a journalist, I find it difficult to turn away from any story without hearing all the details, even when the story is a paranoid confabulation, so I listened and took notes for about an hour. Malone believed that America was known to the ancient Greeks and Chinese. Everyone knew about it, he said. It was an accepted fact. It was the Romans who first tried to cover up America, then the inheritors of their empire, the Catholic Church. It was their private reserve. They hoarded it, used it to finance their wars and their intrigues.

Malone got a little giddy as he went on with story. At one point he sang his own variation on 'This Land': 'This land is their land, this land's not our land. This land's not made for you and me.' It was more than a little creepy. I asked Malone how anyone could hope to keep a continent a secret, and he proceeded to tell me more about the cover-up than I wanted to know. He claimed that the burning of the library at Alexandria was their doing. They were burning the evidence. They conquered and Christianized the Celts and the Norse to put an end to their transatlantic trade. They kept a stranglehold on trade with China, to stop the information leaking out from there. He was on to them, he said. He'd been to the Vatican library. He'd seen the proof there and he had his stones, the stones of a Roman temple on the shores of Cape Cod. At one point he snatched the pencil and notebook from my hand and drew a map and plan of his temple.

I never used these notes. I once thought of making an analogy of a forbidden land and the forbidden body of his victim, but it was too trite. Malone was such a sad case I felt sorry for him. I left him out of my sexual abuse story and set these notes aside. I'd hardly thought about them until Sengeon's call about the Chinese encyclopaedia. Now someone else was talking about a continent called America prior to Columbus's supposed discovery of it. I remembered Malone saying that the Chinese had known all along. Maybe he too had got a hold of this bogus Chinese encyclopaedia.

I started to assemble a few theories that might fit these peculiar facts. I figured some forger with a sense of humour was behind the encyclopaedia. At worst some crazy secret society of historical revisionists was out there cooking up books to justify their version of history. Malone in his paranoia had accidentally fallen prey to this elaborate joke or strange conspiracy. I still didn't suspect anything more sinister. I still felt sorry for the old pervert. I didn't even suspect, yet, that Martin Malone hadn't merely accidentally overdosed.

I did, however, one Sunday when I had nothing else to do, take a drive out to the cape to Malone's former parish, following Malone's map down to the natural harbour where he thought he'd found the remains of a temple. I was surprised to see the site cordoned off and a large dredging machine at work. I hopped the fence and took a look around. There were many piles of rock and debris, but only one was covered by a tarpaulin. Under this one I discovered a pile of white stones. I'm no geologist, but they looked like marble to me, and one stone I could see was clearly fluted as if it had once been part of a large column.

I made my enquiries and found that a large private home was being constructed on this site. The contractor laughed when I mentioned the rocks and referred me to Dr Neuberg of the Harvard Archaeological Department. My interest in the subject appeared to amuse Dr Neuberg. He lectured me boredly, as if he shouldn't have to tell a grown man such obvious things. Yes, the site was of archaeological interest, but only temporary. The marbles, he explained, were ballast rocks. Ships sailing from Europe in the early days of colonization usually travelled lighter on the outward leg and required ballast to keep them stable. All sorts of debris was used; usually it was just river rocks, but the occasional piece of a European church or monument found its way into the ballast. It was useful for identifying the source ports for early transatlantic commerce. This explanation satisfied me at the time. Martin Malone would never have thought of this. He would have taken these remains at face value. Perhaps he already had his own pet theories about American history. Clergymen are prone to these sweeping revisionist ideas. They are professionally credulous. It's a job requirement.

My job requires the opposite. I have to maintain a certain level of skepticism and I tried to do so even when Professor Sengeon finally returned one of my calls about the Chinese encyclopaedia. The encyclopaedia, he said, was out of his hands. The book and all his reports on it had been seized by the bailiff administering one of the many civil suits emerging from my investigation. He advised me not to think about the book. The first tests had probably been contaminated. It was a bad hoax. There was no use following it further. It was the last thing on his mind. He was off to Rome for at least a year. The Mellon fellowship had come through and he'd finally been granted permission to study the Vatican library's collection of confiscated early printing presses.

The Vatican library kept coming up. When we were falsifying the provenance for the encyclopaedia, we'd found a copy of a letter from the Vatican library to build our case. Martin Malone claimed to have seen something in the Vatican library that supported his crazy theory, and now Professor Sengeon had been spirited off there. Was it possible that the Vatican was tied up in this forgery business? It was a wonderful resource, I thought. Where better to set up shop than a library with access to thousands of ancient manuscripts and a secret store of early European printing presses? Maybe some Vatican librarian had found a creative way of supplementing his income.

Sengeon's new lack of interest in the encyclopaedia was suspicious too. There is nothing like not wanting to talk to make a journalist pay attention. I couldn't help feeling that Sengeon had somehow been bought off by his big fellowship and appointment to the Vatican. I wasn't going to let that one drop. I just put it aside for a short time, while I pursued my new interest in the history of ballast.

I did a little reading on the subject and it seems that ballast explains many strange things. Ship's ballast is to alternative archaeology as weather balloons are to UFO sighting, a convenient plausible refutation of the initial evidence. Whenever a stone or ceramic artefact is found where it should not be, in a spot that would challenge accepted versions of history, it is put down to ship's ballast. In the Americas this device is resorted to more often than you'd think. From Gothic gargoyles found in the Gulf of St Lawrence to Phoenician counting beads in the Everglades, these inopportune objects have always been explained away by the magic of ballast. Of the dozens of examples I read of, none troubled me more than the Rio de la Plata find.

The Rio de la Plata dig wasn't news to me. It had been the backdrop of a story I had done years ago about the end of Junta's rule in Argentina.

Thirty labourers had been 'disappeared' from that dig, disappeared being the euphemism for arrested by the secret police, probably tortured, usually killed and never heard of again. Even in Argentina the disappearance of thirty men caused outrage. It was seen as the final desperate gasp of the Junta clinging to power. The workers were all members of the new stevedores' union. The union had been formed in opposition to the existing dockworkers' union, which was corrupt and firmly under the thumb of the shipping magnates, who in turn were staunch supporters of the conservative Junta.

Members of the new union were blacklisted at the harbour and the fledgling union had turned to alternative employers while they built their support and waited for the old syndicate to crumble. Many of their members took work on an archaeological expedition searching for the ruins of two Spanish ships sunk by Francis Drake during the battle of the Rio de la Plata in the sixteenth century. The dig was abandoned after the disappearance of the labourers, though I paid little attention to it at the time. I was more concerned with showing how the Junta's brutal effort to break up the union had finally backfired and how the sympathy for the labourers' families was being used to fuel renewed calls for the end of military rule.

I'd ignored the labourers' families' claims that it was something they'd found on the dig that had got them killed. I thought it confused the issue and diluted the story. When more than ten years later, I saw the Rio de la Plata dig mentioned in the *Scientific American* article on ballast, I couldn't even remember what they thought they'd found. I remembered something vaguely about a Portuguese warship that was being used by Uruguay and Brazil to stir up ancient territorial disputes, but my memory was wrong.

I dug out my old files and pulled back issues of the Argentine dailies to refresh my memory. One of the early Argentine news stories claimed that instead of a Spanish galleon, the dig had actually uncovered the remains of a Roman trading vessel. The families of the murdered men claimed that they had uncovered dozens of unbroken vases, roman amphorae in the silt of the riverbed. Many claimed that they contained olive oil that was still usable. Others added that they'd found tiny votive statues of Roman gods.

I couldn't believe I had missed this background story and checked my notebooks, and sure enough it was mentioned in two or three of my interview notes. One woman said that her husband had brought her a Roman amulet from the dig, but she refused to show it to me. I must have put this down to a crazed sort of denial and edited it out of my story. Even now it was the most reasonable explanation. Many of the stevedores were of Italian descent, still not fully integrated into Argentine society and proud of their heritage. I attributed their version of events to wishful thinking. It would have been a nice turn of events for them if it finally turned out that Argentina was a lost Roman colony.

In the mainstream news articles on the Rio de la Plata dig there were no intact amphora, only potsherds, which could have been from anywhere. In the years since, some of the broken fragments were actually identified as Roman, only to be dismissed and explained away by the magic of ballast. I wished now that I had taken better notes when I'd interviewed the families of the missing labourers. Their testimony had seemed irrelevant then, but it was only too relevant now, so I sent my research assistant looking for the contact information on those Argentine widows. I was particularly interested in speaking to the woman whose husband claimed to have found the amulet.

At this point in my investigation I didn't know what I was uncovering. I was still sure that some sort of forgery scam was involved, but planting fake Roman items at archaeological sites seemed to be a costly way of supporting the authenticity of a few books.

My investigation, such as it was, now proceeded on two fronts. I needed to find out more information on the supposed history of pre-Columbian European contact with America. I also wanted to find out who Martin Malone had been talking to before he was whisked away to California. I made a telephone call to Catherine Malone, Martin's sister, and left a message on her answering machine saying that I'd uncovered some evidence that might clear her brother's name. I spent the rest of the week at the library.

I was surprised to see the amount of scholarship, pseudo or otherwise, that had gone into proving that Europeans made contact with America long before Columbus. It seemed everybody wanted to claim that they had been there first. The Norse had Leif Ericson, of course. The Irish had St Brendan. The Arabs had Abnadazer the Navigator. The Welsh had King David, who had sailed west when his kingdom fell to the Saxons. Every second book claimed that America had been settled by some tribe or other, be they Egyptians, Israelites, Phoenicians or Nubians. The

Russians had sent an army across the northern ice to defeat the Eskimo. The Japanese enjoyed a profitable trade with the Incas. If you believed everybody's claim, America was more of a popular vacation spot than an undiscovered continent.

Most of the books extolling these claims were light on scholarship, long on speculation and fervent theorizing. A publisher called Illuminatus seemed to specialize in these. I quickly learned to avoid anything with their name on it. There were precious few others though. One of the better books was *Discovery and Recovery.* I ordered a copy of my own from my favourite bookstore, and made a note to try to get in touch with its author, Jake Westerfeld. My discussion with Catherine Malone convinced me that I should speak with Westerfeld sooner rather than later.

Catherine Malone wasn't exactly eager to talk to me. She knew about my earlier story on sexual abuse in the clergy, and suspected I was looking for a sequel. I had to call her two or three times. She seemed tired and unwilling to dredge up the past. It wasn't until I told her I had seen the marble columns that she relented and agreed to speak to me.

The man Catherine Malone described was not a crank or a creep. He was as normal as priests get. He'd never had any problems with the community. He was well liked and respected. The accusations of sexual abuse had been a complete surprise. The boy who had raised the accusations had been a troubled boy from a broken family. The type one would nowadays describe as 'at risk'. Martin Malone had helped buy hockey equipment so the boy could play on the school team. He had only served as an altar boy once or twice. It seemed to be more his mother's idea than his own. The last time he'd been to church had been almost six months before the accusation. The Church had been no help during the ordeal. The bishop had urged Father Malone to plead guilty and said the Church was willing to pay reparations. As the investigation dragged on Malone was removed from the pulpit. He spent days alone without seeing anyone and became very depressed.

Malone eventually agreed to let the Church pay off the family and move him to the California monastery. To the end though he maintained his innocence. Catherine Malone had had no contact with her brother while he was in California. None of her letters were answered. She suspected they had never got to him. His death had affected her deeply and she was very bitter.

Catherine Malone was reluctant to discuss her brother's archaeological interests. She didn't want to believe it had anything to do with his troubles. She agreed that he had somehow done something to antagonize his superiors; she just couldn't believe it was all about the stones. Malone had found the stones three years before the trouble started. He'd written a few articles for the local paper and had used his sabbatical to do some research at the Vatican library. He was working on a book and had even found a publisher, but the publisher took liberties with Malone's text, sensationalized it, added wild conjectures that he had never made, and removed long explanatory sections. It was all, they said, in the name of sales. They were in the business of making money and his writing was too, well, academic. They needed to spice it up. Malone had finally cancelled the contract and was looking for another publisher.

It was while he was looking for a new publisher that the sexual abuse allegations first came up. As Malone became more isolated, he'd begun to believe that he was being framed to discredit his discoveries. This was the beginning of the paranoia that I had seen at its height in San Francisco. Catherine Malone didn't have a copy of her brother's manuscript. With some reluctance she told me Martin Malone had sent it to someone called Jake Westerfeld. I was pleased with this little connection in my research. She did give me a copy of one of the articles from the local paper. It showed a smiling Martin Malone standing next to a fluted column taller than himself; this was no ballast. As I left I asked one additional question, already suspecting the answer, and Catherine Malone didn't surprise me. The meddlesome publisher that wanted to dilute and sensationalize Martin Malone's book was indeed Illuminatus.

Jake Westerfeld is not your classic conspiracy theorist. He's too smooth, too glib for that cliché. A successful stockbroker, who uses his personal fortune to finance his publishing firm, he doesn't believe that everyone is out to get him, just a few high-placed individuals in academic and clerical circles. He seems genuinely well adjusted and free of paranoia, which makes it all the more surprising when he tosses out some outrageous idea as if it were common knowledge. In conversation, he makes dramatic and unpredictable leaps of thought. On paper, he is collected, measured and reasonable.

Martin Malone's temple, Westerfeld explained casually, looking at the newspaper picture and nodding, is Greek, or imitation, but probably the former, late Hellenic. It may have been some Pythagorean cult site.

They are, he tells me, very common on the New England coast. Westerfeld remembered Martin Malone's manuscript. He kept it in a large vault somewhere with dozens of others like it. Electronic backups were scattered on secure servers around the globe. Westerfeld happily gave me a copy on disc, but he gave me a synopsis off the top of his head.

Malone had found the remains of a Greek temple on Cape Cod. No one could give him a convincing explanation for it being there. One of the tablets Malone found at the temple had the New Testament parable of the mustard seed inscribed on it in Greek and ascribed to Pythagoras. This sent Malone off to Rome where some dimwit in the Vatican library let him into the restricted collection. Amongst the restricted books Malone had found a papyrus dated to 400 years before Christ containing the same Greek text. He'd also found a portion of the inquisitorial archives that described the burning of twenty heretics in 1420 who claimed the earth was round and that the true promised land was called America.

When I asked Westerfeld flatly if there was a conspiracy to cover up the prior existence of America, he said yes, but a mild one. America had never been widely known in Europe. It had a quasi-legendary status, being in the class of things that some people had heard of but very few had seen, like whales, manticores or Cathay. The medieval church had made the first real attempts to cover up its existence and after the discovery by Columbus a cover-up of that cover-up. I asked Westerfeld why, but he only shrugged. It wasn't his area of specialty he said. He was more concerned with Chinese contact with the West Coast. The best supported explanation he'd seen was that the Romans had resettled a group of Israelite dissidents led by Jesus the Nazarene to America and that the premise of papal power was entirely false.

According to Westerfeld, Malone's manuscript didn't even approach this conjecture, but it was probably enough to scare some cardinal responsible for the cover-up into an overreaction. The anti-Americanists very rarely kill their opponents, Westerfeld explained. Usually they just buy them off or discredit them. If they are really persistent they publish their books in a form that makes them totally unbelievable. Westerfeld confirmed that Illuminatus Press was the usual publishing outlet for these diverted texts. Malone must have really made a nuisance of himself to get himself killed. Westerfeld suggested I watch my step too.

Two days after I spoke with Westerfeld, I received a fax from Sengeon in Rome. He'd been so busy with his research that he hadn't thought about the Chinese encyclopaedia, but something he'd found in the Vatican Museum archives explained so much. Everyone knew that, thanks to its Inquisition's confiscations, the Vatican library had the finest collection of early printing presses. Sengeon also found stacks of blank paper of Renaissance manufacture apparently confiscated during the same inquisitorial raids. If you wanted to, he said, you could print books in modern-day Rome that would be indistinguishable from authentic incunabula. He seemed amused by his discovery, more than anything. It was possible to argue, he joked, that books printed on Renaissance paper, with Renaissance type and on a Renaissance press were in fact incunabula, regardless of what century they were printed in.

For Sengeon the reams of paper and the antique presses explained everything. Some forger had got hold of this Vatican treasure trove. The Chinese encyclopaedia had been forged after all. There was no need to question any historical assumptions. Maybe journalism makes me paranoid, but Sengeon's find seemed to do the exact opposite. Why would anyone go to such efforts to forge a manuscript? There are already too many books. There are warehouses filled with old books that no one wants, and all you need to make them valuable is a mere recommendation from a plausible scholar. Instead of proving that the encyclopaedia was fake, didn't this store of fifteenth-century printing materials instead invite us to question all the historical evidence we had for anything five hundred years ago?

Sengeon's discovery was suspicious enough, but his fax contained another of the strange coincidences that I continued to run into throughout this investigation. Sengeon must have borrowed a fax machine to send me this message. He probably used the fax at the office closest to where he was working that day, which made the sender's name – stamped in tiny dotted text alongside the phone number and transmission time in the fax header – comically ominous. The fax had been sent from the offices of Illuminatus Press.

At about this time I started to receive warnings. The research assistant who had helped me on the *Book of Lies* story was mugged in the parking lot. Thankfully she wasn't hurt, just scared and mystified that in place of her stolen wallet the thief had left a postcard from Columbus, Ohio, with nothing but my name on it. Catherine Malone phoned to say that a lawyer had been round to discuss the prospect of a civil suit against her brother's estate. The lawyer had said she might lose her house. She was distraught. Why was I opening up these old wounds after all these years? Hadn't the family suffered enough? Could anyone really believe they had anything new to add to this whole mess? The lawyer, she said, had said that I would know how to put things right. I had some ideas how I might.

I did not like the possibilities of this story. I didn't like the conclusions I was going to have to draw. I wish I could say that journalists are motivated entirely by the desire to uncover the truth, but that is only part of our motivation. We pick and choose our stories. We don't just wake up in the morning and ask ourselves, 'What story out there remains to be told?' We want stories that make us look good, stories that advance our careers. We like to be believed. Breaking the story that the Catholic Church was trying to cover up pre-Columbian contact with America from Europe would send my career on a radical detour. There would be no going back. It would define my career and there would be no escaping it. It was a huge step into the margins. If this conspiracy were true, I was beginning to feel I would rather not know.

About this time, the feature editor at the network called me for the umpteenth time to ask me to visit Jojo Villeneuve. Jojo was the author of the previous year's surprise best-seller *1001 American Nights.* The network newsmagazine wanted a celebrity feature on her. Celebrity profiles are not really my style, a little too lightweight. But apparently Villeneuve would talk only to me. Not even Barbara Walters would do. The feature editor reminded me with an ill-concealed snicker that the flak jacket and unshaven scruff look of my Belgrade reports was a big hit with women of a certain age. Mexico seemed as good a place as any to get out of the way and make it clear to anyone who cared that I wasn't interested in following up the America conspiracy story, so I finally took them up on the offer.

On the plane down I tried to read *1001 American Nights.* It was truly terrible. I actually snorted at one point. The plot was preposterous, and I've never understood how placing a story five hundred years in the past excuses thoroughly unacceptable relationships between the sexes. The heroine, a young English noblewoman, ends up disguised as a Spanish sailor on a Spanish conquistador galleon only to be shipwrecked off the coast of the southern United States, where she somehow witnesses the massacre at Roanoke. The hundred-year discrepancy in dates doesn't seem to bother Jojo Villeneuve. The history is highly muddled throughout and this is just the most obvious anachronism. The heroine is captured by the savages who massacred the Roanoke colony and only manages to save herself through that Arabian Nights stratagem of feminine wiles and a diverting story. Having caught the chieftain's eye, she continually postpones her execution by amusing him with stories of her travels. The book goes on for several hundred pages of the heroine stringing her chieftain along, until they fall in love and she becomes his queen.

As I read the book, I was very conscious of people watching me read it. I was ashamed of being seen with it in my hands. After having read it I felt a strange compulsion to wash my hands. When we set down on the tarmac in Acapulco, I tucked it into the seat pocket for someone else to snicker through. I wondered how the hell I was going to be able to do this interview straight-faced.

Fortunately Jojo Villeneuve had a well-stocked bar to go with her extravagant personality. She had brought a TV-based conception of how the rich live with her from the trailer park. The house was a movie set, her dress and jewellery straight from a soap opera wardrobe unit, her new breast implants just plain frightening. She told me right off that she intended to seduce me, so I gave her the only excuse she would accept – that I was gay, at which point, she nodded knowingly and did the necessary mental script revisions.

Perhaps it was the constant supply of high-quality Scotch, but I actually enjoyed myself that day. The crew had done most of the background shots already. I had about three stiff drinks and filmed some more set-up footage to put me in the picture. Me following Jojo's gesture to the Gulf of Mexico out beneath her vast projecting concrete balcony. Me walking beside her in the Zen garden as she talks animatedly with her hands. Me sitting beside her in the library as she shows me the historical diaries that are the 'basis' of her novel. When we'd got the set-up footage we needed Jojo and I got down to the business of the interview.

I didn't have to talk much and she ignored my tone of bemused irony as she spun out her rags-to-riches story. She explained that the heroine of her story was her ancestor, and that she, Jojo, had a psychic connection with the woman. Jojo was able to channel her shipwrecked ancestor's thoughts from beyond the grave. Jojo's grandfather had a similar psychic connection with the shipwrecked girl, a connection so strong that she dictated her diaries to him. These diaries were the partial basis of the novel. All in all it was an amusing interview, and Jojo was very pleased with the way it went. There were times when I wondered how much of her extravagant image was concocted and how much was authentic. It really was over the top, but just the right distance over top according to her public I suppose.

When the cameras were off Jojo toned it down a little, just a little. In a whispered voice she told me that her connection with her shipwrecked ancestor wasn't so much a psychic connection as the normal sympathy between an author and her character. I was almost disappointed. Jojo continued to disillusion me, and I saw that she was more wily than her on-camera image exposed. The whole psychic connection thing was something she'd come up with afterwards with her publisher. Her grandfather actually claimed that the diary was a real historical document, but the publisher thought that this was too far-fetched.

In the diary her grandfather had given her, the shipwrecked storyteller was a man, and it was mostly about a tribe of Welsh-speaking Indians, who proved that the Welsh had discovered America. Jojo changed all that in the second draft of her book on the advice of her editor and everyone agreed that her version made a better story. If they liked that, she told them, then she'd edit it again. With each rewrite, they liked the story better, until she had convinced them to pay much more for it, to finance a huge print run and publicity campaign. They were only going to print a thousand copies of the first version, and only on some goofy imprint that the publisher owned just for wackos and conspiracy theorists. The final version, inflated by sex and psychics, was published by a mainstream paperback publisher and was a huge success.

Having seen the house she'd bought with her advance, I congratulated Jojo honestly on her creative skill and her negotiating abilities. I also asked her if she remembered the name of the goofy imprint she had originally been slated for. I was wearily prepared for her answer. She said, 'Luminatis or something like that.' Of course.

I returned home to find that my office had been ransacked. A postcard was left pinned to my corkboard in place of all my various messages and lead notes. The postcard read: 'Nothing is accomplished by this.' No explicit threat was needed, but next morning I heard the terrible news that Dr Sengeon had been killed in Rome in a bar brawl. I found it difficult to imagine Dr Sengeon in a bar, never mind a bar brawl. My excursion to Mexico had been a disastrous mistake. I had gone there to send a clear message to those concerned that I had given up on the story and that there was no need for additional threats and harassment. It had done the exact opposite. It was the last of the awful coincidences that tied this story together. It was stupidly fortuitous. How could I possibly have known that Jojo Villeneuve's pulpy corset buster novel had once been a conspiracy text only suitable for Illuminatus Press?

I have often speculated on how much Jojo knew, whether she knowingly parlayed her grandfather's family documents into a big buy-off or whether she'd just lucked into it. I have never bothered to investigate further. I backed off the story altogether. It was not easily done. After all these coincidences, I barely dared to make a decision. I kept imagining how each story or location I chose might lead back to this strange, irrelevant conspiracy.

I finally took up the flak jacket again and went to Central Africa, chasing a rebel leader through the jungle for an interview. He was a pompous and frighteningly irrational man whose conception of democracy seemed as distorted as Jojo Villeneuve's conception of literary fame. I interviewed him with the same detached irony.

THE AMERICAN SHAHRAZAD

My grandfather Alfred Newton always told me that our family was distantly related to the famous explorer Jorge Villa Nueva. I never knew whether to believe him or not. This is the same grandfather that told me he was four inches taller before the war, but that German machine gun fire severed his legs at the knee and some bits were missing when they sewed the legs back on. I believed this until I was about eight.

The idea that we are descendants of Villa Nueva is a little too coincidental. Villa Nueva is a minor historical celebrity around here. Parks and high schools are named after him. My grandfather immigrated to America and settled here in Florida after the war, some four hundred years or so after Villa Nueva made his journey.

Four hundred years is a lot of time, but it wouldn't be impossible to prove or disprove that he was my ancestor. When I was younger, the idea was very attractive, and my interest in the story was likely one of the reasons I became a historian. Now that I'm older the whole idea of trying to prove that I'm related to a historical figure seems slightly amateurish. Villa Nueva has never been my main research area. It's too glamorous. Besides, it is famous enough to be well picked over. It's one of those areas where you ask yourself, 'Can anyone really believe they have anything new to add?' I stick to the history of early American–European trade patterns for the most part, but Villa Nueva has always been a side interest.

Born George Newton and taking the pseudonym Jorge Villa Nueva or vice versa, in 1579 Villa Nueva published one of the first Indian captive narratives and least credible accounts of the New World called *The Narrative of George Newton.* Its full title is *The Narrative of George Newton intrepide adventurer and explorer, containing a full history of his imposture as a Spanish mariner in the service of His Majestie and his voyages amongst the cannibals and savages of the new world, including observations on their savage manners and strange rites.* According to this much prized document Villa Nueva was born in the Cornish coast town of Newquay in the early 1500s. Somehow he found himself on one of the Spanish conquistador expeditions to the Americas. *The Narrative of George Newton* includes a long foreword explaining that he was working a as spy for the English crown, but that is not the only explanation that has been offered. If Villa Nueva was indeed English, which only a minority of scholars and my grandfather believe, he may have been drawn to the Spanish conquistador fleet by religious associations, his own sense of adventure or mere chance. Most scholars these days prefer to believe that Newton was born Villa Nueva and took an English name when he took refuge in England after being charged with murder and treason by the Spanish general DeSoto.

How ever it came to be, the young Villa Nueva or Newton found himself on a Spanish conquistador vessel sailing from Cadiz some time in the 1530s. By 1569 he was back in Newquay, a talkative old man with a repertoire of strange stories who sometimes muttered words in suspiciously foreign languages. What happened between these dates has never been established conclusively. Even Villa Nueva can't keep the story straight, in fact he admits to falsifying parts of his record. Lying, he boasts, is his one great skill. 'Fabrication and dissimulation have saved my life too often for me to enumerate,' he writes famously. In fact the self-confessed unreliability of the narrator is one of the *Villa Nueva's Narrative*'s great fascinations. Villa Nueva justifies his habitual falsification in the prologue:

> It is my duty to forewarn the reader that this narrative by necessity contains certain untruths and fabrications incurred to accede to the will of the crown and to fulfil certain promises and solemn oaths I have pledged to savage chieftains, by which means I preserved my life and obtained my freedom and which I would not now fain recant merely to endanger my soul. I assert though that the contents of this narrative are honest to the spirit if not always the letter of my true adventures. What inventions I have mingled with my tale, I intend to be as instructive and amusing as those accurate adventures, but they are never so outrageous or outlandish as the true elements of my book and I dearly hope that the wheat of my tale when winnowed from the chaff remains unsullied and true.

So we are warned to take Villa Nueva's *Narrative* with a few grains of salt. It's just difficult to determine how many. It is easier to set the inconsistencies of his story aside and take it as George Villanova would have it.

Whether he was an English spy or a Spanish sailor, Villa Nueva's transatlantic journey was cut short. The crew of the Spanish galleon *Santa Brevita* abandoned him on a beach at the tip of some American peninsula. Villa Nueva variously blames disease, mutiny or shipwreck for his marooning. He told the Indians who found him that he was cast away because he was possessed by demons. For the benefit of his English readers, he insinuates that the Spanish suspected he was a spy and left him there to die. When the Indians found him, he was delirious and his face inflamed from eating the wrong shellfish, so they might easily have believed that he was possessed. They might also have believed that he was a fool. Exactly which Indians found Villa Nueva is a subject of intense speculation. There are descriptions of practices and rituals that ring true to many scholars. Others that leap out as glaring fabrications to pander to his European audience. On the internal evidence alone it is impossible to pinpoint the tribe. They may have been Caribs or Calusa. Villa Nueva calls them the Nunca.

The Nunca nursed Villa Nueva back to health and as he grasped the rudiments of their language it dawned on him that a great debate was raging amongst the tribe as to what to do with him. Some wanted to throw him back into the sea from whence he came, others wished merely to kill him and there was strong support for the idea of boiling him and eating him. Villa Nueva listened to these deliberations from his sickbed and when it became clear to him that his rescuers had settled on the boiling and eating proposal, he resolved to escape. He did not make it far. The jungle around the village gave way almost immediately to swamp and after a night amongst the leeches the natives rescued him once again. Villa Nueva was deposited at the foot of an elevated platform, which held the throne of an enormous man, who Villa Nueva presumed was the chieftain.

This chieftain was the largest man Villa Nueva had ever seen. The flimsy platform of reeds and leaves upon which he sat shuddered if the chief as much as shifted in his seat. Terrified at the prospect of being murdered by these savages, Villa Nueva pleaded with the chieftain, attempting to explain who he was and where he had come from. His grasp of the native language was so slight that his explanation was largely a pantomime. He held his arms out wide, puffed his cheeks and moved in stately slow motion to mime the Spanish galleons, tossed himself around like a struggling madman to show the turbulence of the storm, gasped and flailed as he was tossed into the sea, capered about bowlegged on the hot sand of the beach, pounded imaginary shellfish on imaginary rocks, pulled his face with his fingers and projected imaginary vomit onto the ground and then finally fell down and curled up in authentic exhaustion.

A tortuous silence followed Newton's performance during which he cowered on the ground and awaited the first blows. The silence was finally broken by a series of deep hollow shouts or howls then a clattering of sticks and shrieks. When he could no longer wait for the knife he raised his head. He stared bewildered for a moment at the sight that awaited him. The platform wobbled dangerously, as the chieftain slapped his enormous thighs. The harrowing bellow that issued from his gaping maw, George took to be some sort of savage laughter. The clattering of sticks and shrieks must be a sort of applause. The chieftain beckoned to him to the platform. Two natives took him by the arms and held him up so that his head just reached above the level of the stage. The reed platform swayed and shuddered as the chieftain rose from his throne, leaned over with a slight groan and patted Villa Nueva on the head as one would a good pet.

It was an unlikely way of preserving his life. The natives were so taken with his performance that they had him do it all again immediately. The chief's monstrous belly laughs accompanied the encore from its start and the entire village was allowed to share his amusement, howling with laughter till they gasped for air and fell down on the ground holding their bellies. At first the laughter only intensified Newton's desperation, but a strange elation overtook him as he realized that the natives were laughing, not at the prospect of watching him boil or the futility of his pleas, but at the fool he was making of himself. He began to play it up, flapping his arms more wildly, throwing himself on the ground with more abandon, smearing his face with mud and shrieking with hysterical despair. The natives gorged themselves on his performance. When they were finally able to stand, they led him back to his cage.

This exhibition kept him alive for a week. He performed his act each night for a week. With each succeeding day the chief's mirth diminished just slightly, so that even before the week was done Newton knew he would have to come up with something else. He was learning the native language slowly. Newton had always had a facility for languages and in his cage in the village's central clearing he was surrounded by chattering children at play and their mothers gossiping over their work. Still, he was not picking up the language quickly enough to piece together his explanation. He knew the words for ocean, beach and hunger, but not the words for ship, continent, Spain or colonial empire. On the night that his clown act was greeted with only tired laughter and distracted spitting, and the chief's eyes were unfocused and cloudy with silent, murderous thoughts, he knew that his pantomime's run was over. While he lay on the ground panting from his exertions and listening to the ominous silence, Newton gathered his strength to attempt to relate his story with more precise actions.

Rising to his feet he looked straight into the chief's ruminating eyes and began. He placed his open hands behind his head, splaying his fingers out in what he hoped was a reasonable approximation of a crown. Holding his head erect and motionless, he then walked about before the platform in as regal a manner as he could conjure.

The chief looked quizzically at his courtiers. What madness was the clown concocting now? A porcupine? – they ventured. This was quickly agreed upon. They spoke their word for porcupine and Newton, confident that his mime could not be mistaken for anything but a king, agreed. This must be the word for king. The chief and courtiers congratulated themselves.

George then made little wave shapes with his hands to indicate that his king was across the ocean. The natives interpreted this correctly. They nodded. Yes, we know this story. There is nothing new here. Newton had come from the ocean. Continue, their nods said. Encouraged, Newton tried to show them how forlorn he was to be left alone and how desperately he wanted to return across the ocean. He made exaggerated sad faces and looked around desperately to show how lost he was, then made the wave motions again, pointing to himself.

This passage seemed to require more interpretation. A heated debate broke out on the platform. What was the captive trying to say? What did the ocean and the captive being an idiot have to do with the porcupine?

The chief watched the debate with interest, refraining from weighing in, and then suddenly the solution occurred to him. Newton watched the chieftain's eyes go suddenly wide with wonder as he repeated the word porcupine. Was it true? Was the strange hairy white creature saying he was a porcupine? Newton nodded yes vigorously.

The chief rubbed his belly sagely. The captive was claiming to be a porcupine. But a porcupine so big and so stupid – this was a marvellous story. His attendants added low tones of solemn agreement. If the fat white creature was a porcupine, this was a serious omen.

With a rapt audience now Newton repeated his mime. Around him the Indians murmured interpretations. Each time Newton repeated his mime he exaggerating his distress, wandering around holding his head, and his belly, falling down in a series of elaborate fainting spells. He tried to look as pitiable as possible, then pointed back over the sea and reverted to his king posture to show how it all might be fixed. The natives exchanged anxious glances and whispered prayers until the chief rose and ordered that Newton be put back in his cage.

While Newton fretted in his cell, the chieftain and his attendants agreed tentatively on their interpretation. Newton was a great porcupine who had ventured across the ocean, where the evil creatures that dwelled there had plucked out all his quills. He was now helpless and witless.

Weeks later when George determined the exact nature of the misunderstanding, it was far too late to correct it. It was a fortunate mistake nevertheless. The porcupine had a central role in Nunca mythology and storytelling. Newton always counted himself lucky for this, but credited his own creativity for adapting this mistake to his own purposes.

Over the following nights the chief's questions and Newton's own growing understanding of native vocabulary and syntax came together. The porcupine, he discovered, was a sacred animal. The king of demons, the Nunca called him. Each of the porcupine's quills was a demon that could be sent out into the world to work its mischief or its magic. Each demon, each spine, had a story or in the loose allegory and confined grammar of the language, each spine or demon *was* a story. Newton's appearance on the beach, now they recognized him as a giant porcupine robbed of his quills, clearly delirious and made stupid by his ordeal across the sea, was deeply troubling. Were all the demons out in the world now? This was a terrible thought. Or were the demons just simply gone? This would be no better. If all the demons were gone, there were no more stories. It would mean that the world was ending. Something must be done with the porcupine. He must get his spines back. He must recall his demons.

It was a strange respite. Newton was alive but the natives were in despair. Newton did his best to console them. They hardly included him in their deliberations, but during their frequent interrogations he tried to persuade them that the world was not about to end. 'Could the demons be reclaimed?' they asked him. He assured them they could. But where had they gone? Newton didn't like to leave a question unanswered. Across the ocean, he suggested. The demons, the stories, whatever form they took were across the ocean. This was Newton's instinctive first answer.

This was reasonable, the Nunca agreed. They liked when all the pieces came together, but their joy was momentary. How would they get their stories back then? To the Nunca the word ocean meant the same thing as impassable. Saying that their stories were gone across the ocean was as good as saying they were lost forever. They turned sullen and desperate again and gave Newton the impression of a renewed desire to boil the messenger. Not true, he said, hadn't he crossed the ocean? Hadn't he passed the impassable?

Yes, it was just possible, the chief declared, when the results of their inquiry were made known to him. The big naked porcupine must regain the demons. He must tell them the stories, when the stories were all told, he would regain his quills. They would listen to all the stories and then they would boil him, and once they had eaten him, the great porcupine would be restored. It was not a judgment Newton was comfortable with, but it seemed beyond challenge. Newton became their storyteller.

Every night Newton was brought from his hut (they needed the cage for some wildfowl they had caught and Newton was clearly too feeble and stupid to escape) and brought him to the clearing to tell stories. He began with stories he had heard on his travels, tales of sea monsters and sirens and cities of gold. The chief liked the sea monsters and sirens, but discouraged stories about treasure and cities of gold. It was somehow unseemly or embarrassing and George learned to avoid the topic of gold and treasure altogether. He told Bible stories. The natives cried themselves to sleep the night Newton told them about Jonah and the whale. They thought the story of Lazarus was a great joke. For days afterwards it was all the rage amongst the villagers to pretend they were dead and then to spring back to life. When Newton performed it, it produced the greatest howls from the chief since his classic narrative of the bad shellfish.

This went on for months. Newton lost track of the time he spent there. He recounted nursery rhymes and fables adapting the animals to native fauna. The turtle and the hare became the jaguar and the tree sloth. The lion and the mouse became the alligator and the parrot fish. Chicken Little became an armadillo, but this was not a well received story. The natives did not think that accounts of the world ending were particularly funny.

If ever Newton got comfortable he was quickly reminded that a death sentence hung over him. As soon as the chief thought that he had restored all the demons, they would boil him. He had to be careful not to repeat himself too often. There were a few particular favourites that they liked, St George and the Alligator, the annunciation of Mary, Little Red Riding hood and the panther – all classics in Newton's catalogue, but even these got old.

Newton realized that a story a night was sheer profligacy. He began extending his stories, inventing his own detours and subplots, so that the tree sloth's victory in a foot race with the jaguar was an odyssey of many nights and dozens of characters. Newton's entire day was spent fabricating stories. He had little energy for anything else. It was a precarious existence. His survival depended on concocting ever new stories. Some nights he would rack his brain for a plot. Some mornings he would cry out in despair: 'What story out there remains untold?' By nightfall, however, he always managed to piece something together. As long as he was alive, he judged that he was a success. But life amongst the Indians was only survival. He was not included in their daily life. He was homesick, lonely and despaired of ever returning to Europe.

In a contemplative mood one night the chief asked Newton why he had been on the other side of the ocean. Newton did not immediately understand the question, and the chief, by now accustomed to Newton's overwhelming feeble-mindedness, repeated the question more loudly, slowly and with appropriate hand gestures. When he had lost his stories he was on the other side of the ocean. What was he doing over there? Newton was stuck for an answer for a moment, and tried to recall just how he had finally left his porcupine and ocean tale. No, he ventured, he had merely dropped his quills on the beach and an eagle had picked them up in his beak and carried them across the ocean. A burly attendant cuffed Newton rapidly on the side of the head, dimming his vision for a sickening moment. How dared he contradict the chieftain? No, of course, Newton recanted through the mist of a deafening headache, yes, he had been on the other side of the ocean. What had he been doing there?

'Telling stories,' George answered. It was the first thing that occurred to him. The chief nodded sagely though, as this was a reasonable answer, and Newton's concussed brain strained to make a story out of this. This could work out well for him, if he did this right. Yes, he said, he had been telling stories to the people on the other side of the ocean. But weren't the people on the other side of the ocean the Nunca's enemies, the chief asked suspiciously. Newton could see a horrible thought forming in the chief's grimace. This would sound like treachery to him.

Newton hurriedly made his explanations. Yes, yes, it was true that the people on the other side of the ocean were the enemies of the Nunca, which is why he had been telling them lies. The chief bobbed his head upwards as if to say that he could continue. Newton moved closer and whispered to the chief, looking warily at the attendants as if he wasn't sure that they should hear this. The chief grunted impatiently and Newton explained as best he could. The creatures on the other side of the ocean (it was unfair to call them people) were horrible fiends driven by hatred and greed, but they were incalculably gullible and foolish. The chief nodded as if this truth was self-evident. These creatures had heard about the chief's people and their great superiority and were jealous. If the foreigners ever crossed the uncrossable sea and came to the chief's lands, they would surely destroy them. The chief nodded gravely again. He had always feared this might be true.

All was not lost though, Newton explained. There was no need to despair just yet. Most of the creatures on the other side of the ocean did not believe in the Nunca and their great paradise. Only a few sinister adventurers, criminals and corrupt shamans suspected that the stories were really true. I, Newton said, as your great protector, work amongst the creatures to refute these stories, and to conceal the paradise of the Nunca. George watched the chieftain's face grow wide with great gratitude and unsuspected hope. Yes, that is what he had been doing on the other side of the ocean. He had gone there to tell lies. He had told the chief's enemies that the earth was flat and if they ventured across the ocean they would fall off the ends of the earth. If they did not believe this, he told them that this was a land of man-eating cannibals, who loved the flesh of strangers. The attendants' ill-concealed glances gave Newton pause at this point, but the chieftain quickly urged him to go on. What other lies had Newton told?

Newton hurried his explanation along. Sometimes he told the people on the other side of the ocean that there was no land here at all, only a space in the ocean that was so cold that the water froze to ice. The chieftain stopped him there. This was preposterous. Were the creatures on the other side of the ocean so gullible as to believe that water could get so cold as to turn as solid as the earth? Newton nodded; incredible as it was, the brutes believed even this. The chieftain, Newton and attendants all shook their heads in ritual outrage, thanking their incredible luck not to have been born as stupid as these creatures on the other side of the ocean. Newton told the chieftain that these foreign beasts made war upon each other, and that he, their protector, told the factions false stories to encourage conflict. Newton told the brutes that paradise was to be found above the clouds rather than across the ocean, and they believed this. Newton catalogued his lies, until the chief was persuaded that as long as Newton was there telling lies and spreading confusion, the creatures across the ocean would never think of coming here.

It made only a small change in their plans for him. Newton still needed to reclaim all his stories. He should continue to recall his demons. Without them he was useless to the Nunca, but when he had recovered them all, he would be sent again across the ocean to lie to the creatures who lived there. This was excellent news for Newton, but for one complication. The Nunca steadfastly believed that the only way to transport him across the ocean was by the science of boiling and eating him. Newton protested – There is such a thing as a boat, he told them. The chief was skeptical of such untested magic as this thing called a boat, but Newton prevailed on him to at least consider this radical solution.

More to humour their captive than anything the Nunca built Newton a boat. They hollowed it out of a great log, covered its opening with skins like a coracle and dragged it to the beach. Newton became cocky and overconfident and began listing the provisions he would require, a few cooked armadillos, dried ants, some of that salted serpent he liked so much, some fruit, lots of fruit, two weeks' worth of food, he suggested, would about do it. But the Nunca as always ignored his ritual stupidity. The food would spoil they said, better wait until he was ready to leave. No matter how much he protested that he was ready now they just smiled, shook their fingers at him as if they were scolding a greedy child and returned to the village.

After one of these frequent arguments the natives left Newton on the beach screaming after them in despair and frustration. I must go back! I must get across the ocean! I have to tell lies! I have to go now! When it seemed they had all gone he fell silent on the sand and watched the waves lap gently against the prow of his feeble little boat. A small child emerged from the trees and tugged at his hand. Someone had sent her to fetch him. He was too tired to pull back, and yet she was not strong enough to move him. Finally she looked into his eyes, and said pityingly, as if she were talking to a small pet who could not possibly understand, 'You can't go back yet, fat porcupine. You don't have your demons yet. You can't go back until you get your demons.' She pulled him down so that he crouched before her and she could look into his eyes. 'This is not enough,' she said, stroking the beard that had grown on his chin. This was not nearly enough spines. These were soft and not fearsome at all. How could they send him back like this? Newton let himself be led back to the village, but he cursed the stupid literalism of the Nunca language all the way.

He became spiteful. From then on he only told them stories about the end of the world. He told them that great boats driven by the winds would come from the other side of the world to steal their gold. The chief would protest nervously that they had no gold, but it was no matter; Newton would go on. He conflated the story of Armadillo Little with the boy who cried Jaguar, frightening them all to death with the prospect of the sky finally falling.

Newton invented a story of a college of shamans who lived on an island far to the north. These shamans, he said, invented history. As long as they lived alone and invented myths for the world, the world would go on. But they had been inventing stories too long now. These wizards were becoming increasingly sleepy, and the longer they slept, the longer the nights were, and the longer the nights were the fewer stories they told. It meant that the world is already exhaustive and exhausting. The shamans themselves were shrinking as the world shrank, and soon they would be too small to think anything but the simplest of tales. Later they would be feeble dwarves who slept all the time, eternal night would descend on them all and the world's stories would come to an end.

Newton took perverse pleasure in torturing the Nunca like this. He had come to believe that the Nunca would never let him go. They were addicted to his storytelling. They would never relinquish him. Whether he ran out of stories or kept telling them until he expired, it made little difference. His beard would never be long enough for them. He could grow six-foot quills the length of his spine and they would find some reason to keep him there. If he was going to be stuck there, telling them stories for the rest of his life, he would make them suffer too.

The natives tried to appease him. They fed him better. They sent him a wife. They painted his boat. The people could not understand why their storyteller would tell such horrible stories. Clearly he was a cruel and peevish demon, but self-expression is a feeble excuse. They seemed to think that if they could cheer him up, he might tell happier stories, but he would not relent. The chief was sick with worry. Hunting parties hardly bothered to go out into the jungle. The women took no care in planting. What was the point? The great fat stupid white porcupine had told them again and again that the world was ending. They were beginning to despise him, and yet they still listened. They could not help themselves. The more doomed they felt, the more they needed to hear his stories of the earth being covered with rock, or of huge leaf-eating creatures who would eat the jungle, and especially of the porcupine losing its quills. They took the narrowing of Newton's subject matter as proof. It was true – he had lost his demons. These were the last days and the last stories.

Newton was woken one night once again by the pressure of his wife's huge thighs astride his chest. (The description of the wife and her sexual appetites is missing from many of the modern editions but the original *Narrative* is often shockingly explicit.) This night was different; his wife's wide palm was pressed firmly across his mouth and he was unable to speak. This was it, he thought. Tonight was the night they would finally boil him and eat him. It was true that the hunt had been lacklustre and supplies were low. His wife's brothers entered the hut and bound his feet and arms while his wife kept George pinned to the palm-leaf bed. He did not struggle. What was the point of struggling? Finally his wife removed her palm and her brothers gagged him.

Newton thought he could hear his wife sobbing quietly as they prepared him to be cooked, but when she left to gather garnishes, he realized they were his own cries. His captors basted him with a foul smelling sauce and anointed him with shoots and leaves, then left him to marinate in a deep wooden barrow. It was nearly morning when they returned for him. He had never imagined that he would be breakfast. He had always imagined himself as an evening feast. Still trussed and rendered immobile by garnishes, he was carried out of the hut high above the shoulders of his captors. Newton could see nothing but the darkened sky and a few desperate rays of morning light. Amongst the chants of the villagers who had formed a procession behind his platter, he could hear a few haunting wails, as if the world really was going to end. They were his own involuntary moans of despair.

His captors placed him gently in the cooking vessel. He could feel it rocking above the fire. There was no water in the pot. Why had he always thought he would be boiled? What made him assume this? He'd been spiced and basted; now he would be barbecued, stewing in last night's marinade and his own juices. Was this better? Worse? His senses could get no grasp of what was happening. Did he feel the heat yet? Was he burning? He felt disoriented and nauseous, as if overcome by vertigo or motion sickness. The sounds of the village seemed to grow more distant as he was cooked. A sudden reluctance to die came over him. He rebelled against the heat and the pain and struggled to his feet. When had they unbound him? Had the fire burnt through the cords?

Later he could imagine how he looked, the sun rising behind him over the ocean as he drifted out away from the beach, silhouetting his struggling figure, pink rays piercing between the palm fronds and grass shoots they had glued to his body. Somebody had made sure that the porcupine got its spines back. The truth came slowly to his suffering brain. By the time he sat down, relieved, in the boat, only the faint shadows of the dancing Nunca were visible on the beach.

The provisions ran out long before he was rescued. He had eaten everything in the boat and nibbled away his own vegetable quills, but the sauce had baked into his skin and could not be licked off no matter how he tried. He digested the bitter irony of finally being baked alive by the ocean sun and became delirious with his own ill-remembered stories.

The Basque whalers who rescued Newton took him for a native of the not too distant Americas and rejoiced at the prospect of selling him to some count or duke back home. For the first few days, Newton too thought he was a Nunca. The sailors enjoyed his strange savage imagination and marvelled at his rustic Spanish as he told them the Nunca legends. They asked about gold, and he told them reluctantly that they would have to go far, far inland to find any, amongst the deserts, perhaps. This put off the whalers.

One day a Galician amongst the crew recognized a few words in the savage's own language. So it was true, he said, bragging to his Basque shipmates, who never believed him, his Celtic forefathers had found America long ago. The natives of America were Galician, or Irish or Bretons at worst, but certainly Celts. His people had always known it. Newton realized that he had been speaking Cornish. His mother's tongue, the tongue of his childhood, of nursery stories and lullabies. He began to remember who he really was.

Upon arrival back in port, Newton's adoptive Galician brother gave up his share of the whaling catch to take Newton home. At Vigo, Newton escaped the Galician, left him a few pearls that he'd found stuck to his body when he finally bathed, and shipped out on a small boat smuggling Spanish wine to England.

When he returned home to Newquay, nothing remained of his family and nobody remembered the boy who had gone to sea. What was one more George who had gone to sea? Besides, he was strange and dark-skinned and spoke foreign languages when he thought no one was listening. Within a week of returning homc he was turned in as a Spanish spy. He was interrogated and lightly tortured. It is impossible to say if anyone believed any of his stories and if they did, which. The admiralty archives have some records of a George Villanova providing information on Spanish fleet movements. The home office has notes on the Cadiz Treasure Galleon routes attributed only to the initials JVN.

Whatever George told the admiralty and whatever was believed, he was released as harmless after a few years. He wrote his famous *Narrative,* bought a part share in a small inn with the proceeds and made it prosper in part because of his own storytelling. He may have married. He may have found his brothers. Some of them may be my ancestors. I don't really want to find out. Or perhaps I merely do not want to find out that it is not true. I would rather preserve the possibility that it might be true and never know for sure.

While I was in Italy researching Medici loans for American exploration, I met a woman who told me she was descended from a group of American Indians who spoke a language structurally very similar to Welsh. I had never been to a party like that, hundreds of people moving through a huge Florentine palazzo, mingling, introducing themselves, drifting away if you bore them. I lost track of this woman and kept trying to find her again. Too late I wondered if her Welsh Indians might be George Newton's Nunca. When I next saw her she was telling another man that she had formed a cult somewhere in the Norwegian Arctic. The poor girl was a disciple of that other cult, the cult of fame. Later, I heard her claiming to be a Dadaist poetess. I sympathized. I recognized her desire to stand out, to be exceptional. The same desire makes me want to believe that George Newton, alias Jorge Villa Nueva, was my ancestor. Her strange, desperate fibs served as a sort of warning.

Whether it is misinformation in His Majesty's secret service, oaths made to his Indian captors or merely the undisciplined imagination of Jorge Villa Nueva, nothing in George Newton's narrative is to be taken as unquestionably true. Who knows if Villa Nueva ever visited America, much less was shipwrecked (or marooned or kidnapped) and lived for twenty years amongst the natives of Florida (or the Carolinas, or Hispaniola, or whichever Caribbean island he claims at any point)? It matters to some, but not to me. It is a story I can tell my children as if it might be true, and they can decide for themselves what they want to believe.

TENEBRIAN CHRONICLES

During the eighth century, Viking raids emptied the monasteries of the Faeroe Isles, most of the monks retreating to the relative safety of Ireland. The abbot of St Jerome in the Faeroes, however, had long felt that his community was not isolated enough. He led his order instead northward in search of a more remote refuge. In tiny oxhide-covered boats the monks of St Jerome sailed north and west until they reached the islets of the Jan Mayen ridge. There, on the perimeter of the Arctic Circle, they established the abbey we now call Tenebris.

It's difficult to know anything certain about this northernmost outpost of Celtic Christianity. It was a community defined by silence, isolation and darkness. And these qualities are its legacy. The abbey's own records, the unauthorized *Retrospectives*, are inherently unreliable, and the only confirmed external record of the monastery is a single Icelandic saga. Norse trade traffic must have only brushed Tenebris, because the reference is only a brief episode in the *Skraeleg Saga* and no other saga mentions the hermits of the Mayens at all. In the *Skraeleg Saga* a wandering longboat crew is forced to winter at the abbey. The monks' refusal to speak disturbed the gregarious seamen. They referred to the Tenebrians as wizards and soothsayers, strange monikers for Christian monks, but perhaps, as we shall see, not inappropriate ones. The Vikings were quick to be off again in the spring and apparently no other longboat followed their route to Tenebris.

Despite its isolation, the abbey persevered a surprisingly long time. As the first generation of monks died off, the ranks of the Tenebrians seem to have been bolstered by newly displaced monks from elsewhere in the North Atlantic. The island's population must have been maintained for several hundred years by refugees alone, because there is no evidence that the monastery was known in Ireland or any of its more neighbourly islands.

The abbey's library testifies to Tenebris's complete isolation. Like Iona and Lindisfarne, St Jerome's was a book-producing abbey. At its height up to thirty scribes toiled in the scriptorium, but none of the Tenebris editions ever left the island. A large store of glass bottles was found adjacent to the scriptorium, which suggests at least one possible publication method, but it seems never to have been employed.

Historians, though thankful for the many excellent copies of the Vulgate and early Johanite writings preserved on Tenebris, still marvel that the monks continued to write without any hope of reaching an audience. Motivation, however, was the least of the Tenebrians' worries.

Tenebris suffered the usual solar awkwardness of the Arctic Circle. For the indulgence of a few weeks' midnight sun they had to endure the penance of several months' total darkness. The scriptorium was completely dark for three months every year, making writing impossible. During the months of midnight sun the monks must have written both day and night to have produced all the books discovered in their library. Their scriptorium was roofless. It must have been covered with some translucent fabric or skin to allow the pale Arctic light to drift into the room.

Life could not have been easy for these northern hermits. Some perverse gyre of the North Atlantic drift may have warmed them occasionally, but the islets of the Jan Mayen ridge could never have been hospitable. The saga writer says even the Greenlanders pitied them.

The monks did keep cattle and sheep, and their seed bins show that they worked wonders with the hardy northern grasses. Their refuse pits also contain bones of seals, walruses and some of the smaller whales. So they fed themselves for a while, until the little ice age crept up and choked the settlement. The skeletons of the last inhabitants are stunted and bent from vitamin deficiencies.

The Tenebrian codices themselves are a testimony to the monks' resourcefulness. They used sealskin for vellum, walrus ivory, narwhal horn and puffin feathers for styluses. They evolved a spartan and curiously modern script that is readable in the dimmest light. Magnificent as their copies are, Tenebris's greatest treasures are the manuscripts they copied from. Many of these books, their jewelled covers hacked off to save them from plunder, are unique. A few of the North African texts are now coveted by the wealthiest of bibliophiles and the few libraries in the world that can compete with them.

But these prizes of early Christian literature were not the Tenebrians' only sources of inspiration. The Tenebrian monks lived to write. They were not authors in the modern sense. Their humility precluded invention, but in the darkness and isolation of the Arctic, the monks learned that, though their vocation was not to create but to copy, this does not always require a book.

The solitude, the silence and the alternating extremes of darkness and light must have affected the monks deeply. The black winter months deprived the monks of all stimuli. Without sound, without light, with only the touch of cold stone and the taste of salted seal flesh, their minds groped for other inspiration. Some of their more obscure manuscripts transcribe dream visions rather than any paper text. Hallucinations, like those Byrd underwent during the winter he spent alone in Antarctica, mingled with the mysticism of Celtic Christianity to inspire some of the abbey's more fantastical works.

Alternative Histories

Before its dissolution, the Faeroe abbey maintained an excellent historical chronicle. The monks brought the chronicle to Tenebris, but the new monastery's isolation made it difficult to maintain. Even so, the resourceful monks persisted, relying on meditation to continue the chronicle. All the entries after 768 are the product of dream visions.

The accuracy of the early entries is astonishing. But the monks' visions slowly began to stray from the course of true history. The Hungarian commentator Merovic describes it thus: 'As if to refute their fear that the world is already exhaustive and exhausting, the Tenebrians duplicate its complexities in the kaleidoscopic mirror of hallucinatory mysticism.'

By the time the monks began documenting the future, they had veered far from the true line of history.

Writing was the only outlet for the scribes' repressed creative energy, and the brevity of the chronicle entries gave them too little opportunity to exercise it.

Once the restraining hand of reported fact was withdrawn, the monks found it difficult to confine themselves to just a few sentences a year. Since revealed truth imposed no temporal restrictions, in the last decade of the ninth century the chronicles rushed ahead in history. The entries remain terse and laconic. The remarkable restraint of the dream scholars is apparent throughout, for dreams are rarely as factual as this:

1014 In this year on Good Friday, Brian King of all Ireland and Holy Roman Emperor was slain at Clontarf.

1520 In this year Bishop Mount-Sumen of Mexico was slain.

1758 Shooting stars were common.

The chronicle's style remained remarkably consistent, a catalogue of natural occurrences, catastrophes, battles, the crowning and death of kings and bishops. Most entries are obscure, banal and unilluminating. To us their continuing preoccupation with church affairs and the country that had forgotten them is strange, but not incomprehensible.

The chronicles are remarkably prescient on the troubles of the church; schisms and dogmatic quarrels abound. As many popes are assassinated and heretics burned in the chronicles as in recorded history, though the names and theological reasons do not always correspond.

Interesting too is how mundane concerns from before their Tenebrian isolation creep into the monks' manuscripts, becoming distorted, exaggerated, almost obsessive. The original abbey of St Jerome in the Faeroes had always been in the shadow of the more populous and financially successful abbey of St Murdo in the Hebrides. The abbey of St Murdo attracted many more novices than St Jerome and greater patronage from their families. This may be due to the relative popularity of their specialities: St Jerome was famous for its scriptorium, St Murdo for its distillery. St Murdo built a high defensive walls and hired a small contingent of mercenaries to defend itself against Viking raids. As a consequence, when the raids came, the longboats always made for the much more vulnerable target of St Jerome.

On Tenebris the old jealousy of St Murdo festered. The Tenebrians must have fretted over the success that St Murdo might attain in their absence. Tenebrian envy leeched into their visions. Very few years go by in the chronicles without some small disaster or minor outrage befalling St Murdo: a young girl manages to fool the abbey and takes holy orders, villagers are poisoned by the poorly preserved beer, the abbot is discovered not to know a word of Latin. The most obvious manifestation of this obsessive jealousy appears not in the chronicles themselves, but in a short history on the subject of St Murdo.

The Lamentable History and Heretical Abominations of St Murdo's Abbey manages to invent a heretic named Raymond Lull. The Tenebrian's Lull claimed that the Holy Spirit was present through transubstantiation in any distilled spirit or *aqua vitae*. He also asserted that a mechanical device could more perfectly describe God than man. *The Lamentable History* chronicles how these twin heresies consumed the Abbey of St Murdo. The monks drank themselves senseless every night in the hopes that some revelation would come to them through the spirit of alcohol. They began building demonic machines designed to predict the future and determine the nature of God. An outraged Pope had no choice but to condemn the entire community and to impose a permanent interdict on the abbey. Perhaps the Tenebrians rested better at night after they wrote this. A particular irony of this hallucinatory fiction is that the Abbey of St Murdo was eventually closed due to heresy, not for anything so colourful as becoming drunken engineers, but because of a misinterpretation of John Scotus Erigena's *De divisione naturae* that the local bishop was able to convince the inquisitors was tantamount to pantheism.

Alternative Philosophies

It's possible to see a sort of guilty psychological projection in the heresy the Tenebrians invented for their rivals at St Murdo. The isolation of the Tenebrians engendered a unique philosophy that justified their peculiar methods. Their fundamental belief, which has been termed hyper-Platonism, was that truth lay beyond the reach of the senses, and that it was foolish to try to attain it through their agency. This philosophy made a virtue of necessity. The Arctic night deprived the monks of their eyesight, so they comforted themselves by claiming that the senses corrupted truth and were not to be trusted. There's evidence that the monks 'improved' their isolation by abjuring the other senses, plugging their ears and stopping their noses, though Merovic claims that this last device was the only way to make seal flesh tolerably edible.

The Tenebrians' philosophy explored a particular crevice between skepticism and mysticism. Frequently their writings were unfathomably dour and fatalistic, claiming that the fall of man and the submission of the soul to the despotism of the senses are inevitable and ongoing. Indeed the annals often betray their underlying belief that history is the chronicle of mankind's continual fall into corruption.

This austere skepticism is not so much balanced as complicated by a giddy submission to the mystical. A true, perfect history of mankind lies elsewhere, inaccessible to man as long as he is led along by his corrupt eyes, touch, hearing, taste and sense of smell, but perceptible perhaps to the undisturbed motion of the soul. The Tenebrian technique for this was to endure a winter of darkness and virtual silence in meditation and prolonged sleep, accumulating dreams and visions that could be poured out in the short summer of ecstatic writing. As the years passed the nature of this writing wanders further and further from the original goals of St Jerome's scriptorium. The monks could not confine their mystical inspirations to history. Almost inevitably, the mystical visions expanded the Tenebrians' subject matter, until their output became quite encyclopaedic.

Alternative Cosmologies

For a community isolated at the farthest reaches of the world, beyond the borders of what was even to the most expert geographers the known world, and with apparently little interest in venturing anywhere beyond their archipelago, the Tenebrians showed a surprising interest in both geography and cosmology. Most Tenebrian cosmologists pursued a strain of theoretical geography, whose main goal was to determine the shape of the earth. A series of regular polyhedra called Platonic solids were their favourite forms. The atlases of Tenebria abound with pyramidal and cubic earths. All these earths had sides of equal shape and size, of which the known world occupied only one.

In the later days of the abbey, the cosmologists of Tenebria seem to have settled on a dodecahedral earth, a Platonic solid with twelve pentagonal sides. This shape was preferred for many reasons. Primarily it aligned well with their philosophical hyper-Platonism. The pentagonal sides demonstrated the golden ratio, a theoretical constant that defied mere senses. The dodecahedralists had to refute an earlier Tenebrian theory that the cube was the inevitable shape of the earth. In Plato's hierarchy of Platonic solids, the cube represented earth, while the dodecahedron represented the invisible element of ether. The dodecahedralists argued that since the true earth could not be apprehended through the senses, the physical 'earthy' earth must be a deception and a distortion of the invisible but true ethereal and universal earth. By this logic the dodecahedron became the accepted form of the earth.

Whatever their opinion on the topology of the earth, Tenebrian cosmologists were united in the view that the universe is relatively fixed. The sun and stars do not budge. The earth, however, is far from motionless. It is falling, plummeting downwards away from the sun into darkness. Some of the *Retrospectives* describe the peculiar feeling of vertigo the monks would suffer during the winter months, when their eyes had no visual clues to deceive them that the world was still and they would become acutely aware of the earth's free-fall through space.

Alternative Geography

Tenebrian geographers used the process of divine sensory deprivation to complete their maps and accounts of terrestrial geography. Like their historian colleagues, Tenebrian geographers had no reliance on fact, and could entertain a wider scope of study than conventional geographers. Tenebrian maps show some very respectable representations of the Americas, including some major rivers, the Great Lakes, the bay that would eventually be called Hudson's Bay and a surprisingly accurate plotting of the Northwest Passage.

Nor did the monks confine themselves to the single known pentagonal face of their dodecahedral earth. The best Tenebrian atlases include maps of the other eleven faces of their 'globe'. These other planes bear frequent, subtle correspondences to the known face. A coastline may be reversed, a peninsula on our maps becoming a bay on another face, an isthmus a narrow strait, a glacial fjord a long stringy cape reaching into the sea. These contradictions or reflections took a thousand forms. They might appear in relief – a deep valley becoming a cliff on the imagined continent, or in climate – a polar sea becoming a desert, a dry plain a profuse rainforest, or a hundred other ways a map can be turned inside out and folded, and bent.

Perhaps the most famous and certainly most readable of the works of Tenebrian geography is a 'travelogue' that describes the theoretical travels of a Tenebrian monk around one adjacent face of the dodecahedral earth. In his preface the author is careful to point out that he has never left the Tenebrian archipelago himself and that the traveller is merely a device to facilitate the narration, but it is easy to forget this as you read his account. The narration is so earnest and enthusiastic and full of unnecessary detail that it is difficult to believe that the author didn't at least believe he had made these journeys.

He praises the wines of the centaurs, which he describes as light and delicately flavoured, a wonderful accompaniment for the dandelion leaves and blackberries that are the staples of the centaur's vegetarian diet. It is as if he had brought back a few bottles himself along with the recipe for centaur's salad.

When he becomes nostalgic and sentimental for the hospitality of giants, you imagine the bosom friend he made and left there in that country. The giants, he writes, are a simple, honest people, who preserve the old ways and live close to the land. Their memories are so short that they forget their own kin if they do not see them for a few days, and so they treat everyone, strangers and neighbours alike, with the same generosity, trusting that they must have met before. When the travelogue writer advises that the difficult and uncomfortable ride to the top of the Amazonian high plain is well worth the effort, you are inclined to believe him, and pencil it in for your next holiday. It is a trek, he says, that cannot be undertaken on foot and you must persuade an Amazon to carry you up the slopes on her back, but once there the vast expanse of the Amazonian Piano Grande 'fills you with a sense of awe of God's superfluous imagination. It is a mountain meadow woven like a fine lady's needlework with peonies, poppies and wild tulips. This spectacle of colour spreads as far as the horizon, bounded only by clouds.'

Alternative Zoology

The tales of travel to the pentagon next door seem to have inspired another great expansion of Tenebrian scholarship. The travelogue writer took great pains to describe the populace of this neighbouring pentagon, the centaurs, fauns, unicorns and giants that were his hosts during his grand tour. These descriptions reawakened in a new generation of Tenebrian scholars the great tradition of the medieval bestiary. The peculiar aspect of Tenebrian bestiaries is not the fantastical beasts they claim exist. All medieval bestiaries have their share of centaurs, sphinxes and sirens. It's the creatures the Tenebrians declare to be fabulous and non-existent that distinguish the Tenebrian encyclopaedia. Having examined the number of animals that are supposed to exist, Tenebrian zoologists all conclude that there are too many for this world. It's not only more than are necessary. It's more than it deserves. It's as if, suspicious and perhaps a little ashamed about their own rampant imaginations, the Tenebrians decided to compensate. This leads to mass imaginary extinctions. There are six Tenebrian bestiaries and each successive one seems to compete with the previous to declare more creatures unreal.

All Tenebrian zoologists affirm that centaurs and fauns are real. All believe in unicorns but not in horses. Two believe in lions, but not house cats. A third claims all cats, wild and domestic, are figments of sensory indulgence. Insects gradually become fewer and fewer with each new bestiary. In the last, only black flies and bees are given any credence. The last bestiary author is the stingiest with his approbation. He even claims that cows are fabulous animals, when the archaeological record shows that the Tenebrians still maintained a small herd at the time of death.

Alternative Hagiologies

That uniquely Roman Catholic blend of history and biography which documented the lives of the saints was not ignored at St Jerome's in Tenebria either. Of course the Tenebrian hagiologies were filled with highly speculative saints. There was, for example, St Peter of Giammai who founded an orphanage and school for wayward boys. His miracles include flying and purging the coast of his homeland of pirates. The Tenebrians also canonized a St Doolittle, who, a century before St Francis, preached not only to the birds, but also to the cats and dogs and in addition heard their confessions. A shadowy Tenebrian version of Joan of Arc is their Santa Alicia, who, like St Joan, led an army to defeat a tyrannical monarch. She too was a mystic to whom God spoke through all manner of animals including rabbits, dormice and even, in a slip up of Tenebrian local colour, a walrus. Most sympathetic of all to us modern readers is a certain St Carlo who underwent a sort of temptation by chocolate in order to purify himself and attain his piety.

Alternative Poetics

In most mystical literature, for example the dream poetry of Anglo-Saxon England or the writings of St John, allegory and symbolism are the dominant literary tropes. Platonism and allegory usually go hand in hand, but this is not usually the case in Tenebrian literature. Tenebrian poetics argue against this at every turn. 'The representation of things unseen by things seen does a great injury to God,' writes one Tenebrian scholar. 'A clean cloth does not make the soot of the fireplace clean. Instead the dirt mars the white linen, and so those things that are divine and perceptible only to the spiritual senses are marred and sullied when represented by objects of the sensual world.'

What's most amusing about this passage is that the earnest literary critic goes on for several pages after this apologizing and decrying the inadequacy of his own simile. Objects of the divine senses are not the same as white linen. It is a gross misrepresentation to suggest so. His apology is many pages longer than the simile itself. He ends in a defeated tone that is almost pathetic, suggesting that all writing may indeed be folly and that in an unfallen world, writing would be unnecessary.

At several points in the history of the abbey's Tenebrian exile there was a debate as to whether they should continue to write at all. Many Tenebrian literary theologians believed that the essential form of any true story was not in words or in earthly events but in the body of an angelic messenger, whose meaning was pure and lucid to God, but which was inevitably distorted and refracted by human interpretation. When an angel appeared on earth, its meaning (the monks used the Latin word *sententia*) was dragged through the mud of human history or human language and grossly marred. If this continued long enough, the angel would retreat to the celestial sphere and abandon all hope of communicating with mankind.

This curious pessimism combined with the belief in eternal return, according to the unreliable *Retrospectives*, caused frequent seasons of crisis in the abbey. As angels return to the earth and continue to be distorted by human language, the Tenebrians reasoned, the same errors are repeated and worsened. They asked themselves, 'How can we believe that anything we have to say has not been said before? How can we believe that we are not compounding old errors with new?' Despairing they would never be able to purge themselves of sensory distortions to access the true divine message, they frequently descended into creative apathy. During these seasons of pessimism little new work was done at the abbey, and the monks contented themselves with copying old texts in a resigned attempt to accelerate the exhaustion of stories and hasten the final impact of man's fall. These passions never persisted. The monks' restless imaginations always resurfaced and blossomed into yet another generation of Tenebrian mystical writing.

A Fugitive from Tenebria

Though the Icelandic saga is the only confirmed external reference to the Tenebrian community there are those who suggest that the sixteenth-century travel narrative by a Cornish sailor, George Newton, is a crypto-

Tenebrian text. Newton claimed to have been held captive by American Indians and that he was forced to recite stories for their amusement. The religion of these Indians appears remarkably similar to the Tenebrians' peculiar form of Christianity, especially the aspect of stories as spiritual entities or angels. Some of the Indian dialect given in Newton's narrative could also be a phonetic representation of archaic Irish Gaelic and High Church Latin vocabulary.

Two *Retrospectives* refer to a shipwrecked sailor who refused to be integrated into their order and whose barbarism, love of drink and indiscriminate sexual appetites were incompatible with monastic life. It is tempting to identify Newton with this character from the *Retrospectives*, but Newton's dates disagree with archaeology by a century or so. The abbey would have been silent for a hundred years by the time of Newton's voyage to the Americas.

The Last Days of Tenebris

The Tenebrians' disregard for conventional chronology makes it difficult to tell how long the abbey persisted on the penumbra of the Arctic Circle. Early researchers, assuming complete isolation and the unequivocal monastic rule, naturally gave the monastery a single human life span of seventy years. Archaeology has extended their stay. The monks kept a cemetery on one of the archipelago's smaller outlying islets. The soil, seized by permafrost, yielded to digging machines to reveal a surprisingly large number of graves. These graves are the best measure of how long the abbey of St Jerome flourished on Tenebris. If we can believe the dates on the headstones, the last monk was interred there around 1340. From 1250 to this date there was a gradual decrease in bone size, as the barren islands became more so. Volcanic activity in the region submerged many of the islands and seriously diminished others in the late 1400s. Simultaneously the Little Ice Age began to edge its glaciers over what remained. So we can establish a fairly secure *terminus ad quem* for the Tenebrian community.

All the bodies buried in the Tenebris cemetery were male, confirming that the community was sustained by refugees alone. New members might have been deposited by disdainful Viking traders. North Atlantic storms might have shipwrecked a few flimsy skin coracles, making novices out of their fisherman pilots. But weather and dwindling population finally did the abbey in. Its silence was absolute for four centuries.

Jenkinson and Barents both managed to miss the smaller Mayens when they explored the region in the late sixteenth century. Baron Nordenskiold stumbled on them fortuitously in the year 1869, the exact year of the last entry in the Tenebrian Chronicles. He searched fruitlessly for the inhabitants who he assumed had just recently finished the article.

The Retrospectives

Of the documents Nordenskiold's expedition is said to have carried off are some charts related to the Peri Reis map, a translation of the Revelation into Inuit and the furtive *Retrospectives.* The *Retrospectives* were chronicles in which the monks documented the history of their own abbey and of its inhabitants. These texts were influenced by a certain amount of wishful thinking. In them, the rediscovery of the abbey and their return to civilization was just around the corner.

The suppression of idle wish-fulfilment may have been one reason for the abbot's numerous decrees against such writing. There also seems to be a general belief though that the self is not a fit subject for meditation and mystical dictation, and that wish-fulfilment, like self-expression, is a feeble excuse for the use of sealskin and precious light. The subject should not contemplate itself, its own history or its own future. Even revelation cannot penetrate the self-interest and sensory illusion that governs self-reflection. By this thinking, even this very text is questionable.

THE COLLECTOR

I've been asked to write a short biographical essay, a sort of memoir, a history of my successes and the growth of my business. I yawn just thinking about it. What's the point? There are hundreds of books by us so-called business leaders. How can we believe that anything we have to say has not been said before? We boast of our origins, humble if not plain abject. We expose our great ambition and our positive philosophies, but does any one of us give away the secret? Does any one of us know the secret? We all think we do, and I am old and bored enough to provide my own version. You can take it for what it is, but it is really only meant for one man, a man who long ago stopped listening to me.

I have yet to meet a successful entrepreneur who isn't a collector of some sort, who did not, early in his life, come upon a single fine example of a certain type of object and almost instantly covet a room of objects just like it. It used to surprise me how many of my clients and partners told the same story of that childhood discovery, how one object's uniqueness touched them beyond anything they had previously known and yet how that object excited a need to find more like it, as if multiplying it would define and complete it, or somehow affirm its reality. I have seen articulate men and powerful speakers reduced to wordlessness trying to describe the paradox of that first specimen's awesome strangeness and the necessary existence of more just like it, the need to continually relive the thrill of discovery and ownership it gave them.

It is such a common story that it no longer surprises me when an associate tells me over dinner that he has a prized collection of fossilized camels, or a casual conversation on a long flight turns to my row mate's collection of Negro League baseball gloves. I have my theories about the relationship between our collections and our success, best illustrated by explaining how my own collection began.

My humble origins are the banal constant of every business journal article and every preamble to the conferment of an honorary degree. I grew up on Fogo Island in northern Newfoundland. My father repaired boats. My mother worked part time for a lumber company and most of my schoolmates would grow up to achieve similar, more or less happy lives. But none of them found the bottle that I found. As an eleven-year-old, I did not know that the Labrador Current finished its brusque sweep of the Davis Strait at my doorstep, nor that it was fed at the north end of the Labrador Sea by the East Greenland Current. I should have known these things, growing up in a community that still scraped much of its subsistence from the sea and in the Viking-crazy decade after L'Anse aux Meadows had been uncovered, but I was an averagely ignorant child. I didn't care for much more than iceberg spotting, beachcombing and poking washed-up sea animals with sticks. It was during one of these multidisciplinary outings that I discovered the bottle.

The bottle, I now know, was manufactured at the Pärnu glassworks in present-day Estonia. It originally held a type of aquavit distilled for centuries in Pärnu, and though the bottle is embossed with an image of the Swedish warship *Vassa*, after 1721 the spirits it contained were known as Peter the Great Vodka. Whether the vodka was Swedish or Russian, the bottle's last liquid contents were not vodka or aquavit, but Polar bear blubber. Residue of this blubber has helped preserve and complicate the dating of the note inside.

The note is fascinating, but it was years before I could read it. When I first found it I did not even know what language it was written in. It was as opaque and inscrutable as the bottle itself, which, though originally clear, was blackened on the inside by bear grease and buffed on the outside by the friction of North Atlantic ice floes. The bottle was so dark I didn't see the note inside. My first impulse, when I saw the bottle there entangled in seaweed amongst the round shore rocks, was to smash it. Few things are more pleasant to a young boy's hand than the high arc of a lofted object or to his ear than that predictable explosion of glass. I will never know what stopped me. Some small spark of curiosity delayed the sure pleasure of bottle smashing. Something must have told me this bottle was different from the whisky bottles tossed from the fishing trawlers off the coast or the screech jugs hurled by my older schoolmates off the headlands on death-wish Friday nights. I rinsed the bottle off in a tidal pool and held it up to the sun, admiring the cumulative effect of the ocean's buffeting as much as the embossed warship on the bottom. Both of these things made it old, and its being old made me want to keep it.

Before I satisfied the growing impulse to show someone my 'cool old bottle' I had to empty it out. Scavenged bottles never have their stoppers. They're always empty or clogged with debris. This one seemed full of sea junk, bits of seaweed, bark or something, but as I pulled all this away I found the cork. I used my penknife to pry it out. This was a struggle of some ten minutes, but when I finally tossed the shredded cork aside, I saw the bottle was not empty. It took me a further half an hour with a hooked stick to fish out the paper that was curled around the inside.

The paper, brown and oil-stained, crammed with indecipherable black characters, changed the meaning of the bottle. It transformed it from a cool old bottle into a sort of emblem. I kept my message in a bottle locked away, showing it to no one for years, steeping it in significance. It triggered the sequence of events that made me what I am today. Because of that message in a bottle I learned a little of half a dozen languages, and conceived a passion for acquisition that has fuelled not only my collection, but also my business dealings. This single object has meant more to me than anything I have ever owned. But after all these years, even now that I have deciphered the words, I have no idea what the note truly signifies. I cannot decide whether the writer was insane, truthful or just pulling the leg of the imagined discoverer of his note.

The author of the note was Jonas Gjudson. He was either Finnish or wrote in Finnish because he assumed a Finn would find his message. Gjudson was stranded on an ice floe when he wrote his message, but it is not a rescue plea. It is a confession. Gjudson was an explorer whose ship became trapped in the Arctic ice while searching for the Northwest Passage. The ice slowly ground his ship to splinters, leaving him and his crew on the Arctic ice. One by one the crew succumbed to frostbite and starvation. Gjudson confesses that he has just killed the last remaining survivor, poisoned him with arsenic in his aquavit, perhaps poured from the very same bottle that carried the message.

The Northwest Passage was a Gjudson family passion. Jonas's father Ulrich had disappeared twenty years before trying to discover it. Jonas Gjudson believed that his father had found the Northwest Passage on that voyage, and that a secretive Venetian conglomerate had murdered his father because the Passage jeopardized its lucrative overland route to China. The man Jonas murdered was an old friend of Ulrich Gjudson, an Englishman named Matthew Jenkins. Jonas despised Jenkins, and had always suspected he was a Venetian agent. When his own expedition failed, Jonas blamed Jenkins, and finally exacted his revenge with the poisoned aquavit.

By the time Jonas Gjudson wrote his confession, he knew that Jenkins was no spy. The conspiracy against him and his father was merely the fabrication of his boyish imagination, calcified by time and paranoia into fact. Jenkins's papers contained several letters from the elder Gjudson to Jenkins. One letter begged Jenkins to look after the boy and his mother if anything happened to him. Another gave instructions on how to find and decipher coded messages concealed in five books in his library. These messages would exonerate Ulrich Gjudson if ever he were imprisoned and accused of treason. Jonas Gjudson, now grown, faced with his own death on the Arctic ice, realized the terrible error of his childhood. His entire fantasy of the Northwest Passage had been based on those books. He destroyed those books himself, believing them to be evidence the Venetian conspiracy could use against his father. By destroying them, Jonas had condemned his father to death. And now following some half-conceived theory about the Northwest Passage from one of those books, Gjudson condemned himself and his crew to death. He had killed the man his father trusted to protect him.

That is the terrible, implausible content of my first message in a bottle. Distilled by an addled mind, fertile imagination or some arcane conspiracy of the past, it is as strange as I ever wanted it to be. I have no desire to research its origins. I have never been tempted to track down more information about Jonas Gjudson, his unfortunate father and the friend, Jenkins, who was powerless to save either of them. (I am curious about the books though. I would hunt them down if Gjudson hadn't said he destroyed them. They would make a fine collection too.) The message in this bottle is that the universe is vast, incomprehensible and expansive. It gives me confidence that there is no natural limit to my own expanding ambitions. This is the connection between collecting and successful entrepreneurs.

I kept my message in a bottle wrapped in an old sweater inside a locked steel box at the bottom of my closet. I took it out only occasionally, not wanting to spoil its strangeness through over-examination. It became a sort of totem, a talisman for a world outside my little village, a world that had never before interested me, but was now crucial. This one message in a bottle might have been enough for some people, but not me. It was too much and yet not enough. It was a prize specimen, a singular object, but to me it hinted at a world of singular objects. When I lay in bed at night I imagined my bottle bobbing its way across the Arctic Ocean to me, scuffed by ice floes, seized by congealing ice each winter, slipping free each spring to continue its journey, rolling endwise across nighttime seas. And in daydreams of my bottle's voyage, I saw more bottles, dozens, hundreds of bottles populating my imaginary ocean, racing along like sticks in a creek race, criss-crossing each other, some smashing, some falling to the ocean bed and sinking into silt. All of them, I knew, contained messages. The world had five oceans of messages in bottles, hundreds of proofs of the world's strangeness. And I coveted them.

I never stopped going down to the shore to look for bottles, but I knew I would never repeat my lucky find. I always knew that I would have to be rich. So I became rich, in order to collect bottles. I always think it's funny to say that, but it is a simple truth. I amassed my fortune for the single purpose of expanding my collection of messages in bottles. But the message in a bottle provided more than motivation. It provided the intellectual means. It instilled in me the ideal moral conditions to achieve what I wanted, the imperial mindset of all collectors, the belief that they deserve to have more. It is a sad truism that great men succeed because they believe they deserve to succeed. Little men fail because they believe that to exceed a certain boundary is to be greedy. They believe there should be limits, that there is such a thing as excess. A great man never believes in any limitations. His collection tells him that it can never be complete. There are no limits. He is not morally bounded by any measure of 'enough'. There is always more out there.

Today I am rich by most people's standards, but there are still many men wealthier than I, men who could buy up my enterprises without stretching their credit. I don't compete with them. I know the world is wide enough for us all. I can expand within my own space indefinitely. My business or businesses involve the oil industry – transportation, logistics, support services, infinite divisions of small tasks. Offshore oil is my focus, for the simple reason that I like to have my people near the sea. I have offices near most of the world's great bottle hunting grounds. It's a nice parallel task and has not distorted my business unduly. The collection and my business grow very nicely alongside each other.

My second message in a bottle did not come directly from the sea. I bought it at auction. The bottle was one of the hundreds of bizarre objects in the collection of a nineteenth-century Danish Curio Museum. At auction the big money was spent on the skeletons of a dwarf couple and the stuffed Himalayan 'yeti'. The yeti was a clever conglomeration of bear, elk and albino mountain gorilla parts sewn together by some gifted taxidermist, but this did nothing to diminish its value at auction. It went for more than half a million. You may think it's more than it deserves, but the idea that someone applied such expertise and imagination to a fake and someone else went to a similar effort to debunk it makes it as valuable and as collectible as an actual yeti. A collector of famous frauds snapped it up.

I often go to such auctions now for the company of other collectors. It is good to be amongst your kind, but the Danish curio auction was my first. Riley, an employee who'd shown some interest in my first bottle, accompanied me that day. I watched with pleasure as other collectors acquired their Indian erotica and their mummified Vheissan spider monkeys, but Riley was disappointed. The message in a bottle did not attract many bidders, and I was able to take it home for just a little more than the reserve price. Riley had expected something more dramatic, more competitive. He couldn't see that competition was not the point. This misunderstanding of his has caused more than a few problems since.

I was not there to impress Riley. I claimed my message in a bottle and have been very pleased with it. This bottle now shares a certain notoriety and ill repute with its housemate the fraudulent yeti, but this was not always the case. There's nothing about the bottle to suggest that it's a fake. It was originally found in the Faeroe Islands. The bottle is Venetian, made in the eighth century. The message inside is on vellum. I've since had the vellum analyzed and it turns out to be sealskin. Initially only the message was implausible.

The text on the sealskin describes, in good medieval church Latin, a year in the life of a certain northern abbey. It declares itself to be the 667th annual volume of a chronicle of the Abbey of Tenebria. Primarily a list of deaths, illnesses and new novices, its most interesting part is the introductory gloss, which abstracts the previous several hundred years of the abbey's history. The abbey was formed in the early ninth century by a group of Irish monks who, driven out of their Hebridean monastery by Viking raids, fled northward to a group of islands 'beyond Thule', which they call Tenebria.

On Tenebria the monks continued the work of their old abbey, transcribing church texts and chronicling the history of the world. The abbey's northern location made this difficult. There were months when they were totally without light. This not only stopped them from writing, it also had strange psychological effects. During the dark Arctic winter the monks would hallucinate and imagine they were seeing events in the outer world. They emerged to light each spring to document these visions in their histories. If the message in this bottle is to be believed, there are some six centuries of alternative history inspired by the monks' nighttime hallucinations.

The whole story is improbable. How the monastery survived after the first generation of monks expired is half explained by the chronicle. There are entries about shipwrecked fishermen being taken into the monastery, and there is a cryptic reference to novices who were 'fished from the shoals of savages'. We have to imagine the abbey mounting recruitment raids on Inuit Greenland and seizing the occasional washed-up European, but it is a stretch.

Half a century after the first Tenebrian *Chronicle* and its bottle became famous, an Orkney kelp baron and minister's son named James Urquhart began selling the Tenebrian histories he found in the family manse. The new *Chronicles* cast a shadow of fraudulence on the whole story that has never been removed.

Urquhart's Tenebrian histories were far more outlandish than the original *Chronicle*. They described grand conspiracies to conceal the existence of America, angels who came down to earth to reveal the secrets of the pyramids to shoemakers, wars fought beneath the earth in the tunnels formed by ancient volcanoes. The fantastical histories were gobbled up by collectors throughout Europe and the Americas. Brigham Young University apparently has the largest collection of these now.

Urquhart became quite wealthy. A man after my own heart, he used his wealth to finance his own collection (wives apparently). But the bubble soon burst. No one could disprove the authenticity of the texts themselves, but the bottles were suspect. Sealskin vellum may be acquired in the Orkneys, but medieval blown glass bottles are more scarce. An island glass blower, disgruntled with his meagre share in the profits, confessed to making the bottles for his neighbour, the kelp farmer, and the thriving trade in bottled alternative histories came to a halt.

The kelp baron's father was probably the genius behind the Tenebrian fakes. Before his exile to the Orkneys, Urquhart senior was a minister in Edinburgh whose unconventional beliefs got him chased from the pulpit. Influenced by Swedenborg and perhaps some personal version of Leibnitz, the minister preached that the world was merely one of an infinite number of possible illusions and that if it were possible to free oneself of the tyranny of the senses one could perceive these other realities. This fantastical skepticism is too close to the Tenebrian world view to be mere coincidence. It has persuaded most historians that the monastery never existed, that the original *Chronicle* and the histories are all fakes.

I reserve judgment. There's nothing about my Tenebrian message in a bottle to prove it's fake. It is a beautifully paradoxical object, valid yet implausible. In the years since I bought the original *Chronicle*, I have obtained a few of the later histories too. They still keep turning up along the North Coast of Scotland. It seems the Orkney squire got rid of his stash before he was exposed and moved to Australia. My people pick them up in the fishing villages, from trawler captains and oil rig operators in the North Sea. My employees are always on the lookout. They know they can earn a nice bonus if they turn up some gem. I have the *Chronicles* of year 1014, in which Brian Buru is killed, and 1758, which mentions Halley's comet. These messages in bottles belong in the second tier of my collection, but I still value them.

Despite my love of auctions, I still get many of my messages in bottles from the sea itself. Besides my operations in the north of Scotland at the tail end of the North Atlantic Drift, I have businesses in many of the world's great bottle-hunting grounds: Kamchatka, Tasmania, Tierra del Fuego and the Comoros Islands in the Indian Ocean.

My young friend Riley made the best catch of all himself. Riley is a meteorological statistician, a man with uncanny instincts. He claims he can smell a cyclonic storm and feel low pressure systems in the arches of his feet. One summer in the Comoros, Riley watched some fisherman haul a blue bottle out of their net. At the sight of the bottle, the fishermen began slapping their foreheads with their palms and wailing as if some great calamity had befallen them. The bravest of the Comorans plucked the bottle gingerly from the net and threw it with all his might back into the ocean, but this did little to calm the nerves of the fishermen. They continued to howl and curse the ocean.

Riley watched this all with great interest while the blue bottle bobbed harmlessly some twenty metres away. When they were exhausted from tearing up their nets trying to destroy their boat, Riley tried to get an explanation out of the fishermen. The Comorans declared hysterically that the bottle was cursed. This same bottle turned up every few years to curse whoever had found it. Everyone associated with the bottle would be visited with calamity. Your nets would tear. Your boat would rot. The fish you caught would poison you. Your wife would leave you. Your unwed daughter would get pregnant. Tourists would discover your village.

Nothing could undo the curse. It stayed with you until someone else pulled the bottle out of the ocean. By that time, if you were still alive, your life was already ruined.

Riley sensed a nice bonus in that bottle. He tried to take it right away, but the villagers would not let him touch the bottle. They didn't want it anywhere near them. They wanted the ocean to take it away, so Riley stationed a man at the end of the pier to keep an eye on the bottle until nightfall. When the sun went down and the only sound was the wailing of the cursed fishermen and their families, Riley fished the bottle out of the ocean again.

Riley was right. He always had good instincts. The bottle did contain a note. It earned him a substantial bonus, though not as substantial as he would later come to feel he deserved. The bottle is a gorgeous cobalt blue with a pure silver stopper. It always amazes me that every person who ever found it eventually convinced himself to throw it back into the sea. It is so obviously valuable. It must carry a powerful taboo. Since acquiring it I've done some research and found that the legend of the cursed bottle is not isolated to the Comoros. It is well known in Madagascar, Zanzibar, the Seychelles, Oman and on the other side of the Indian Ocean in Sri Lanka and India's Gulf of Kutch. The Somali current stirs the Indian Ocean like a cauldron and spins the cursed bottle around all these shores.

The note inside the cobalt-blue bottle is written on papyrus. The calligraphy is exquisite, unmarred by moisture or time. I have had half a dozen scholars examine it and all agree that the characters are Persian. Some of my experts claim that the words are meaningless, others suspect it is a code. At least two scholars claim to know the code. They say it is a cryptic symbolic language used by the dervishes of a small Sufi sect for translations of sacred documents that should not be spoken aloud. Both scholars refuse to translate the message. They will only paraphrase. Their translations are vague and roundabout. What's there is just a semblance, a faded cipher of what was intended or envisioned.

According to my two Persian experts the message is written in the pompous and bombastic tone of the djinn, the demons of Arabian legends. This djinni (or genie) declares that he was captured on paper, tricked by a calligrapher, who, disguised as a concubine, tricked him into telling the story of his origins and his powers. Neither of my crazy Persian scholars will tell me what this story is, what these powers might be. They claim they don't dare read that part. Speaking the words of this story aloud will release the djinni. Everyone knows, they say, that the written word is the enemy of all djinn. Bottles and written texts are the only containers that can hold them.

My two dervish experts aren't about to release the all-powerful djinni from his double prison. I myself have no fear of releasing this dreaded genie, but I'm not about to learn Persian at this time in my life, never mind Sufi cultic codes, so the world is safe as long as the bottle is in my possession.

In the ten years since he found the cursed bottle, Riley has left my employ and set himself up as a sort of rival, not in business – meteorological analysis was never more than a sideline, but in collecting messages in bottles, an arena that I consider my private reserve. I had to fire Riley about a year after his great find. He'd been forging messages in bottles to make up for what he felt I owed him for the Comoran bottle. I found him out easily enough. He didn't have the means to be a successful forger. It costs more in time and money to fake a message in a bottle than to buy an authentic one at auction. Riley's bottles were never quite right. His notepaper was always from the wrong century. I think he's realized that was a dead end. These days I enjoy turning up at auctions to outbid him.

I owe so much to Riley though. It is a shame he had to leave the company. He frustrates himself by trying to compete with me. He doesn't seem to have the spirit of the true collector or entrepreneur. It is too personal for him. He wants what I have, not what is infinitely available for him to claim. Riley also pushed me into a mistake, encouraging me into another hobby, a sideline of sorts, and an error of judgment on my part. In the course of my collecting I have assembled quite a group of experts to help me investigate my bottles. I have excellent calligraphers on staff and linguistics experts on retainer. I am a patron of several of the world's leading paper-makers and glassblowers. My contributions to certain scientific institutes make mass spectrometers and carbon-dating equipment available to me whenever I wish. It just happens that all of the resources necessary for the authentication of messages in bottles are the exact resources required to construct a credible fake message in a bottle.

I began my small publishing business, as I like to refer to it, as a way of testing my employees. Whenever one of my agents turns up with a bottle, I send him his bonus cheque immediately, but I make sure that he soon finds one of the fake messages in a bottle assembled by my team of craftsmen. The test for the finders is whether they remove the additional note within the bottle, which, in a very good facsimile of my old friend Riley's handwriting, explains that if you want to screw that old bastard Hughes, give him this fake bottle. The world is full of honourable men. A surprising majority of the bottles turn up with the note inside. Those that bring me my fakes without a note find that they are soon reassigned to one of the colder stations, Kamchatka or Tierra del Fuego and I begin a rigorous investigation of the first bottle they found.

It can be quite amusing to invent stories for bottles. There's an art to it, matching bottles to messages. Bottles and messages are symbiotic creatures, dual objects. They live off each other. The message and its medium must be sympathetic. The container must add something to its contents, as the buffed and opaque aquavit bottle adds obscurity to my Arctic explorer's note, as the baroquely decorated blue bottle complicates and embellishes the coded calligraphy of my genie in a bottle. It is difficult to achieve this synthesis in a fake message in a bottle. This sympathy is difficult to premeditate, but I feel I have had my successes.

In a nineteenth-century gin bottle I enclosed the confessions of a former first mate of a South Sea freighter. Dismissed for abandoning ship during a squall, he curses the moment he left the bridge, but curses more the ship that did not sink to validate his cowardice.

In an Argentine wine bottle I slipped a single sheet containing the proud last words of a South American assassin. From his exile on an island off the Pacific coast of the continent, he stands by his decision to murder the general who betrayed the cause of liberty to become a dictator. In his final words the assassin commits himself to his country with the confidence that history will make him a hero. The general never existed, nor did the country. The general's name is an anagram of my own, the country a hispanicized version of my hometown back home in Newfoundland.

In a thick, murky brown porter bottle I stuffed the memoirs of a dissolute Franciscan monk. In the best church Latin I could muster, the friar narrates his various romantic conquests with lewd detail and winking asides. The friar claims to have slept with a hundred and forty-four women. Among them are the usual blushing novices, and insatiable mothers superior, burly barmaids and not a few worried ladies who came to him to confess their barrenness, but to whom the friar miraculously provided a surrogate heir. The Franciscan Lothario doesn't pretend that he was motivated by anything but his own pleasure, but he justifies his seductions by claiming he is doing God's work by exposing corruption in women.

I bought a bottle recently that has made me think twice about falsifying messages in bottles. I outbid Riley for it at an auction in New York. It was a clear wine bottle, with cork and wax intact, and a single slip of paper was enclosed. An unopened message in a bottle always means more to me than one whose contents are known. It preserves the mystery, the romance of finding a message in a bottle on the beach. In my excitement, I probably paid too much, but I am an old man now. What else do I have to spend my money on?

After the auction I brought the bottle home and opened it carefully in my study. I was not pleased with what I found. The message is a verbatim copy of the note I wrote for the South American assassin I invented. Placing the two messages beside each other I could detect minute differences, but the penmanship appeared to be by the same hand. I knew that the calligrapher who made my note, a quiet, scholarly old Argentine gentleman, had died several years ago, or I would have flown him up immediately to question him.

All I could do was analyze and hypothesize. The bottle was historically appropriate, not completely unlike the one I had used, but not, after all, too difficult to get hold of. The wax was very convincing, saturated with just the right amount of seawater to make it seem plausible that it had floated in the ocean for a century. The provenance was shaky though. It was predictable and orthodox back through various antique dealers to a dubious curio shop in Santiago, Chile, but after that we have a nameless twelve-year-old Chilean beachcomber, who cannot now be located.

I have my doubts about this. What twelve-year-old would leave a message in a bottle unopened? Perhaps beachcombing children are more cynical these days, but I can't believe that the child knew that opening a bottle with a message diminishes its value a thousandfold. Maybe he thought that no one would believe him and he brought the bottle to an adult intact so that he would be believed. And if that adult were an antique dealer with a little knowledge of bottles and auctions.... It is all a fraction too improbable.

I want to believe that I imagined and wrote as a work of fiction a letter that existed secretly in reality for a hundred years, but only a monstrous vanity or ignorance makes it seem possible. I have plenty of both, but it's too far-fetched for even me to seriously entertain. The only logical explanation is that somebody faked this message in a bottle. Perhaps my old calligrapher was paid off. Perhaps the note is a rough draft for my original that just fell into the wrong hands. There are a few possible suspects as to whose hands these might be, but I most naturally suspect the hands that raised a paddle at the auction and bid me up to the top of the bottle's range. Now as I recollect that auction, I imagine a smug grin on Riley's face even as he lost the bidding to me.

This incident has convinced me: I have to stop inventing my own messages in bottles. I have taken it as a warning, whether cosmic or personal. I feel slightly guilty about it in retrospect, as if I did some disservice to the collection, as if my fraudulent messages in bottles insulted the authentic ones somehow. It is difficult to explain why. I know they are mere objects, but if they represent, as I have always believed, the vastness of the world, its incomprehensible detail and variety, then there would be no need to invent. The duplicate assassin's statement seems to say as much, seems to rebuke my lack of faith in the world's vastness.

I have more reason lately to believe that the Chilean fake is the work of Riley, since another dubious bottle has turned up and further muddied the waters.

I find it mildly ironic that my work in the oil business has brought me back to Newfoundland. We opened an office back home two years ago to service the Hibernia oil fields that are just beginning to open up off the Newfoundland coast. We have some old hands in the operation there, members of the so called Old Collectors' Club, men who have worked with me long enough to joke with me about the message in a bottle they are going to find and the fortune I'm going to have to pay them for it. I got a call from one of these old collectors last week. He didn't sound like a man who had found a treasure, but he said he had something, and he overnighted it to me here at head office. I understood his disappointment when I saw it. It was not a romantic's ideal of a message in a bottle. The bottle was nothing but a big glass pop bottle, Pure Springs ginger ale. I remember bottles like this from when I was a kid, before they replaced them with plastic. The message was hardly more promising, a single sheet of loose-leaf paper, folded roughly in half, the holes torn, ripped from a high-school binder, by all appearances. I could imagine its contents as well as its finder must, some pornographic graffiti by a juvenile hand, the signatures of a grade-school frog-and-firecracker cult, at best the dismal confessions of a closeted small town homosexual.

I felt sorry for the veteran of the Old Collectors' Club. He was not the sort to take this sorry example of messages in bottles as a good omen. He was not the kind of man who, having won ten dollars in the lottery, takes it as proof that he has a chance of winning a million the next time. He was the kind who believes that he had one chance at best to win anything, and that it had been wasted now on this pop bottle and loose-leaf. I sent him twice the usual bonus before I had even opened the bottle. Perhaps in retrospect that was not the wisest decision. It seems less the whim of an indulgent employer today than a bribe.

I have been collecting messages in bottles for many years now and I have seen many strange things, but I could not have been more surprised by the message in this bottle. The sheet of paper was three-quarters filled with ink, stumbling, ham-fisted penmanship, unsure of its angle of attack or its spelling, ugly but somehow familiar. The signature at the end told me why. It was a passable counterfeit of my own adolescent scrawl. In it I confess to murdering my boyhood friend Doug Biller. I allowed myself a moment of anger, uttered an ugly-sounding curse one of my Persian scholars had taught me and read the message again. I could read it a few thousand times more; it would still tell the same story.

One late Saturday night at the point above our little hamlet, my friend and I sat on the rocks with half a bottle of screech he had stolen from his older brother. We argued, about a piece of junk bicycle that he was supposed to sell me, and in our drunken tussle I pushed him down the slope, onto the rocks and into the sea. My confession, scrawled on a page ripped from a school notebook and stuffed in the bottle from which we'd drunk home brew, took the same dive into the sea.

It's all a lie of course, but it's a terrible accusation. I did have a friend who drowned when I was in high school. I seldom think about him any more, but we were close, and I've never really had a good friend since.

It makes me very sad to think Riley is behind this. It has always been too personal for Riley. It's such a disappointment, that he should take up collecting, but miss its essential message that the world is endless and full of possibility. It makes greed and rivalry stupid and petty. I don't know what I will do with him, whether it is worthwhile destroying him, being drawn down to his level, or whether there is some gesture I can make to make him see what it is all really about.

I took a good long walk this week along the beach where I found my first bottle, that story of a father and a deluded son. I did a lot of thinking about my life, my accomplishments, what is left to accomplish. I never regretted remaining single, not having a family, but it makes me a little sad to think that what I have learned will die with me. I have sent Riley a message, by bottle of course, but I am not optimistic. What is the use of writing? What will this accomplish that a hundred other arguments have not? I don't know. Perhaps he's growing older too, perhaps a little wiser. Perhaps I have appealed to his self-interest just enough.

If the currents are right he should pick it up within the month. I'll be waiting here until then and we will discuss the future and the past.

WHY ARE THERE NO PENGUINS?

It is as reasonable to represent one kind of imprisonment by another,
as it is to represent anything that really exists by that which exists not!

– Daniel Defoe, Robinson Crusoe's Preface
to the third volume of *Robinson Crusoe*

'Why doesn't the ice melt?' the boy asks.

The question alarms me. Why should he be thinking about the ice melting?

I gather my thoughts before answering the boy. 'Whatever do you mean?'

'Why doesn't the ice melt in the sea?'

I see what the boy is after now. I attack it Socratically. 'Why doesn't the sea freeze like the ice?' But the boy is no longer put off by questions as answers to questions.

'Yes,' he says. He can see it's the same question and still expects me to answer. It is a fine question too. Indeed I'm proud of the boy for asking, but I'm careful not to frighten him. I must answer the question in the spirit it was asked, in the spirit of a boy's natural curiosity, not as if it was something of direct concern.

'At times the ice is melting, but just as frequently the sea is freezing. It is a slow process in each direction. Some days the floe may shrink a few centimetres. Some days it may grow a few.'

'Is it growing or shrinking today?'

'Growing. Most definitely it is growing. Today the sea is freezing around the ice floe. It is a cold day. The sea is definitely freezing.'

The boy sniffs the air with his pointed little nose and looks around with childish indifference. He shrugs and says nothing more on the subject of our floe melting. He asks about penguins again.

'Will we see penguins?'

I don't mind explaining about penguins for the umpteenth time. I'd rather he think of penguins than fret about the integrity of this ice floe. He knows we won't see penguins. I have told him over and over again that penguins only inhabit the Antarctic region.

'We will see more puffins, and beluga and right whales, and as we drift closer to Svalbard and the Greenland current, we will encounter narwhals and walruses and perhaps some polar bears. The narwhal has a long tooth that extends from its mouth. It is known as the unicorn of the sea. The walrus ...'

'But why are there no penguins here?'

'They aren't native to the Arctic. They only inhabit the regions of the south polar sea.'

'They eat fish don't they?'

'Yes.'

'And there are lots of fish here.'

'Yes, these seas are full of cod and great shoals of herring ...'

'And they like cold weather and snow.'

'They do.'

'So *why* don't penguins live here?'

It is a great effort not to laugh at the boy's grievance. It seems a great injustice to him. All the conditions are right for penguins – there should be penguins, as if snow and ice and fish were the direct cause of penguins, that if a boy could only assemble enough snow and ice and fish in one place, he could conjure penguins.

I have no good answer for him. I have been to any number of lectures at the Geographical Society on the subject, but to me this explanation of chance and brutal competition for the phenomenon of species distribution seems inelegant. I tell the boy that each creature on this earth has its place. He knows this is not an answer, but lets it go by. He is a good lad, much too wise for his age. He knows not to press too hard. He'd rather hear a disappointing answer than have me admit that I do not know. Even so it will not stop him from asking again in a few days.

He is silent for a long time.

We left Bergen two summers ago in the *Bifrost*, sailing north and east through the Kara Sea in search of the Northeast Passage. The *Bifrost* was beset by ice in October of that year off the Taimur Peninsula. The *Bifrost* was a strong ship; I counted on it surviving the pressures of the ice, enabling us to continue eastward once more the following spring, but the ice drifted west and northward all winter. In May we were still fast in the ice. Even then we could have saved ourselves. That summer we could have made our way across the ice to Franz Josef Land or Novaya Zemlya by sleds and small boats. Instead I let my mania for the Pole override all good sense.

In truth, it had always been my secret desire to make an attempt for the Pole. I had always suspected that the currents might take us north, but not this far, not so tantalizingly close. Few have ever been to these high latitudes. The Pole seemed within reach. Surely it was worth our effort to try for it. We had already endured one winter on the ice and had provisions for another. The long Arctic winter would be easy to bear a second time if we slept with the knowledge that we had conquered the Pole.

I led a party northward by dogsled in June of last year, but illness and storms forced us to turn back. By the time we returned to the *Bifrost*, only the boy and I were left alive. I can only guess what happened to the six men who we left on ship. Most likely, they panicked when the pack ice began to press in on the boat and they set out on foot to find us. The sea or the storm enveloped them somewhere. They did not find us, nor did they return.

The *Bifrost* was in no shape to carry us anywhere, but the boy took shelter in the cabin for the darkest weeks of the winter, and when the perpetual night finally broke, began this journey by dogsled towards the ice edge. Having reached open water, we can proceed no further. The kayaks were lost long ago. Now we depend on the ocean currents to carry us towards safety.

There are still many more hours of darkness than light, and few audible stimuli to compensate. I fill the silence with observations. I take water temperature, air temperature, and barometer readings. I record the length of the day and the night, the angle of the sun, the phase of the moon, the position of the stars. There is precious little to do. I write letters. I write my many notebooks. What is the use of writing when no one will ever see these notebooks? It serves no possible purpose, but to occupy my mind and hold back the sea of despair that is creeping in upon me.

My other occupations are equally futile. I inspect the equipment rigorously and endlessly. I inventory the supplies, which are not seriously depleted, but are no longer plentiful. I find myself sleeping for hours and hours, as my body conserves energy and of its own accord tries to make this uneventful time pass as quickly as possible, but I have vivid dreams that make me feel that I have lived other lifetimes. I frequently wake up, surprised to find myself still here on the ice. The reality of this situation here cannot match the vivid reality of my dreams. This may as well be another dream, another possible, but by no means definitive, existence.

The boy is tedious today, fed up with all this, irritated and irritating. Though he has asked often already and heard the same answer, he cannot help asking again if will be home soon.

'How much longer?' he asks plaintively and petulantly.

I have to remember to be glad he is merely weary and that he has not yet considered being terrified.

'We must be more than halfway there.' This is a reassuring thought, since we are more than half way through our provisions.

'We left the *Bifrost* on the twenty-eight days ago, journeyed southwards towards the ice edge, where Captain Ibsen will be looking for us. Captain Ibsen will be at sea by now. He will sail northward to the ice edge and search using the maps and charts I left in my study for this purpose. It is only a matter of a few weeks now.'

The consistency of this story seems to satisfy him, as much as he can be satisfied.

I am far more worried now. The drifts are no longer carrying us closer to the Pole as they did for the first few weeks. The ice is now drifting away from the Pole, west and south towards Iceland. For years I half suspected that the currents north of the European and Asian land masses moved north and westward. The old Tenebrian maps and Delrina's alchemical ranting about the Pole's telluric energies suggested such a current in the polar sea. I showed the boy before we left, confiding my secret plan to make for the Pole, if we were beset by ice, but I never supposed that the current would be so powerful as to carry us so far west and to feed, so disastrously for us, into the southerly East Greenland current.

In the spring when the search ship comes north, Ibsen will not find us anywhere along the route I charted. Following my meticulously drawn maps he will search fruitlessly far to the east. Ibsen will never find us here. I have begun thinking about alternatives, while the supplies are still plentiful and desperation does not impair my judgment.

The best hope for survival is to wait for the new freeze in the autumn. As soon as this floe freezes up and connects with the great winter sheet of Arctic ice, we should waste no time, packing up the sledge and making for Bjørnøya. If we plan well and make good time, we might make it there before the pack ice breaks up again. Anyone who knows my diplomatic and military career also knows full well what sort of reception I will receive in those islands. How happy our old enemies will be to see me drag myself to the shores of their most remote penal colony, the worst place on earth, but my only salvation. A long captivity awaits me there. My life will depend on my friends' and country's ability to win my release. By sledding to Bjørnøya I will be trading one captivity for another, but I can hope to survive imprisonment in a dark cell. On this Arctic ice there is the certainty of starvation and frozen death. And there is the boy to think of.

Sledding out to the penal colony at Bjørnøya has weighed too heavily on my unoccupied mind. It has seized my imagination, and I have been ill. My medical journal reminds me of the dizzying heights my temperature reached in the last few days. Each time I woke, I dutifully recorded it. It peaked a few days ago and seems to be returning to normal now. I did think I might die. My medical friends tell me that the human body cannot withstand sustained high temperatures; the nerves will overheat and the brain will boil. It seemed an awful punishment to die of a fever in such high latitudes. I did not die, but while the fever raged I tossed and turned in my furs and dreamt. I dreamt in such lurid vividness that it was difficult to separate truth from reality.

My old enemies had finally caught up with me. I was lying on the dirt floor of a cell in Bjørnøya prison. In my cell, just as here, there was no light and I was unable to move about, but these deprivations were compounded by the taunting of my captors and the poverty of the food. Distant shrieks and groans reached me from neighbouring cells. The furtive tracks of rats across my thin blanket, broke the tempo of my sleep. I would die in that cell. It seemed certain. Malnourishment would destroy me if not some plague carried by the rats or merely the beatings I earned with the continued defiance of my captors.

As I lay there dying, rats gnawing at the sheets, hunger gnawing at my gut, despair gnawing at my hope, I formulated elaborate escape plans. I imagined that the next time they dragged me out for interrogation, my hands would have grown too thin for the shackles and I would slip out while I waited unattended in the interrogation room. I would steal provisions and a boat, ah, if only for a boat. With a boat I become another man. A boat for me is like a horse to some men, the pen to others. It is the shape of my freedom. If I escaped with the boat into the ice, they would not follow. They are cowards, afraid of the ice, the polar bears, mere cold.

They prefer to stay in their barracks and be killed by treacherous comrades rather than pursue me out here onto the ice.

In this feverish dream I revelled that I had escaped the prison and found freedom in the Arctic ice. I scoffed at the fools for thinking they could hold me, until the fever finally broke and I awoke. In the disorientation of waking, the furs that encased me, the condensation of my breath and the ubiquity of ice seemed to confirm my dream. I had escaped the prison and I was on the pack ice. Minutes passed before I could separate dream from waking reality. I had never been in that prison. It had been a mere dream. I had been lying free here on the pack ice all that time.

I am not a young man; the irony of life does not tickle my imagination or make me philosophical. I accept it as grim necessity that to escape sure death on this ice I must now escape to that prison of my dream.

We lie in our beds now amongst the furs, as we do for twelve hours of each day. It helps us to preserve our energies. I would sleep longer, but I feel that we must pretend there are still such things as day and night, so we obey the chronometer and take to our beds with it should be night, wake when it should be dawn. That is not to say I sleep these twelve hours. The constancy of night confuses the body. It does not know when to be active or when to rest. I lie here half awake listening to the boy's breathing. Occasionally I hear him cough, a high-pitched cough, brought from the front of the throat. It's worrisome. I have only a few medical supplies and my medical knowledge is limited, but I console myself that it is not a deep, wet cough, in the lungs. There's no need to worry unduly. But it is still a cough.

In my mind's eye I can see the cough syrup in the medical kit, a thick brown elixir in a dark bottle beneath the gauze, beside the disinfectant. Should I wake the boy to give him a spoonful? It is probably not worth it. If I wake him, I'll only make him aware that he's coughing. I wait and listen. There are long silences in between his clusters of coughs that make me think it has passed and that mercifully the boy has fallen into a deeper sleep. As these silences stretch out, I realize how tense I am and begin to relax each muscle one by one, allowing my own body to consider sleep. A single cough ends this false silence, and I feel my body clench again.

I rose last night to retrieve the cough syrup from the supplies, digging them out from the piles of rations and ropes at the back of our canvas and ice cave. When I reached the white box of medical supplies, I already suspected that would not find any cough syrup there. This was an entirely new kind of hallucination for me, a hallucination of memory, a perfect visual record of an object that had never existed. The mind is a curious apparatus.

I suppose that the mind conjures these visions to preserve its reason, as if the mind knows it cannot tolerate the emptiness of the Arctic night. The hallucinations began when winter set in. The sun had disappeared below the horizon for good and at the brightest point of the day cast only a reflection against the clouds in the distance.

The first hallucinations were mere lights and geometric formations in the night sky. I mistook them first for aurora borealis, but the lights were too bright and the formations too distinct and symmetrical. Luminous shapes: circles, diamonds, exact squares combined together in symmetric formations like snowflakes. These visual phenomena spread to the corners of my peripheral vision, until my eyes twitched, trying to hold them all in view. The patterns collapsed and reformed. They intersected each other, in great baroque constellations of excruciating detail. I began to catalogue them all in a journal, but it was exhausting. There seemed no end to their combinations. I tried to dismiss them by closing my eyes, but the bright lights and shapes shone just as vividly on the backs of my closed eyelids as they did against the night sky. Only in sleep did the lights fade or mutate into the more traditional narrative forms of dreams.

The first realistic hallucination appeared days later, a goldfish, just a small thing perfectly shaped and a bright tangerine colour, frozen stiff in the snow. For a minute I groped clumsily in the snow with my sealskin mitts to try to pick it up. I was about to take the thick mitts off to pick up the tiny fish when it dawned on me that it could not be real. Since then, my mind's recreations have steadily become more complex and challenging. The formations of light only recur when I am near exhaustion, about to drift off to sleep. They return like the dramatic theme of an opera's overture, repeated once again in the finale to remind me it is all of a piece.

The boy's questions bring me out of my reverie.

'What does the Pole look like?'

I'm momentarily annoyed by this, by the necessity of explaining or being logical.

'It looks like this, just like this, ice and snow.'

He's excited by this. 'Are we at the Pole then?'

I have to laugh, and tell him, 'Sadly, no, this isn't the Pole.'

He's a scientific little lad though, not so easily put off. 'But how do you know?'

'The instruments, the compass, the charts ...' It's a half-hearted answer and it's met with silence for a few moments.

'But then,' his voice serious in query, 'how will people know if you reached the Pole?'

I answer, unreasonably snappish. 'We would tell them: that's how they would know.'

More silence, then, quietly, sheepishly even, he asks, 'What if they don't believe you?'

I never answer him.

Last night I dreamt or imagined that I was back at the whaling station at Bergen in the final stages of preparation for this expedition. Ibsen accompanied me as far as Bergen on the steamer along with the meteorologist, Jensen. The *Bifrost* was anchored further down the coast waiting out a storm. The old harbourmaster hosted the three of us along with a collection of other stranded travellers. He suggested we amuse ourselves by inventing stories about ourselves.

'We were all strangers here, never likely to meet again, why bother each other with our tedious lives. Let us see if we can't imagine more exciting lives for ourselves.'

It was as good a way of passing the time as any. My friend Captain Ibsen alarmed everybody by telling everyone he was an agent of a foreign government. He told his story so convincingly that I'm sure some of our fellow passengers would have reported himself to the police, had I not laughed so heartily and clapped him on the back when he was done. Jensen told us all that he was actually a writer of adventure stories for children, and if he revealed his pen name everyone would recognize it immediately. I was racking my brain for a suitably outlandish story, when one of the other travellers told everyone he was an Arctic explorer who was about to make a dash for the Pole. Again everyone laughed. I was outraged to see Jensen and Ibsen join the mirth. What could be more absurd than an adventurer obsessed with the Pole? I never did get to tell a story of my own.

My hallucinations or dreams communicate very succinctly. I cannot avoid now the realization that I have made a terrible and probably fatal mistake. It will torture me the rest of my short life here on the ice. Ibsen was right. I was a fool to try for the Pole. The dwindling ice reminds me of the vanity of my motives. What did I hope to attain? Fame, that feeble immortality, is unrealistic. Who remembers Hall or DeLong and the others who died before me on this same fool's mission? And science, that's a shabby premise. What science can be done at ninety degrees latitude that can't be done at eighty-five? There is no use denying it now. It was vain and ignorant to try.

What will Ibsen do when he reaches the Kara Sea and finds no trace of us? Will he try sail further eastward past the Taimur peninsula, the peninsula that we ourselves could not pass? He won't be so reckless as to be beset by ice as I was, but perhaps he will be able to pass that way all the same. By following the *Bifrost*'s planned route he will instead be sailing further and further away from us. I should have left some message after that first winter. Novaya Zemlya was within our reach. We could easily have made our way there and left a cairn with a message, but I would never have persuaded my crew to return to the ice again and trek north with me.

Now I must count on Ibsen puzzling it out for himself. How many times have I spoken to him of my ambition to attain the Pole? Dozens of times. He must surely remember. How many times has he cautioned me against it, saying only a fool would try? The Pole cannot be reached by boat. Only a monstrous vanity or ignorance makes it seem possible. Besides, he would argue, there are better methods these days. Hadn't we both attended Andrée's lecture to the geographical society about his balloon? Wasn't this, inevitably, the way the Pole would be conquered? – but I would hear nothing of this. I was fixated on currents and drifts. He must know now that I have pursued my folly. But how can I expect him to know that these uncharted western currents have carried us so far away from our intended course? He cannot guess. I cannot count on any rescue from that quarter. I must depend on my own ingenuity.

The boy is quiet now, asleep maybe. I have just told him again, 'We left the *Bifrost* twenty-eight days ago and journeyed southwards towards the ice edge, where Captain Ibsen will be looking for us. Captain Ibsen will be at sea by now. He will sail northward to the ice edge and search using the maps and charts I left in my study for this purpose. It is only a matter of a few weeks now.'

He is a good boy, patient, uncomplaining. I don't know if I could have borne the cold, the boredom and the ceaseless danger at his age. How old is he anyway? I'm no judge of these things. Ten perhaps? He is still boyish, a child. He has none of the bluff and swagger of the potential man in him. His hair is fair, straight and beginning to hang long in front of his blue eyes. I shall have to cut it for him soon. His skin is still soft and his cheeks rosy from the cold rather than raw and chapped like my own haggard face. He seems immune to the elements. He is a great comfort to me here and I am thankful for his company. He asks to be told stories and poses challenging questions that amuse us both. When I am most distracted and worried about the growing areas of rotten ice around our encampment, he asks me if we will see penguins, and I must argue with him until he laughs at my gullibility. For all these things I am eternally grateful, but I never believe that he is really here. It is important that whoever reads this understands this. The darkness and isolation may have triggered all these visions and dreams, but these hallucinations have not affected my ability to reason.

The boy isn't really here. I know that. I admit that I forget occasionally, am drawn in my imagination's fiction. But when I am required to, I am able to summon reality. The boy is not here. He is at home, safe with his mother, or safer than this. As my supplies dwindle I put more hope in him. The search ship will have sailed by now, but if they follow my instructions exactly, they will be searching hundreds of kilometres east of here.

Only the boy can put them into the right course again. Captain Ibsen knew that everything was in my library. The boy will know which cabinet to check. The boy will know which charts, which journals conceal the crucial clues. He will guide Ibsen to Mortenson's ship logs and Antropov's account of his ordeal on the Arctic ice floes. Ibsen knows enough Latin to decipher the Tenebrians' maps. Surely too he will see through Delrina's abstruse iconography to understand that his alchemical scribblings and his ranting about telluric forces are merely charts and descriptions of ocean currents.

The riddle Antropov wrote on the frontispiece of that peculiar Chinese dictionary he gave me will help. 'When is the sea itself a ship?' The boy guessed the answer to the riddle right away, and he'll explain it all to the good captain. The sea is a ship when it is the frozen ice floe – the ice floe that saved Antropov's expedition, the ice floe that has kept me alive so far. Trust Antropov to choose such a gift, a book whose subject matter is its own creation, from a man saved from the sea by the sea itself. He grew wise and contemplative in his old age. It is a shame that the hostilities put an end to our correspondence. No matter, the boy knows the answer to the riddle. He will put Ibsen on the right track. They will be here soon, as soon as they realize that I have taken to the ice and the ice has taken westward, they will be on to me. Yes, between Captain Ibsen and the boy they will put all the pieces together.

I have begun an investigation of the currents around the floe. I have crates of empty bottles now and only a few full ones, so I am trying to put them to good use. I place a numbered card into a bottle, then venture as close to the edge of the ice as I dare to hurl the bottle out into the water. It is a fruitless endeavour, I know. The bottles move in the same currents as this island of ice. They will go nowhere. Occasionally I see one of them bobbing out in the water, a dark green break in the monotony of white slush. At night I see green bottles when I close my eyes. The hallucinations are fewer now daylight has returned for a few hours a day, but as I fall asleep I still see shapes and geometric formations in the darkness and dream very vividly.

I miss the boy. He was a good companion. I barely see him any more. When he does return he's less real, just a vision, a fleeting shape out of the corner of my eye that disappears as soon as I turn my head his way. He doesn't talk to me any more either. He doesn't ask about penguins. Occasionally I hear a high-pitched scream, that makes my heart stop, as if he has fallen into the sea. This is hardly a reassurance. I miss his ceaseless questioning, about when we will be home. I long to tell him. 'We left the boat on the twenty-eight days ago, journeyed southwards towards the ice edge, where Captain Ibsen will be looking for us. Captain Ibsen will be ready to sail by now. He will sail northward soon, but we have already made up most of the distance ourselves. It is only a matter of a few weeks now.' I sometimes hear myself repeating this comforting sequence to myself. By now, I am no longer certain of the number of days and the degrees of latitude and longitude. I do know that I can go no further southwards or eastwards. The ice has broken up to the east, making the partial refuge, the purgatory of Bjørnøya unreachable. I must count on Captain Ibsen and the boy's detective work now. It is my last hope. I cannot call the messages in bottles a hope, only a distraction.

As I was looking out for ships at the ice edge this morning, I put down the binoculars for a moment to rub my eyes, and glimpsed something bobbing in the loose ice at the water's edge. It was one of the dark green bottles I have been throwing out into the open sea. It offended me to see it floating there, just metres from the ice floe. I fished it out with the net I have been using to catch fish. I was about to hurl the bottle back into the water, when I became curious to see what I had written. I haven't had the discipline to make the message the same; sometimes I add more detail than others. I unstoppered the bottle and removed the message. The message was in French. I did not recall writing any notes in French. But why shouldn't I have? The writing did not look totally unlike my own. It is difficult to maintain any standard of penmanship with these huge seal skin mittens. But I could not have written this message unless I am madder than I have thought so far. I say the message was written in French, indeed it looks for all the world like French. I can even pick out specific words, but the message makes absolutely no sense to me. I cannot decipher it.

It is worthwhile considering where this bottle might have come from. If it did not drop from the hovering city of Laputa then it may indicate that the currents here are more complex than I imagined. Perhaps my own bottles might escape the orbit of the pack ice. I've tried to draw some new charts of the Arctic currents that might explain how this bottle arrived here, but it is no use. I can't persuade myself entirely that I didn't write this myself during one of the longer nights. I hope that I did not write this, not merely for the sake of my sanity, but certainly for that too. That I could write something like this and forget it is very troubling.

When I was a boy I had a book called *The Three Musketeers*, or at least I thought I had such a book. I lost it at some point. I must have left it outside one day or forgotten it when we moved to the town house near the harbour. Years later I recalled it and went looking for it amongst my old toys and the books that I had given to my brothers. My brothers had no recollection of such a book, though they liked the sound of the story when I described it, and they were eager to read it once I found it again. Neither my mother nor my father could remember the book either when I asked them. They laughed and told me I had a vivid imagination. In fact no one I have ever spoken to about it has remembered a book called *The Three Musketeers*, and more than a few have told me I should write the story down. I might, should I ever return home. I would gladly spend the rest of my days in the warmth of my study, writing adventure stories. *The Three Musketeers* is a phantom book, a story I imagined so vividly as a child that it became a memory. I owe imagination that book. Today my fancy took back its debt.

I have been running out of paper. You would never have thought it. Ibsen laughed when he saw the multitude of notebooks that I brought on board at the beginning of this voyage, but I had great plans. I had notebooks of geographical observations, zoological observations, meteorological logs, a ship's log as well as my own private journal. All these lapsed long ago, except for this one journal, which is now the sole caretaker of all my thoughts, dreamt and undreamt. It hardly seems worthwhile differentiating the two now, any more than it seems worthwhile separating water from ice.

As my paper ran out I recalled the notebooks Jensen, the meteorologist, had left with me. Jensen was one of the first to succumb to the fever that decimated our expedition and doomed this trip to the Pole. Before he died he made me promise to bring his notebooks back with me. I assumed they were his meteorological observations. When my own supply of paper ran out, I resorted to filling the empty spaces in Jensen's notebooks. He was profligate with his paper, only writing on one side. I wrote on the back of his notes. This sustained my journals for another few weeks. Towards the end of Jensen's first notebook, I found that Jensen had filled the back of the pages himself, not with weather observations, but with a novel, a boy's adventure story. It reminded me of Stevenson, and I recalled that Jensen had said something that night in Bergen about meeting the Scottish author in London.

Rather than regret the loss of blank paper, I was happy to find this story, to have some sort of distraction, a momentary mental escape from this prison of ice and water.

Jensen's story is told by a young boy. He may be ten or twelve; it is difficult to tell. He seems a precocious child, studious, absorbed by books. The boy's father has disappeared mysteriously. It is hinted that he has been kidnapped or killed. He may be involved in some conspiracy or some adventure, some voyage of discovery. The boy does not know what to believe, but suspects that all the necessary clues are hidden in the father's library. A certain mysterious captain is trying to get his hands on five particular books in a locked cabinet. The boy believes that the captain is holding his father prisoner and that the books contain certain damning evidence against him, though reading it myself I was sure that the captain was only trying to help find the boy's father. To protect his father, the boy destroys the books, by the unusual means of eating every page. When the first chapter of Jensen's book closes, the boy has consumed the five books of his father's most guarded cabinet.

I read Jensen's book with a deepening sense of despair. It was clear to me that the boy had made a horrible mistake. I rifled frantically through Jensen's notebooks in search of the following chapters, but they were not to be found. I am doubly stranded.

I don't know when Jensen told me this story. He must have told me it, or how could I have incorporated it so well into my desperate hallucinations? How can I trust my memory after all this? I do not know what to believe any more. Perhaps, as I have imagined for so long, I do have a son waiting back home for me who can help Captain Ibsen solve the mystery of my disappearance. It is too improbable though, that Jensen's story and my memory are so similar without one being based on the other. I am in such despair. The more I force myself to remember, the more certain I am that I don't have a son. I would remember something about his mother, would I not? I would remember my wife too? Oh, how could I have deluded myself? What is true, then? If the boy is merely a figment of my imagination or of Jensen's, what of Captain Ibsen? Did I really leave him with instructions to come looking for me when the ice broke up. Is there a Captain Ibsen? Nothing is certain. The ground for all this is as uncertain as this slushy, drifting ice. No solid fact can be built on any other, lest that supporting fact melt off into hallucination or break away like false memory.

The boy is asking about penguins again. Over and over, he asks the same question: 'Will we see penguins?' I no longer bother to answer him. How can he think of penguins while the ice rots beneath us and the provisions are reduced to scraps? Oh, if there was only some way to shut him up for a moment. I trudge through the wet ice, as far as I can from the encampment, over the ice hummocks that protect us from the worst of the wind, but he follows me there too, incessantly repeating his questions about penguins and the shrinking ice. I cannot tolerate more of his interrogation.

On the bare ice beyond the hillocks, I spied a bright patch of colour amidst the grey of the ice – a goldfish. I groped at it with my mittens, but was unable to grasp it. Neither could I get it with my bare fingers, which grew numb and insensible the moment I took off the mittens. I returned to the tent, resolved not to think about it, but its resistance infuriates me. It mocks my powerlessness. I may not be able to extract myself from this forsaken floe, but I will have that cursed orange fish. I will take a hatchet with me and pry it out.

KEPLER'S ORBIT: CHAPTER I – THE INTERROGATION

From his chair in the centre of the room Kepler gives the room a grudging professional evaluation – an interrogation room, dark, undecorated, except for a few ominous stains here and there on the floor and walls. To his left, just outside his reach is a steel tray of instruments, scalpels, ice picks, a mason's hammer, something for him to contemplate while he sits there. Kepler's arms are cuffed behind him, binding him to the chair. He gives the chain a good yank, more out of disgust than anything.

Kepler is angry. He's angry with *them* for resorting to this and he's angry with himself for letting it happen. He never thought they'd be such cowards, ambushing him in an alley, like muggers, preferring blackjacks and blows to the head, rather than brave speeches and accusations. Kepler had a speech of his own ready for the day they finally knocked on his door, a speech as much for his wife and the boy as for his enemies – useless now, he regrets.

He understands now that he humiliated them. He stood just outside their reach for too long. Just by living and breathing he was taunting them, and so they've resorted to a dark alley, the overwhelming advantage of numbers and a blackjack swinging in low over his shoulder for its target just above the ear.

He feels the bruise throb now as he clenches his jaw. He'd like to run his thumb along the purple welt to feel the tenderness and the sharpness of the pain again, but his hands are tied firmly behind him. The cuffs, the interrogation room and the throbbing behind his ear are an insult. If this is the way they want to play it – low and dirty, he thinks, grinding his back molars, that's the way it'll be. If they were men about it, brought him in clean and looked him in the eye as they did it, he might have laid it all out for them. But if it's like this, they're going to have to work for it. They're going to have to burrow a little further into the dirt, get a little grime in under their fingernails and in their nostrils. If they want a confession, they're going to have to claw it out of him.

But something is not right. Kepler's heart is racing, his veins bursting with rage. He twitches and fights the urge to lash out ferociously and smash the chair beneath him. This is the wrong way to go into an interrogation. Nothing is accomplished by this. An interrogation is a marathon, not a boxing match. You want to be calm, ready for it to come to you, not seething with the desire to drive your fist through something.

Kepler breathes deeply and slowly through his nose to slow his heart rate, but he can still feel his blood coursing through him, surging like a throttled engine. His body is racing away from him. What the hell is going on?

Suddenly Kepler knows exactly what it is. They've shot him up with something, primed him to talk. He snorts and shakes his head at their stupidity. Did they really think this would work? Kepler knows all about the little vials and needles. He knows something maybe they don't even know. They can make you talk. They can make you bubble and twitch with energy so that you have to spit it out, but they can't make you tell the truth. If you get the truth with these things it's one of two ways. Call them power of suggestion and exhaustion of the imagination. The mere suggestion of this voodoo truth serum tricks the subject into spilling his guts, or he just runs out of things to say and has to resort to the truth.

Kepler knows something now. They've let him in on a little secret. It gives him a crucial toehold in the tug-of-war that's coming. Time is important to them. Truth drugs are dangerous and messy. You don't use them if you can help it. But they need him to talk sooner, not later.

Here's another thing Kepler knows. They hate silence. All interrogators do. If you sit there and stare them down or even look at your feet, they'll beat you senseless. But if you keep talking, even if it's nonsense, they have to listen. They keep sifting through the garbage that you're shovelling at them, looking for that scrap of truth in it. They have to wait for your excuses will trip you up. Your excuses *can* trip you up, if you're not careful or if you're too careful. If you try to fit your story to the facts you think they know, sooner or later, you're going to give them something they don't know. Half lies are no good. Only complete lies will do. Lies that make them blink in disbelief, lies that make them look at each other like they can't believe your guts, lies that make them think you've lost it, or maybe they really have got the wrong guy.

Kepler is ready for them when they swagger into the room. He's reined in his heart rate a little, has his pulse throttled back as far as the drugs will let him. He feels strong as he faces his interrogators. There are the three of them, two tough guys and a pretty-boy officer. One tough guy pulls up a chair and shoves his ugly mug in Kepler's face, trying to look menacing. The other thug paces behind Kepler, like a wrestler waiting to be tagged, anxious to have his share of softening Kepler up. The officer stands by the wall in the shadows, outside Kepler's peripheral vision. To look at him Kepler would have to move his head, and take his eyes off the thugs. That would be a mistake right now.

The thug in front of him speaks in a hoarse, breathy voice. 'We paid a little visit to your house today. Just to ask after you and say good morning to your lovely wife.' Evidently he'll be asking the questions. The mention of his wife is supposed to scare him, but he's working the wrong angle there. She is Kepler's wife only in name now. She's betrayed him in so many other ways, she'd jump at the new opportunity, but Kepler has told her nothing. There's no use telling the thug that.

Kepler gives them the face they want, distraught and hopeless. There's no use being defiant. That'll just get his face tenderized and maybe a rib or two broken. That'll come soon enough. The thugs want to scare him, so Kepler tries to look scared and broken. There's no use beating up a broken man.

And Kepler talks. He more than talks. He babbles. 'I'll tell you everything,' he says. He slumps in the chair, looking tired and beaten. 'I'll tell you everything I know. It was a mistake, a stupid mistake. I should never have done it.' You always start with this. They want you to admit you deserve to be here, so Kepler rants. He tells them he's sorry, that he's an idiot, a weak fool. He repeats the same vague self-accusations. He looks willing, his eyes always on the bully in front of him as if he didn't know that the pretty-boy officer was in charge here. Kepler squeezes his eyes tight in contrition and wails until the thug is tired of this meaningless confession. The thug knows Kepler is sorry. He just needs to hear what he's sorry for, but he can't get a word in while Kepler blubbers and curses himself.

There must be a signal from the baby-faced lieutenant, because the thug finally changes his tactics and says, in what's supposed to be an understanding voice, that Kepler'll feel better if he tells them the whole story. Kepler sniffs and takes a dozen deep ragged breaths before he begins.

'I knew Catherine's family had money, but not this much, enough to hire its own justice,' Kepler says, sounding as awed and terrified as he can. 'Not that it would have stopped me, the money I mean. I didn't marry Catherine for money. They can have all the money back. I'm sorry. I'm so, so sorry. It's just a big mistake.'

Kepler babbles on again, cursing his stupidity, begging for forgiveness. The silent guard behind him has stopped pacing and the interrogator in front of him has a baffled, disgusted look, but the officer is out of Kepler's line of vision and you can't hear an eyebrow raise or a knowing smile crack. The talking muscle is asking him what the hell he's talking about. Kepler works up a sweat that looks like panic and keeps spilling his story.

'I know it looks bad,' Kepler says, 'because of the fake name on the marriage licence, but it's because ... Well, you guys must know why or I wouldn't be here. It's because I was married before ... Jesus, what an idiot ... a couple of times before. It's a weakness, I admit. I don't plan it out. It just happens, and there's the hassle of divorce, the papers and the lawyers, the money. And the time, the time. I couldn't wait to marry Catherine. I was so in love with her. I'm still in love with her.'

The talking muscle is looking confused, on the angry edge of confused. He's looking to the officer for permission to smack Kepler, just to release some energy. He's worried about dosages and bad reactions. Did they give him too much of the gift of the gab? Kepler's eyes dart back and forth, as if terrified, between the interrogating thug and the officer. The thug stands and raises a threatening hand. Though he's been punched, chopped, kicked and thrown by men with more muscle and technique than this chump will ever have, Kepler cowers and tries to look like he fears that smack more than anything else in the world. When the blow lands, he recoils, snivels, gushes out more of his confession.

'I'll give back all the money, maybe not right away. It'll take time. It was never about the money. I loved Catherine and I wanted to marry her and with my previous marriages, it was just easier to do it under another name and start living my life.'

They go over and over this, Kepler repeating the same story about the string of marriages and the assumed name. He glosses over the assumed name, as if it's a minor detail. He doesn't want to emphasize it. It's not the substance of this confession. But the thug grabs it, can't resist the bait.

'Where did you get the name?'

'What name?' Kepler snivels, so confused now.

'Kepler, you idiot. Where did you get the name Kepler? Where did the ID come from?'

Kepler looks up hopefully, looking happy to find new information to give them. 'It was a friend's name. John Kepler. He was an oil engineer. He died in Venezuela and his death was never registered at home. I figured I wasn't hurting anyone.'

They aren't buying this, this suggestion that he's not Kepler, but some sap who borrowed Kepler's ID as part of some scam to marry a rich chick. They aren't buying it, but they haven't discarded it yet either. Kepler did once fake his death in Venezuela and disappear for a few years. It's not outside the realm of plausibility that an old friend, a stupid old friend maybe, might have borrowed his identity for an illicit marriage.

His interrogators spend an afternoon trying to shoot holes in this story. Asking him quick questions and delivering quicker blows to the head when Kepler is slow to reply or seems to stumble in his story. Kepler makes a show of falling apart, but sticks to the story. The officer disappears for fifteen minutes at a time and returns occasionally with some documents. He'll be checking the background on the story. Pulling up marriage licences, trying to find this Catherine he's invented. At the end of the afternoon, Kepler has a post-traumatic-stress look on his face. He's talking to the muscle as if he's an old friend, like he's glad to get it all off his chest. He doesn't know how long this has bought him. And here in his shoulder is the sting of a needle again, and a sudden blackness.

Kepler wakes up on the small cot in a dark cell. His hands are unbound and his body throbs with a dull unspecified pain. He can't remember returning to this room and has no idea how long he has been asleep, but it feels like days. He feels his stubble with the palm of his hand, and smiles, no, not days, probably not even hours. They've put him out for a few minutes, given him the false sensation of a long sleep, and they'll be at it again soon. These people know much of his resistance is just professional pride. Nobody in Kepler's line of work would allow himself to cave in on the first day, but if they hold out a few days, a week maybe, then they feel they've done their professional duty. So the interrogators make a few hours seem like a few days, a week seem like a month. By the end of the week your circadian clock is so messed up, you don't know if you are awake or asleep anyway. There are better methods these days. Kepler knows a few of them, but this usually works in the end too. Your mind loses its grip on reality and then on the principles that keep you silent. You could be dreaming all of this. You might be talking or you might just be thinking to yourself. 'Let's see if it comes to that,' Kepler mutters to himself.

He's back in the interrogation room in less than fifteen minutes. The two thugs look pissed. They know the marriage and assumed identity story is pure fabrication and they're angry that he had the guts to even try to pull it off. Kepler hadn't thought of that, a mistake of timing. It looks cocky. They've checked out the background facts and they're insulted at the story's flimsiness. He'll pay for this mistake in the usual currency. Mentally he calculates the length and severity of the beating they're going to want to deliver. He saves his next confession for when their anger's spent. If you are going to be tied up and beaten for a certain amount of time, you don't want to waste a confession by talking before the beating is over.

Kepler's slumped over in the chair for real now. He's trying the trick of counting the bones in his body to retain his focus and block out the pain, but he can't get past a few metatarsals before some urgent pain calls his attention to another part of his body.

Kepler has a decision to make. He hasn't had the luxury of thinking about it between blows to his body. Now, while the thugs straighten their shirts and admire the product of their labour he considers it quickly. Beginning with such a bullshit story was a tactical error. He should have started something almost believable and spiral out into implausibility. By the time he was making up stupid stuff like multiple marriages and mistaken identity, the interrogators might have thought he'd lost it. They might just believe that the beatings knocked any sense out of him and that if he had anything useful to tell them, he spilled it several rounds ago. Kepler's bigamy and assumed identity story has upped the ante. Catching his breath there on the chair he decides to play it like that was his last act of bravado and now he's ready to give up.

Kepler lifts his head slowly. He can hardly see from the swelling around his eyes, but he manages to give the thug a look of resigned defeat, 'Okay,' he croaks, 'you want Operation Vespucci? You can have it. It's too late now. I'm out of the loop. My work's done.'

The thug nods, grudgingly. He hasn't heard of Operation Vespucci, but he'd rather not give that away.

'You know that my group supports the creation of an autonomous indigenous state in the Chiapas region of Mexico and northern part of Guatemala. You probably also know why.' Kepler makes a show of wincing and gathering energy to continue. 'I won't bore you with the details. Maybe you also know that I've been meeting with Vatican officials and the odd cardinal every now and then. You probably want to know what that's about.'

Since no one has interrupted his tale with a question or a fist, Kepler figures he can keep going. He hesitates just slightly. He's about to go out on a limb now that might not support the implausibility he's about to foist on them.

'There are some documents that we came across in Avignon, left there by the Avignon Popes during the so-called Babylonian captivity of the papacy.'

This revelation is greeted by moist expressions of disgust, as if they might have guessed this all along. This is a good sign for Kepler. He's been counting on their paranoid theories about the Catholic Church, their desire to see conspiracies woven into the most banal events.

'What was in those papers? Where are they now?' the thug asks. His eagerness to believe momentarily overcomes his eagerness to beat Kepler to death.

'The Avignon papers proved that the Popes knew about the American continents for centuries before their discovery by Columbus. They had an arrangement that put Inca and Aztec gold in Vatican coffers and sent European heretics to America as slaves.'

The thug is looking at the officer like, What the hell, do we have to listen to this crap again? but Kepler is going to give them the Freemasons. The Freemasons are the sweetener in this hard-to-swallow story, but he waits for the thug to hit him again anyway.

'Don't give us any more of your crap, Kepler,' the thug warns. He's almost winded gulping down these lies.

Kepler doesn't even raise his head. He just whispers out his story, like he doesn't care if they believe any more. It's all he's got. 'The Templars and their inheritors, the Scottish Rite of Freemasons, knew all about this nice little arrangements of the Popes. They blackmailed a portion of the profits out of the Church for years.'

Snorts from the thugs as if they knew all along that the Freemasons were at the bottom of this.

'The Templars finally got greedy. They manipulated the French, Spanish and Portuguese governments into discovering America and destroying the papal monopoly of American trade.'

The thug's face betrayed his attempts to suppress his outrage. He always knew the Catholic Church and the Freemasons were no good, but this takes the cake. Kepler can hear the captain pacing somewhere behind him in the shadows. Kepler has counted on their prejudices making them weak. They want to believe what he's telling them.

As if to refute this, or as if they too had realized how uncritically they are taking this, the big thug is in front of him again and provides two quick blows to Kepler's ribs. They arrive so quickly that Kepler doesn't have time to tighten his already weakened stomach muscles. He convulses forward, rocking the chair so that he's about to pitch forward onto the cement floor.

The other thug catches him and crouched down, his face right in Kepler's face, he asks, 'Are you screwing with us again, Kepler? You want to screw with us again?' It's the first time Kepler's heard the other's voice. It's thin and squeaky and somehow scarier than the other's slow grunts.

Kepler doesn't have to fake his agony.

'No, I swear,' he manages to wheeze. He's already imagining the next working-over when they figure out he's lying again, but what can he do. 'I swear. It's what we had.'

The blows to the ribs seem to satisfy his interrogators' professional conscience, and they let him continue.

'We used these papers to persuade the Church to support the creation of the Chiapas autonomous state. It's why all these old treaties are suddenly being discovered that support aboriginal title in the southern Mexican states.'

The interrogators pace and look pensive as if they had been completely apprised of these treaties and their consequences. There's some whispering amongst them.

'And you still have these papers?' the interrogator asks.

Kepler hides his distress at this question. The last thing he wants is them rummaging through his library for these imaginary papers.

'I've never seen the papers. I've just been told. I was handling the negotiations. Somebody else will be doing that now. I'm expendable.'

'Who will be handling the investigations?'

'I don't know.'

'Will it be Humboldt, perhaps?'

There's that name, Humboldt. Kepler has seen copies of their files on him. He's seen the hypothetical links they've made between this Humboldt character and himself, but he knows of no one called Humboldt, no one with this alias and no one who fits the profile in those files. He may be a phantom.

'Maybe,' he answers. 'Maybe Humboldt, maybe someone else. I don't know.'

There follows a series of questions like this. Their technique is lax. They're so eager to believe this story that they're feeding him answers. They are just going through the motions. Occasionally in a token gesture of professionalism they knock him around a bit and leer at him, but overall they are buying the story, and soon enough Kepler is back in his cell in a vicious chemical sleep.

Later, impossible to tell how much later, he's back in the interrogation room. There's no preliminary beating this time. It's not necessary, the last beating is still sinking in. The blows planted on his body blossoming into glorious bruises and acute pains. It's possible now for Kepler to tell where he really hurts, where the blows that counted landed. He's shocked at how weak he feels, how raspy his breathing and how feeble his voice.

'You want me to tell you about Humboldt,' he says, without raising his head. There's a low mumble of assent. 'Sure,' it says, 'we'll try that one for a while.'

Kepler speaks raggedly. He can't take a full breath any more, but he gets it out, slowly. 'I met Humboldt once at the airport in Tuvalu. We were both supposed to pretend to miss our flights and spend the night on the island. We'd rendezvous and exchange information. Your operatives trapped us there. They fabricated some sort of local uprising that kept us confined to the airport. The twelve non-native passengers from flights through Tuvalu were crammed into a sweltering room inside the terminal. Humboldt was one of them, I guess. I had no idea what Humboldt looked like. I assumed that Humboldt knew who I was, but I couldn't be sure.'

Kepler stops to breathe, wince and gauge the effect of this opening. No one seems to be limbering up his knuckles in preparation for some exercise. Kepler can't see the pretty-boy officer but the talking thug looks interested. To keep this interesting Kepler has made several concessions to reality. He was held up in Tuvalu for half a day once, but he was there on one of his very rare enforced vacations. There may also be a person named Humboldt. The officer and his thugs think so. Kepler is just adding to his legend.

'Whoever Humboldt was, he must have suspected, like I did, that one of your men was in the room with us. Neither of us gave anything away. Everybody chatted away and complained about the delay. After about an hour in the room, someone suggested a game.'

'Who suggested it?'

Kepler pretends not to understand the question, as if he's drifting away and losing it.

The thug asks more forcefully. Punctuating the question with a poke to Kepler's cracked ribs.

'I don't … I don't know who suggested it, one of the priests maybe. There were two missionary priests. It was one of them. The old priest suggested we tell stories, entertain ourselves the old-fashioned way. I just rolled my eyes and let them carry on, but then I realized that this was our opportunity. Humboldt would know it too and he'd try to communicate with me. I had a compact audio recorder and ten hours of tape. I just let the tapes roll while everyone told their little stories.'

The interrogators ask Kepler a dozen questions about the stories told in that room. They want descriptions of everyone. They pick at little details in that room. The thug is asking most of the questions, but the pretty boy is interested enough now to get to the point. 'Which one was Humboldt?'

'I don't know,' Kepler says, 'maybe one of the Chilean engineers or the bad-ass priest. No, not the old guy who suggested we play the game, the other. A big guy, quiet, with dark West African skin and huge hands.'

'What made you think he was Humboldt?'

'He had that look, you know that calm. That blank look.' Kepler knows they know that look, the studied blankness that Kepler himself has perfected. 'He used certain words, expressions, keywords, ancient codes. They could have meant nothing. He might have been Humboldt. He might have been one of your guys.'

'What was his story?'

Kepler complies, the winces and quick painful breaths were real, but the story is entire fabrication. 'The priest told this weird story about the guy who discovered something called mitochondria, some stuff that's in human cells. He said the guy discovered it had different DNA than the rest of the cell, like it was some other organism that had been absorbed by the cell. I thought it was weird how the priest kept repeating the word cell – like it should mean something.'

'You thought he was trying to tell you something.'

'I thought he was trying to say our one of our cells had been infiltrated.'

'Was it?'

'I don't know. I just kept the tape recorder running.'

'How did the story end?'

'What?'

The thug can't take any more of this stupidity. With one swift kick, he knocks Kepler's chair back a few feet. 'How did the goddam story end, about the guy who discovered this shit in human cells?'

'Oh, he went crazy. He thought the stuff was trying to kill him.'

The thugs look at each other, as if they understood something now. There are some tentative follow-up questions. 'Did you believe the story?'

'No.'

'Was it code, a hidden message?'

Kepler guesses so.

'So what did it mean?'

'Maybe. Maybe there was a mole. I don't know ... I handed the transcripts over. There are experts who are paid to decipher these things.' This is a lie too. They don't have experts to do anything. The organization isn't that big. If there is a code to crack he has to do it himself, but it doesn't hurt to let his interrogators think the organization is bigger and that he knows less than he does.

No one is challenging the Tuvalu story yet, but they're not showing any sign of satisfaction. They want more. Just to keep him on edge, they tell him they visited his house again.

'That's a nice little study you have there, nice and private, a lot of nice books.' The thugs don't expect answers. This isn't small talk. They're not giving him a breather. They're reminding him that they have him at their mercy, reminding him that he doesn't know what they know. And they keep asking, 'What's with all the books anyway? You read too much, Kepler. Come to mention it you write too much too. You should leave the books alone. There are already too many books; you don't need to write your own.' Is this a hint? Do they recognize the Tuvalu story? Do they know Kepler had ripped it right out of a book? Kepler hopes to God that the officer doesn't share his taste in literature.

There's a long silence, as if they aren't sure what to do next. The thug finally moves on. 'What about the other guy, the engineer? What was with him?'

He gives them the Cuban engineer. 'The Cuban? He was just a little guy, olive skinned, pointed nose, black eyes, thick curls of black hair with silver streaks.

'He told the story of how one of his professors died. This professor was this really stiff guy, but smart, a real star, built impossible bridges in Argentina, aqueducts in Iceland. The professor wanted to be Leonardo da Vinci. He used to write backwards with his left hand like da Vinci. This was supposed to develop the right side of his brain or something.'

The thug asking the questions has that dangerous look, like he thinks maybe Kepler is winding him up.

'I'm not saying it worked. I'm just repeating what this little engineer guy said,' Kepler says quickly. 'Anyway the professor had some gorgeous wife that all the students were hot for. The professor and his wife were really jealous of each other and used to have these noisy fights in his office. One day the professor turns up dead and they find all these death threats in his desk drawer. Some people say he wrote them himself in his crazy left-hand writing. Others think his wife or one of the students he'd slept with wrote them. No one knows for sure, but the wife is the one who was arrested.'

The officer has been silent so long, Kepler is surprised to hear his voice. It's a quiet voice, neither high nor low, just slow, careful and interested. 'What do you make of this story, Mr Kepler?'

Kepler hears his own relieved voice. It's true he's relieved to be talking with the captain, not just because he's less likely to fly off the handle. He's the one Kepler has to fool, the only man in this room he truly fears. Kepler turns to look at him now, again he's surprised by how young he looks, the smoothness of his shaven face, the tidiness of his uniform. There's a look of patience and intelligence in his eyes. Kepler pretends to silently appeal to his mercy and superior understanding, but by this point Kepler almost believes the officer can save him.

Kepler, thinking momentarily of his own wife, says, 'It's another betrayal story, another turning.'

'Was Humboldt telling you there was a mole?'

'Maybe.' Kepler drags it out. 'That's what I thought ... at the time.'

'You suspected there was a double agent in your organization?'

'I was starting to suspect.'

'Was Humboldt a double agent?' This catches Kepler off guard. He doesn't know what to answer this.

'For us?' Kepler asks.

'For you,' the officer answers. His voice is smooth and precise, like a measure of potent and expensive alcohol.

Kepler gulps, flustered. The wrong answer could end this. 'Yes,' he says finally. 'He was our double agent.'

They follow this line of questioning for a while. How long had Humboldt been working with them? Kepler doesn't know. How long had Kepler been working with Humboldt? Kepler says four years. This sounds like a safe answer, and it doesn't trigger any immediate repercussions. They don't ask too many questions about Humboldt yet, and Kepler is relieved. He doesn't want to contradict anything they believe about this phantom. Right now that seems like the fastest way to another game of concussions and fractures.

They get back to the Tuvalu meeting. They ask him about the other ten stories, just to be safe. He goes over them all, making some up as he goes, ripping others off from airport novels and magazine articles. It goes on for hours as they have him repeat the stories over and over, trying to trip him up, getting him to contradict himself, but Kepler isn't as beaten as he pretends to be and any slip ups he blames on bad memory, the fuzziness of his brain now.

After his willingness to give them Humboldt, they are surprised at his stubbornness when they convene again in the cosy interrogation chamber. They thought they had broken him. They'd left him untied and brought a table in to write out his confession, but now Kepler is being evasive again, never giving a straight answer. Instead of a simple yes or no, he tells them tales of agents who believe the earth is flat, operatives that claim to use tunnels beneath the earth to traverse entire continents, a conspiracy to conceal a utopian colony on an island at the centre of the Arctic Ocean.

The interrogation is about to get ugly again. He's asking for it. He goes to great lengths describing the package of books he received last week – a Chinese encyclopaedia and an alchemical treatise. Kepler is halfway through this list when the hammer falls on his outspread hand. Kepler doesn't see the hammer until it is upon him. For a few bewildered seconds he can't identify the source of the excruciating pain. When he sees his hand upon the table, it doesn't look like it belongs to him. It looks like another object. Instead of a thumb there was merely a mess of blood and crushed flesh. The sight of it combines with the searing pain to extinguish his consciousness. As his eyesight becomes black and red he hears the officer speaking.

'Let us have a talk with the boy,' he seems to say.

These words haunt his unconsciousness. The boy – what might they do to the boy? The boy's mother would betray Kepler if she could, but she has nothing on him. The boy might do so out of ignorance. What does the boy know?

Again Kepler's on the cot. He feels worse than last time. He's not cuffed to the bed, but it's so hard to move he might as well be. He can feel the end coming now. He's surprised at how quickly his energy and imagination were sapped. He knows he's only been here days, if that, but he feels drained. But then he never expected that his captors were capable of such brutality. He sees his bandaged hand and recalls the hammer of the last interrogation session. A shiver runs through his body, and he finds he can move at least enough to get to the side of the cot and heave the long, fitful stream of bile onto the floor. When the vomiting stops he curls up on the cot to retain warmth.

He manages to think dispassionately that the hammer is a new one for him. The brute with the hammer probably thinks he's clever. But torture is torture. Originality is a phantom given credence by ignorance. The hammer has probably been used before for this purpose. His torturer has just revived the ancient art.

His captors have let the drugs run out. Kepler is awake for once by his own devices. For once he has time to concoct a story. They'll want to know about Humboldt. That's where all their questioning has been leading. They only want Humboldt.

Kepler looks a beaten man when they bring him back to the interrogation room. They don't bother binding him to the chair. They just cuff his hands to the table in front of him. He's not pretending when he holds his trembling hands out to be cuffed. The drugs, the beatings and the sleep deprivation have taken their toll.

'We've been to see your wife,' the captain says. The fact that the officer is doing the talking is ominous now. It means that he too thinks the interrogation is moving into its final stages. 'I spoke with your son as well. He's a fine boy, the little scholar. He misses his father. I'm sure you're looking forward to seeing him again.'

Kepler can't tell whether this is a threat or a promise. He shouldn't be this stupid, but it really is ambiguous to him. The mention of the boy makes him nervous. They'll know by now that the woman is useless. She'll have happily told them anything they want to know, which is exactly why he's told her nothing. The boy is another story. Will the boy be smart enough to keep his mouth shut? Surely they won't hurt him.

There's something sinister about this expression 'the little scholar'. What does it mean?

Kepler can't help turning his head to look at the officer. Again he's surprised by the how young he is, how tidy his uniform is. He looks like he'd never hurt a fly. Kepler's wife is probably falling over herself to tell this pretty boy all his secrets. But Kepler fights back his disdain, the anger bubbling in him. The captain is in control. He's the one Kepler needs to distract for as long as possible. He wonders if he has delayed long enough. Would if be safe to capitulate now?

Kepler looks up at the young captain. He makes himself totally abject. His eyes silently appeal to his mercy, all fear and incomprehension, like he hopes the captain can prevail on the two thugs to relent. But he knows better. Kepler always knows that they are lackeys and they do nothing without the captain's order.

Normal service is resumed and the big man asks the rest of the questions. They come fast and furious now, as if they're on to him, and aren't going to allow him to waste their time with digressions and shaggy dog stories.

'How did Humboldt communicate with him?'

He's ready for this, and has a story. 'On paper, handwritten, hand delivered. I used to ...'

'Who were the couriers?'

'Professors, students, people attached to the academy. We used the ...'

'Do the couriers know what they are carrying?'

'No. They don't ...'

Again they cut him off. 'Were the letters in code?'

A simple 'Yes'. He's got the message. They're impatient with his stories. Stringing them along now will only aggravate them. He'll answer questions for a while and wait until they are ready for another detour.

'Did you decode them yourself?' Kepler can feel the silent thug breathing, not so silently, behind him. He hears something heavy being slapped into a thick open hand – the hammer. They know the right answer to this question. If Kepler gives the wrong one, the hammer will fall again.

'Yes. I decoded them myself.'

The voice of the officer emerges from the peripheral shadows. 'Your organization doesn't have a cryptography group, does it?' Kepler imagines that the thug couldn't have pronounced the word cryptography.

'No,' Kepler answers.

'Do you use book code?' the officer continues.

'Yes.'

'Are the books in your library used as the key books?'

'Yes.'

'Which books?'

'All of them.'

'All of them?' There's a distinct note of skepticism in the officer's smug voice.

The thug is taking a few experimental swings with the hammer behind him. There's a slight swish as it passes through the air behind his ear, and he shudders and twitches involuntarily.

'Keep still,' the thug whispers in a gust of halitosis.

Kepler doesn't know if he's kept his nerve or lost it, but he keeps lying. At least he thinks he's lying. He's starting to lose track now. It's starting to go wrong. In his exhaustion he's deviating from the plan, mingling truth and lies.

'There are a lot of books in your library. Your son showed me around. He seems very proud of them. I find it hard to believe that all of them are there for the purpose of ciphers.' The officer is pointing out that he knows things. Kepler shouldn't dare to lie.

'There are hundreds,' Kepler says. 'They were in the house when I arrived there. I believe that Humboldt has the same collection.'

There's silence as they consider this answer. The thug in front of him takes a tight grip on his wrist, holding it to the table. The other thug allows Kepler to see the hammer again. Kepler wonders if he could recant now. If he could tell them he's made up everything, that Humboldt doesn't exist, that the books were his own father's and have nothing to do with the organization, but no, they believe in Humboldt. Kepler is stuck now with all his lies.

The questioning continues. 'What do you do with the notes once you've decoded them?'

'I destroy them,' Kepler manages.

'Destroy them how?'

'I eat them.'

The thug's hand springs up from Kepler's wrist to his throat, flinging his head back as far as it goes, and Kepler's choking to speak.

'I swear to God it's true. I'm not making this up.' His eyes wild, desperate.

He's sure now that they are going to kill him. He didn't think they would, but then he never thought it would ever come to this. The struggle has been so civilized, and then they'd brought him in. He'd always thought that he was harder than they were and that was his advantage. Now he's seen how savage they can be, he believes they would kill him and he's suddenly very afraid to die.

'You see, Kepler. We've grown impatient with your tall tales. You've played a few too many games for your own good. Now you have to work to make us believe you.'

'It's true,' Kepler whispers hoarsely. Again he hears the cold head of the hammer being slapped into a fat palm. 'I swear it's true. The notes are on rice paper. The organization is paranoid. They don't want half-burnt fragments in the fireplace.' He's racking his brain desperately for something that will make this all stop. 'You can ask the boy. The boy has seen me. Go ask the boy.'

There's another long silence in which Kepler sees how wretched he's become. He can't believe he has given them the boy. His cowardice overwhelms him. To make them stop, to make them go away, he has sent them the boy. He almost wills the hammer to fall now, not on his hand, but his skull, but it doesn't. The hand at his throat relents and is eased away. Kepler sees the captain nod to the thugs.

'And there are only five books used for the codes. The boy will know them,' Kepler says slowly, his surrender complete.

'Another visit to the little scholar then,' the officer pronounces smugly.

The thug behind him puts his hammer down and comes around to face Kepler, his face a happy grin as he kicks the chair. Kepler feels himself falling helplessly backwards, then a burning flash as his skull hits the concrete and then all he sees is red.

Set against the scarlet red curtain of his vision, the unconscious Kepler sees the faces of the boy, the interrogator and the officer as if illuminated from below. The officer is somehow also Humboldt and he's reciting nonsensical syllogisms – If Kepler is a liar, is he telling the truth when he says he is lying? If Humboldt is a man, and all men are books, then Humboldt is a library. The boy keeps taking books down from somewhere behind the curtain as if he is looking up supplementary evidence for these hypotheses. The thug merely laughs at each statement as if each was a fabulous joke. The whole nightmare stinks of his torturer's breath.

And again, mercilessly, he is roused back to conscious. Kepler wishes one more time to die. Broken, he thinks to himself. The word seems too apt. He is broken. They have broken him. He will tell them what they want to know now. The moment he sent them to the boy to save himself, he was theirs, and they know it now. Any doubt about this evaporated when they left him alone in the room with the captain. The thugs are no longer required.

Kepler sits again on the uprighted chair. He looks up gratefully as the captain unlocks the handcuffs. He knows that this is half the point of the torture, to make him look to the captain for mercy, but he has overcome that conflict. He is thankful that the captain is here alone.

'You didn't think we would harm the boy, did you?' The captain says, as if Kepler's fear makes him the brute. 'He deserves better than you, much better. It seems he has done his duty. He has destroyed the books.'

It takes a while to sink in. When it does, Kepler is too shattered to be thankful. With those books they would have had the whole organization at their mercy, but it is hard to care. They will surely kill him now.

The captain seems to know what Kepler is thinking, and looks at him with mock concern. 'Oh, don't worry. You haven't outlived your usefulness yet. It would have been better if you had talked to us sooner. It would have been easier on us all, but some people still care for you, I think. You have friends, a son. You are not unloved.'

So that is it, thinks Kepler. He's bought enough time. The boy has destroyed the codebooks. The organization will have done the rest. Somewhere out there the plan has been put into action, and Kepler's information is no longer valuable. For his captors, he has other uses. They won't kill him now. It serves no possible purpose. He's useful as a hostage and this is fine with Kepler. The endless interrogations will stop now. They'll leave him alone, giving him time and opportunity. Torture and interrogation and watchful vigilance are time-consuming, and now that Kepler's organization is in motion, the officer and his friends aren't going to have a lot of time on their hands.

They have given him something else too, a new brutality, a new focus. Kepler lies in the cot and feels his anger congealing inside him, hardening him. He despises his own weakness and he vows to overcome it. He has betrayed the boy. He has failed him, but he will not let that act of cowardice stand. Someday he will break out of this feeble prison and the smooth-faced captain will have something to answer for.

THE POLYGAMIST

Bigamists get no respect. People seem to have no idea what goes into it. They haven't a clue how difficult it is to maintain more than one wife. They just think it means being half a husband to two women. And if people can't appreciate what it takes to be a successful husband to two wives, it's impossible for them to understand what I've achieved. There may be only a dozen men in the world, other bigamists, who truly understand what it takes to be married to five women simultaneously. I'm telling this story for them. Only they can grasp the scale of what I've accomplished. They'll appreciate my achievement if no one else.

When I talk about bigamy I don't mean those religious freaks who have six wives in the same house all happily making them dinner every night. That's not bigamy. That's just sick. There's no skill in that. That doesn't take any talent or imagination, just a bunch of other wackjobs who believe in the same twisted world-view you do. Real bigamy is the good old-fashioned sailor's tradition of a woman in every port. A real bigamist is a man who manages to be married to several women simultaneously without any of them figuring it out.

What is it that makes a good bigamist? It's not good looks, clearly, and it's not power and wealth. You don't have to be a genius either. I am past believing I am wiser or more sensitive than anyone else. You know what distinguishes a bigamist from an ordinary man, and a good bigamist from some sap who gets caught three days into his second honeymoon? – imagination. Imagination is at the centre of what it means to be a bigamist. Bigamy puts a huge strain on a man's imagination. Successful bigamists are very creative men. I don't think it's going too far to say that we are artists.

I didn't think too hard about these things when I was young. I've become more philosophical as I've got older. I've started to ask myself how I came to be a bigamist. What sort of man becomes a bigamist? What was it that drew me to this peculiarly demanding calling? It seems to me that we're blessed with a unique creativity and a hyperactive imagination that can't be confined to a single course of action. Bigamists have a flexible sense of their own personalities. We're like actors, like the very best kind of actors. The best actors don't just *play* the role they've been given. They aren't pretending. For as long as they are on the stage or in front of the camera, they *are* that character. Bigamy is just like that. You become the husband that each wife wants. You don't just pretend. You are that person, and each wife demands that you be a different husband.

A real bigamist never marries the same sort of woman twice. Why would you marry two women who are alike, who expect the same things from you, who want to shape your life in the same way? What would be the point? You might as well just marry once and save yourself the effort. It seems to me that it's also a sort of betrayal, marrying two women who have the same idea of an ideal husband. When a woman marries a man she expects that man to be hers alone. It's cheating to be that same husband to two different women.

A real bigamist seeks out different kinds of wives. He needs wives who demand different things from him, wives that require that he be a different person. To be successful at this you have to be creative, adaptable and alert and you must believe. There are times when the strain is going to seem too much, when you are going to feel like giving it all up and settling for the certainty and the leisure of a single marriage. If you are going to get through these crises, you have to truly believe that each marriage is important, that the vows you took to each woman are binding – to love, honour and cherish, etc. You have to believe all that for each wife. Even the 'forsaking all others' applies. You can't for a moment think that you are cheating. You've got to know that you are being faithful to every woman you marry. Each wife exists in an alternate version of your life and each alternate husband is loyal to his bride, forsaking all others.

I don't know if it's the same for other bigamists, maybe some bigamists have it all planned out, but I for one was surprised to have become a bigamist. I married my high-school sweetheart, Steph, the summer after I graduated from university, just as we had always planned, but before that I married Mireia. I met Mireia in Montreal, where I was going to school and she completely overwhelmed me. She was the most exotic thing possible and I wanted her the moment I saw her. Mireia had this fabulously sexy accent. Her family had either fled Peru and taken refuge in Chile before coming to Canada or fled Chile and taken refuge in Peru. I could never get it straight, and I tried. It exasperated her when I asked and I'm sure she changed the story sometimes. I don't think she really wanted me to know, and I thought it was mysterious and intriguing either way. Her parents were in Paraguay or Uruguay when I met Mireia anyway and she lived alone in Montreal.

Mireia was so tragic and so adult that I felt naive around her. Back in high school I had been the daring one, going off to university while everyone else got jobs at the mine or the mill. Back home I stood out. Mireia made me see how ordinary I was. I looked at myself through Mireia's eyes and saw a goofy undergrad from Northern Ontario. There was nothing, I thought, that she could see in me. The strange truth was that Mireia was attracted to all the flaws she exposed. She told me she adored my freshness, my honesty, my lack of sophistication. She got a kick out of going skiing in the Laurentians with me. She liked that I played hockey every Tuesday at midnight and that I had never eaten Indian food or Thai food or even seen a bagel before the age of sixteen. She thought I was wholesome. I had never seen that myself. I was used to being the big fish in a small pond. I was head boy of the school and Steph had been the first girl in our class to go on the pill. I organized the grade thirteen class trip to Whistler. I was the one who had defended Bobby Armitage when everybody said he was gay. Back there I was big-minded and cosmopolitan. In the city with Mireia I became more small-town than I ever had been.

Mireia thought I was a bit clingy. She didn't like that I always wanted to be around her, so I was surprised when she asked me to marry her. I said yes of course. You don't say no to a woman like that. She was the most amazing woman I'd ever met. She was gorgeous, obviously, but in a strange, un-Canadian way that was irresistible. She had incredibly thick black hair, bobbed very short and swept behind one ear. Her features would have been harsh, if she'd had my own pink-white skin, but hers was the colour of baked earthenware, warm and sun-soaked, and beneath, her cheeks had flecks of perfectly defined and countable freckles. I was one of the few who knew that her icy blue eyes were not tinted contact lenses and that her body was strong and firm all over, like an unripened exotic fruit.

Even Mireia's moods were sexy. She was deeply sad and prone to fits of inexplicable anger. She would scream at me in Spanish that I never understood, and then demand that I make love to her to prove that I was hers alone. It was in one of these fits of unexplained jealousy that she asked me to marry her, or actually, dared me to ask her to marry me. I asked and then we went to bed. In the morning she blew up at me again, screaming at me to get out of her apartment and never to come back. I lied to get her into bed, she said, and I never meant to marry her. We were married next month in a Catholic Church full of incense and a small crowd of Chilean or Peruvian relatives whom I have never seen since.

I moved into Mireia's apartment, but still spent a lot of time at the house where I paid partial rent in exchange for a reserved spot on the sofa. Now that we were married, Mireia was even more angry and distant. She often kicked me out and I needed that spot on the sofa back at my old apartment. Mireia liked it when I went away for short periods. I was studying mineralogy at school and there were lots of field courses, on which I spent weeks in Northern Quebec and Ontario picking away at the Canadian Shield and the Laurentians. Mireia was always tragic and sentimental when I left, but I knew she was glad to see me gone. When I came back, she loved me extravagantly. She called me her man of the woods, her rugged Canadian boy.

The summer after Mireia and I were married I went back home to my summer job with the Ministry of Natural Resources and the intention of explaining everything to Steph. It should have been simple, but when I got home, it all seemed so stupid. I tried to imagine myself explaining what had happened in Montreal and describing Mireia, but it sounded crazy. It sounded like I had made it up. In fact, the whole time I was back home, it was as if I *had* made it up. It didn't seem real at all. The moment I saw Steph again, I knew that I loved her and that we were always meant to be together. I hadn't been myself in Montreal. The thing with Mireia was totally out of character. Steph and I spent a wonderful summer together. She liked the city habits I'd picked up. I introduced her to spicy food and red wine. Everything went back to normal. We were the coolest couple in town again and everything was going to be the way we had planned. Before I returned to school, we set our wedding date.

The plan was to divorce Mireia before I married Steph. I figured I might even be able to get it annulled. It would be as if it had never happened.

I never actually got around to divorcing Mireia, though. It never came up. The right moment never presented itself. You would think that it would just come out during one of our fights, but our fights were never normal fights. I don't get to say much. Mireia does most of the talking. I just get to look sheepish or outraged, whatever seems to be required by this particular rage of hers.

I don't know if there is something wrong with the registration system. Maybe our old rector back home was lazy. Maybe there was some miscommunication between Ontario and Quebec on marriages. It should never have been allowed, but I married Steph at our local church without a problem. She'd been working already for three years and her Dad gave us the down payment for a little house out by the lake. I worked at the MNR full time and we were a happy, small town couple. Steph liked to say how we were a shining example for the town. I was her sophisticated city boy, bringing civilization to Northern Ontario, and she was the luckiest girl in the world. By Christmas though, I was worried about Mireia. She could chase me down pretty easily if she wanted to and I didn't want to contemplate the idea of my two wives meeting each other. I wasn't yet a confident enough bigamist to talk myself out of that situation. I decided I better take a little business trip.

In Montreal Mireia threw the most violent of her fits at me. She gave me no chance to confess between all the accusations and insults she hurled at me. We were both in tears when she finished, with me holding her wrists tightly to stop her from slapping me. Then we made love in the old bed. I stayed a week. I told Mireia I'd been up north doing some work for the geological survey. At the end of the week, when I still hadn't found the courage to tell her I wanted a divorce, I told her I had to go away again, and that I didn't think I could guarantee I could be home much, for, say the next few years. This didn't provoke the reaction it was supposed to. It backfired completely. Instead of initiating the argument in which she finally dumped me, it seemed to soothe her. She seemed to like the idea that I wouldn't be around very much. This, apparently, was just what she wanted from me. Again, I left Montreal just as married as I had arrived.

Back home Steph informed me I'd been speaking Spanish in my sleep. Improvising, I claimed I'd studied Spanish at McGill when I'd thought for a while of going into the Foreign Service. Steph's eyes widened at the words 'Foreign Service', as if this was a glorious, romantic idea, exactly the sort of grand ambition she expected from me. 'How cool would it be if you were a diplomat?' she said wistfully. That wide-eyed look, that unconcealed gaze of admiration had the same effect as Mireia's condescension and bitterness. It made me want to fulfill her expectation. Her desire to see something in me changed me, or revealed something. The husband that Steph wanted, the person I was for her, needed a career and a life more cosmopolitan than the MNR could provide.

Steph's reaction helped me realize that there is something decisive and deterministic about the woman you marry. By deciding who you marry, you decide your whole life. You choose who you are going to be.

That night as Steph and I discussed how we would handle me working in the Foreign Service, I was filled with awe and gratefulness. I felt fortunate to have the opportunity to be such different people, to live more than one life. I took the diplomatic corps test the next chance I got, finished high enough to choose a career stream and applied to the foreign intelligence department. When I told Steph she gazed at me with the molten eyes of some beguiled Bond girl. Growing up where we did, where people go into their fathers' businesses and only leave the country once in their life for that family vacation to Disneyworld, I had become something totally new and unique. Maybe originality is a phantom given credence by ignorance, but Steph always reminds me to be thankful for that ignorance – I should call it naïveté I suppose – still exists to reflect on me.

My intelligence training took me to New York, where I was supposed to learn how to look and act American. I met Katerina in the elevator of the Park Avenue Ritz. She smiled at my good tuxedo and diamond cuff links. I thought she was a shallow, blonde American princess, and felt compelled to get her into bed as a sort of revenge for her being rich. It was a strange, unexpected sensation. I had never felt that shallow before. It was as if I had found out something new about myself.

I didn't manage to fool Katerina for long, or perhaps I never fooled her at all. As I dragged myself out of her bed on the fifth or sixth morning she asked me what sort of swindler I was. I almost asked her what sort of swindler she wanted me to be. She was that obvious. It was far too easy to see what she wanted. She was sick of glib society boys and presentable suitors. She wanted to rebel and her best idea of how to do so was to find the wrong man.

Katerina was actually much younger than I'd first thought. Her clothes, her demeanour and her confidence with money had made her seem much older. But over that first week in her hotel suite a clearer picture had emerged. She gushed about a debutante ball in her recent past. She rolled her eyes like a teenager whenever she mentioned Daddy and Daddy's money. Maybe her family's money embarrassed her. Maybe having things come so easily bored her. Over the years I came to understand that she needed drama in her life. She needed crises. She needed things to happen, things that had to be overcome. Daddy's money smoothed out the road in front of her, removed all obstacles, leaving her nothing to fight against and feel heroic. From the start I must have known that this is what she wanted from me.

Katerina pretended to believe I was in publishing. I told her I was in New York meeting with my board of directors and wooing prospective authors. This explained what I did during the day. I made up some story about a big scandal book that I was bringing out. I blamed my temporary money problems on the lawyers' fees required to fight the many injunctions against its publication. By our third meal together the bill was going on Katerina's gold card.

I was still pretending to be the highly leveraged publishing magnate when I proposed to Katerina. She put her hands on her hips and challenged me to show her the ring, but the tremor of excitement in her voice told me she had already decided. She could already see the trouble that I would be, the drama that I would make for her. Hours after proposing I left for Timmins. When I returned to New York, Katerina was still in the same suite at the Plaza. I walked in to find her lying on the bed wearing nothing but the huge diamond solitaire she had bought herself. I held both her hands in mine and swore that when the big deal went through, I would trade the ring in for one twice as big. I had a crazy sense of vertigo as I promised this, as if I could see myself from the top of the room. Like a good-hearted rogue who didn't know the depths of my own unscrupulousness, I half believed it, but I also knew up there behind the camera at the top of the room that I never would pay for that ring or anything else I gave Katerina.

Katerina didn't want a big society wedding. A big wedding to the suspicious stranger would have caused a bigger scandal, but it would also have given her family a chance to intervene, and Katerina wasn't that strong-willed yet. Instead we eloped. She bought us two tickets to Reno and we had the traditional Nevada chapel wedding. We honeymooned at her family's Lake Tahoe lodge. On the morning after the wedding Katerina was sullen and reproachful. I didn't really love her, she said. I was just using her. Every word out of my mouth was a lie. She was going to get her Daddy to annul the marriage. I protested that I had never loved anyone else like I'd loved her. This was absolutely true. I loved the others differently. Still I had to get back to Canada to finish my Foreign Service training, so I sneaked out of the Tahoe lodge the next morning while she was still asleep. I was in the car with the keys in the ignition when I realized that I wasn't doing this right. I returned to the lodge and relieved Katerina's purse of half its cash and credit cards.

My unspoken deal with Katerina is that I can spend a month or the value of a mid-sized car before she cancels the credit card. That first time I charged flights to New York to resume my intelligence training and then the flight back to Timmins. The balance went to diamond earrings for Steph and six months' worth of mortgage payments on the house. I may have been a cad to Katerina, but I was still Steph's knight in shining armour. Steph was overjoyed with the earrings. A gift from Tiffany's ... she'd never dreamed. The box was kept like a trophy on her bedside table. I promised her next chance I got I'd take her to New York. She actually shook with pleasure. I had touched upon one of every small-town girl's most cherished dreams. It takes so little.

Before I returned to my training I dropped in on Mireia, bringing her a big round boulder I'd picked up at the side of the road. I told her it was from a terminal moraine in Northern Quebec and that this was what I'd been working on for the last few months. I spewed about ten minutes of geological nonsense while she arranged the rock artfully on her coffee table and told me she would rather have had jewellery. She was lying, of course. She liked to expect jewellery and instead get something hokey and pseudo-sentimental like a rock that represented my life's work away from her. I spent a week with Mireia before she got tired of forcing me into arguments and generally being unreasonable and asked, wasn't I going away soon?

I knew already when I put the money down on the Timmins mortgage that my intelligence career wasn't going to last very long. The stress of the first few months of my marriage to Katerina made me realize that bigamy is not a hobby, something you can dabble in on the side. It's a career you have to dedicate yourself to full time if you want to do it justice. I stayed with the Foreign Service just long enough for them to send me to Venezuela. Steph was pregnant with our first child by then, so she stayed behind for a few months.

I only stayed in Venezuela for a week, long enough to for someone to redirect any letters from Steph to a post office box in Montreal and vice versa for my replies. I then faked an anxiety attack and was sent back to Canada on long-term leave. My letters to Steph hinted at all sorts of intrigues, and swore her to secrecy. Her letters were dutiful and admiring and made me long to be beside her to watch her belly grow round.

I spent those next six months in and out of Mireia's bed. I took to telling her that I wanted her to move with me to a little cabin I wanted to buy by Lake Nipissing, where we could start a family. She made it clear that she'd been waiting a long time with grim expectancy for this sort of proposal. Finally, when I had waxed a little too poetic about the blackflies and the cold lake water, Mireia kicked me out again.

I returned to Katerina. I'd phoned her once or twice since I left (collect from bars where the sound of shouting foreigners was exaggeratedly obvious), begging to be forgiven. I kept telling her how sorry I was. I'd been swindled out of my money by a deceitful employee, and I'd only borrowed her money to help get my publishing company back on track. Each time I called I invented another author whose breakthrough debut I was just about to clinch the rights to.

Katerina was prepared to half believe it all when I finally came back to her. She hadn't filed for divorce. She hadn't got the marriage annulled. She'd convinced herself that she had a fatal weakness for me, and that she would always wait for me to return. It gave her a burden to worry about. It gave her a past and made her seem more interesting. We spent a month at the house in Connecticut that was nominally our home before I left her once again in the conventional way, with more of her money in my pocket and a vague excuse.

The months when I was supposed to be in Venezuela established the pattern of things. Steph thought I was on some secret mission, Mireia thought I was up north scratching at rocks, and Katerina assumed I was off swindling someone else. After a year of distress leave, the foreign service let me go. Katerina's money supported Steph and me. Mireia never wanted any of my money. Whenever I tried to pay for things she accused me of trying to buy her. If I looked especially hurt by these unfounded accusations, she'd let me do something wholesome and unglamorous around the apartment like repaint the walls or install a dishwasher.

I rotated myself through my three wives, spending a few months in each home, explaining my departures to Steph as secret foreign postings, to Mireia as mineralogical surveys in distant rough locales and to Katerina as wild doomed business adventures. In addition to this seasonal migration through wives, I spent at least one long period away from each of them. Mireia was my first wife, so I deserted her first. She was becoming increasingly disappointed with me returning unscathed from my survey expeditions. I decided to put myself in imaginary harm's way. When I told Mireia that I was going to the Amazon on contract to a mining company, her strange pool water eyes filled with tears. She seemed to think I'd chosen South America for her, as a demonstration of my devotion. She was already imagining what her horrible continent would do to her wholesome Canadian boy.

The idea came from a newspaper story about the disappearance and possible abduction of four Canadian mining engineers in Amazonia. I flew immediately to Sao Paulo, composing a letter on the plane. There were rumours of an Indian uprising in the area, and there was talk that drug runners had an airstrip there, I wrote, so it might be dangerous, but she needn't worry. Nothing ever happened to me, I declared, with as much small-town bravado as I could muster. Her love made me immune. In São Paolo I mailed the first letter immediately and bribed a post office clerk to send a second package of undated newspaper clippings a few weeks later. Mireia would have imagined quite enough peril in the Amazon for me, but the newspaper stories about the lost engineers gave these phantoms some solidity.

The next three years I devoted to Katerina and Steph. I felt no remorse at deserting Mireia. I knew that she was cherishing my loss. She would have thought that she was responsible for my disappearance. She had driven me away. Her visions of savage tortures and grim deaths only flattered her sense of her own tragic capriciousness and power and restored the ideal of my haplessness and valour.

My Amazonian disappearance gave me the opportunity to hone my bigamy skills by living with two women in the same city simultaneously. Katerina had convinced her father to buy a small publishing house in Paris dealing mainly in translations of esoteric texts and alternative histories. They installed me as the publisher in the faint hope of keeping me from wandering. I wasn't totally happy with this arrangement. I don't like authors. Their creativity is second rate, and I didn't want anything to do with books. There are already too many books. But the arrangement worked out in other ways.

Steph was ecstatic when I told her we were moving to Paris. Within a week she had rented out the Timmins house and was already investigating respectable lycées for the boys. Katerina and I stayed in her family's sprawling apartment in the eighteenth arrondissement. Steph and I found a terribly romantic apartment in Montparnasse. I told the boys that Mondrian had lived in the building, which prompted Steph to sign herself up for art lessons. My days were spent with Steph and my nights with Katerina. Katerina presumed I was at work during the day, but there wasn't much for me to do at the publishing house. It ran better without my intervention and when she phoned to find me out of the office it just served to feed Katerina's obligatory constant suspicion.

My espionage work, for reasons that were abundantly apparent to Steph, could only be done at night. She had no problem with sleeping alone. It allowed her to fantasize about the dangers and intrigues I was exposing myself to. Besides she was seeing more of me during the day than she had ever done in the five previous years of our marriage, and I had brought her to Paris.

Before the seventh anniversary of my second marriage, none of my wives had ever met each other. Katerina and I often ate at the Le Porc-épic Fâché, but this was the first time I'd taken Steph there. The waiter winked as he handed us the menus, and asked saucily if I would like the usual. I assented slyly, as unflustered as any master spy. Steph's eyes widening and her eyelashes fluttering with excitement as she watched me order. She loved all of it, loved that I had brought her here to a restaurant she could not imagine affording and yet at which I seemed a regular. She loved every layer of mystery and intrigue I added to her life. Katerina sauntered into Le Porc-épic as the crème brûlee was arriving. I spotted her out of the corner of my eye as the maître-d' took her coat, but I pretended not to see her stride across the restaurant to our table. I let her surprise me with a big fat movie slap across my cheek. She called me a bastard, said that she knew I was a lying cheat, but to do this under her nose. It was an insult. It was a classic scene. There's no need to embellish such things. Can anyone really believe they have anything new to add? Katerina played her role perfectly. I am sure she savoured that slap for months.

Steph was on the edge of her seat, clutching the armrests as if this was all theatre. I stayed seated, astonished by my own composure as I slipped into the American accent I use with Katerina and introduced Steph as Josée Villeneuve, an author whose book we were about to publish. Katerina scoffed and stormed out, before Steph could utter a word. I followed Katerina to the door, making the necessary consoling and explanatory motions and sounds, but I was not going to leave with her. I wasn't going to spoil my anniversary. Katerina preferred to stomp off alone anyway.

I told Steph that Katerina was connected to Quebec separatists. She didn't expect me to divulge state secrets, she protested, but she gulped and nodded at each spoonful of the story. The tale was a sort of anniversary present. Katerina was the niece, I whispered, of a French cardinal. At his death this cardinal had left Katerina certain Vatican papers that seemed to prove that the French had been in Quebec for much longer than historically presumed. This so-called pre-Cartier file allegedly showed that they had been there two hundred years before the discovery of Canada by Cartier. Certain French princes of the blood had been fobbed off with Canadian protectorates to tidy up claims in France, and most importantly, the Algonkian and Montagnais tribes had signed treaties that made them French citizens. I didn't need to tell Steph that this was all a huge fraud, but it was the sort of thing that could throw Canadian constitutional negotiations into a crisis. Aboriginal title was the federal government's ace in the hole in negotiations with Quebec. If Quebec could claim that those same aboriginal inhabitants were French citizens, everything would have to be re-examined. I explained to Steph that my assignment was to secure the pre-Cartier file, so that our government could suppress it or begin the process of debunking it. To do this I had to secure the trust of Katerina. When I'd finished Steph cracked the crust of her crème brûlee with a distracted but vigorous stroke of her spoon and asked her only question: 'Did you sleep with her?' I gazed earnestly into her wide eyes and assured her there were some things I would not do for my country. The sex that night was embarrassingly grandiose.

That evening was one of the high points of my career as a bigamist. It also marked the end of our time in Paris. Katerina's father fired me from the publishing house and Katerina fled back to the U.S. I scurried after her to try to save our marriage. Katerina wasn't easy to appease. I had to promise to stay with her for six months at the family's Colorado ranch. It was a tortuous six months trying to walk the line between penitent straying husband and only half reformed rogue. Katerina didn't want me completely domesticated.

During those six months, I discovered that Katerina's father was my secret ally in keeping the marriage together. He was afraid that without a prenuptial agreement, a divorce was going to cost him. Since the marriage he'd also been hiding income in several accounts in my name. The revelation saddened me. I didn't need help. It diminished the risk and tarnished the glory of my three marriages.

I had already sent Steph a very official-looking document, apparently from the foreign office, saying mysteriously that I had been detained overseas. I later sent an Amnesty International flyer with my photograph superimposed over that of a detainee in Myanmar. It was all too easy. Even sending Mireia a letter via a Colombian hospital, saying that I was recovering and should be able to return home in three months, did little to raise my spirits. I needed a new challenge.

One of the few escapes from Katerina's compound was the occasional trip to the liquor store. Katerina trusted domestics to buy and cook the groceries, but buying the weekly supply of gin for her martinis was beyond them. My trustworthiness being somewhere just above that of the domestics, the job fell to me. The compulsion to keep driving was stronger every time I left on this two-hour errand. I would have disappeared on one of these shopping trips one day had I not met Kym at the liquor store. She caught my eye between rows of bottles and licked her lips outrageously like a stripper. She struck me exactly as the sort of fling a bought upper-class husband would choose. I paid for her sixpack at the cash and followed her beat-up Datsun back down the highway, turning off on a dirt road that ended in her trailer park. When I left her trailer about an hour later, I instinctively checked my wallet. Kym had written her name and phone number with eyeliner on the lone bill she left me. I take this moment as the epitome of my career as a bigamist. I had succeeded in seducing authentic, literal trailer trash. It was a feat of sleaziness I never thought myself capable of.

For the next few months I let Kym buy the household booze and met her at her trailer instead of making the trip all the way into Boulder. Her commission for this errand was not insignificant, but I took great pleasure in being fleeced of the money. I was leeching in much the same manner from Katerina. It had a fine karmic circularity. From certain artefacts in the trailer and the odd paranoid question from Kym herself, it was clear there was a boyfriend somewhere. The whole time I was with her I was bracing for the inevitable confrontation. It came about two months after I bought Kym our first sixpack. All the intelligence training in the world cannot save you from a righteous ass-kicking at the hands of a jealous logger. I took the punishment like the straight man I had become in this relationship. Kym liked me dumb, rich and gullible. For her I was a victim. It helped her self-esteem.

The phone call to the house came the next week. Inevitably Kym was pregnant and most certainly it was mine. As always, I did the right thing. I took the keys to the Grand Cherokee and a modest number of credit cards and left Katerina again. It was about time. I had paid my dues for Paris.

Kym insisted on a traditional Vegas wedding. I concocted another fake identity and made the usual solemn vows. Wedding vows made me proud and nostalgic. Those same words every time. It reassures me that there is nothing new. The wives may change but the wedding vows are still the same. Each time I say 'I do' I get that same solemn tingle of excitement and expectation. Even as I repeat them I feel renewed. I feel richer.

Kym and I drove from Vegas to Northern California where I set her up in an old farmhouse and waited for the child to be born. The child looked nothing like me and everything like the logger, but I undertook to believe Kym's unnecessary assurances that it was mine. A few months after he was born I told Kym that I had to go away and make some money. The story I had in mind was a variation on the mining stories I always told Mireia, but Kym immediately guessed that I was going back to Katerina to wrest a suitable support settlement from her. I had to admit that she was right. You have to trust a woman's intuition on this.

In fact, I really intended to go back to Mireia. My Amazonian captivity had lasted long enough and a few months of ranting and simulated nightmares would convince her that I had suffered enough in the hands of the natives. I concocted a wild story about the deal I'd made with my captors. I had promising never to reveal the tribe's whereabouts and to protect their territory with lies and misinformation on my maps. I hardly ate for two months in order to look emaciated enough for my reappearance.

Denial is an ever-present part of a bigamist's life. You have to be able to rationalize things, to yourself not the least, but there comes a moment in any bigamist's life when his power of self-deception lets him down, when facts fall through the safety net of excuses and denial. My return to Montreal was that moment for me. It should have been another triumph. I felt at the height of my powers. I was now married to four women, deceiving them all. I was a trapeze artist with four women in the air, throwing and catching them expertly and assuredly, but then I dropped one.

When I arrived in Montreal, Mireia had moved. This was my first surprise. Mireia had lived in that same apartment for years. She never moved. I spoke to the landlord and found that she left almost a year ago, moved to a new house in the suburbs. This couldn't be right. Mireia would have never have moved out of the city. She was a city girl through and through. She detested the suburbs. I checked the phone book and found no entries there under her name or mine. I was stymied for approximately four hours, trying to think of her friends' names, her relatives, wondering how one placed those 'Any persons knowing the whereabouts' ads in the newspaper. One of my old friends at foreign affairs finally tracked her down for me. It turned out that Mireia *had* moved to the suburbs, changed her last name and moved to the suburbs. I rented a car and thought gleefully of how I would tease her about abandoning her principles.

That, however, was not all she had abandoned. I should have known by the address, by the well-mowed lawn in front of the house, by the Honda Accord and the SUV parked in the double driveway. I should have known when she answered the door in workout gear. I should have known when I heard the unmistakable shrieks of early childhood behind her. But I didn't.

'I'm alive,' I said, as she answered the door.

It took her only a moment to reply, 'No, you're not.' Her face was concerned and apologetic but not quite as concerned and apologetic as I felt I deserved.

She never thought I was dead. That much was clear. She would have shrieked and cried and staged high-calibre Latina hysterics had she ever thought me dead, but that was not what the papers in the manila envelope she handed me said. According to these papers I was dead. Mireia had petitioned to have me declared legally dead. I was still reeling from the shock of being dead, when she landed the sucker punch. She had remarried. She was now Mireia St Clair. It was all very humbling, and somewhat baffling. I had never thought Mireia capable of such things. Not of leaving me for dead in the jungle and annulling our marriage. I didn't doubt she was capable of that, but of marrying some sport-utility-driving suburb-dwelling schmuck who wanted her, of all things, to bear children. It was profoundly disorienting and left me in no condition to argue when she asked that I go away and not come back. I didn't even have the presence of mind to propose that she cheat on this new husband with me.

I spent a week in a hotel drinking, watching TV and wondering what to do next. Mireia's betrayal completely blindsided me. How had she become that suburban housewife I'd seen standing at the door? She looked more like Steph than the Mireia I loved and married. It was as if our whole life together was a lie. What was I to do now? It was too early to go back to any of my other wives. Mireia's desertion left me at a loss, but it hadn't thrown off my bigamist's finely honed sense of timing. Kym and Katherine needed more time to be pissed off at me. Steph needed to worry a little while longer about me starving and sleep-deprived on the damp floor of a detention cell in some rogue state. I was sensitive to these needs and didn't want to be selfish or to think short term.

I could never say why Steph needed to worry about me or why Kym and Katherine needed to be convinced of my worthlessness. For all my experience, women are still a mystery to me. I understand what they want, but never why. I understand my own compulsion to satisfy these needs only a little better. It is something about experience, about personality and of expanding my horizons, about being, as the army recruiters used to say, all that I can be, however contradictory this all might be.

During my crises of confidence there in that hotel room, I began to wonder if I was really cut out for all this bigamy stuff. This was my first failure. Before Mireia left me, I had thought that I was invincible. I thought that I could keep all the balls in the air, and none would ever fall. Mireia's defection had shown that I wasn't the perfect bigamist, that I could lose a wife. Could it happen again? If Mireia was capable of leaving me, abandoning me in the jungle at the mercy of cannibals, why couldn't Steph? Why couldn't Steph decide that she'd had enough of worrying about me and raising the boys alone and just give up?

When I began to think about calling Steph, I knew it was time to get out of the hotel room. I couldn't let one setback knock me out of the game. I had to dig deep and run back out onto the field.

My walk took me to my old neighbourhood around McGill, and I returned there each day for a week, wandering the old streets, scoping out the old hangouts. I was returning to the places where I had first known Mireia, trying to retrace my steps, maybe unconsciously trying to find her again. She wouldn't be there. It had been more than ten years since I left McGill. No one I knew would be there. None of the old places existed. They'd all changed their names and their décor. It made me feel old, but I kept going back, and after a few days of walking the old streets I began to feel at home again. I began to recognize places and people, not individuals, of course, but types. Being a bigamist has a lot to do with understanding types, being able to identify the type of woman you are about to marry and becoming the type of husband she requires.

As I sat in the new cafés and drank in the new bars around the university I slowly began to see that they were still the same places. They might have changed names or locations or décor, but the same types of place existed. There would always be a pretentious hangout for arts grads and politicized idealists. There would always be a cheap drinking hole that engineering students were in the process of taking over from the locals. There would always be a strip of three pick-up joints where undergrads got their one-night stands out of their systems. There would always be the hip ethnic restaurant du jour and a de facto gay hangout. These places always existed. They were essential types. They merely changed their address, their décor and the lettering on the sign. The people were the same.

What a rush, what a relief, to remind myself that people still conformed to type. The costume might be different and the code words changed, but the same universal types existed. I might not find Mireia here in our old haunts, but I would find Mireia's type, which was all the same to me. Ten years ago this sort of thinking would have seemed cynical, but I'd aged, matured and developed my philosophy of bigamy. I understood that it was about me, about exploring the different aspects of my personality, that each woman was a direction that I could travel. There are only so many directions. Another Mireia could take me further down the path the old Mireia had abandoned.

I found the place Mireia would have hung out in, if Mireia were still herself, or herself of a decade ago. I hadn't realized the problem with this yet. Ten years makes a difference. Ten years of Mireia's handiwork had changed me. Any new Mireia would see that. She would see a battle-scarred veteran of the emotional wars, a cagey old-timer, not the green rookie Mireia had discovered. She would see that she couldn't fool me, couldn't string me along, couldn't be the femme fatale she needed to be, as long as someone else had revised my innocence. All this became plain later, after I met Sophie.

Sophie was the sort of girl who is attracted to a man with ten years of head games under his belt, a man made complicated by time and complicated women. Sophie was a type of girl I had never dared to date, never mind marry. Girls like Sophie always saw right through me, saw that my innocence was as big a sham as my experience. They never dated guys their own age. They were too smart, too future-focused, too eager to be beyond themselves. They always dated guys ten years older than themselves. They were greedy; eager to appropriate that older man's experience. Because they were out of reach, I'd convinced myself I never wanted them, but now I *was* ten years older than Sophie. I was what she was looking for, and suddenly I was looking for her too.

In the coffee shop where I lay in wait for my new Mireia, I ordered Bridgehead coffee out of solidarity with my imaginary South American captors. Sophie, standing in line behind me, congratulated me on my political correctness in a way that blended equal halves of honesty and irony. I bought her a coffee and we sat down together at the corner table beneath the smug figure of Ganesha. As we spoke, I transformed myself, becoming more what she wanted with every word. It was easier to do than ever and it was gratifying to know that I still had other selves to draw on and develop. For Sophie, I became a former mining engineer who'd worked in Peru for five years. I'd seen how mining wrecked habitats and played havoc with traditional aboriginal ways of life, and I was disgusted. I was writing a book about it now and consulting for a few NGOs. Sophie couldn't have invented better herself. She was idealistic and ambitious, young and anxious not to be. She wanted to be more than she was. She needed to steal experience and hoard it away. I could feel her devouring my years as we spoke.

She was beautiful too, of course. I have never married a woman who wasn't beautiful, but it was invigorating after all these years to see a new kind of beauty. Sophie didn't embellish herself the way Katerina did with diamonds and spa treatments or Kym thought she did with piercings and body art. Nor did she conceal herself the way Mireia had done as a way of creating some mystique. Sophie had something of Steph's natural, unpretentious beauty, but she was uncomfortable with it. She hadn't quite figured out how it went with her ambition and intelligence. She didn't yet trust that they were compatible, but I was designed to help her reconcile her diverse charms.

She made love to me like the act itself saved the rain forest. Our relationship grew tangled and complex very quickly. I was living in her apartment within a month, paying half the rent and making all the meals while she was in class. We both agreed it didn't make sense for me to get my own place, since I was returning to the rain forest in a few months, so I stayed in her apartment, revelling in her youth and yet another new self. To fully explore the role, I actually even started writing the book I had told her about. After the disappointment of Mireia's desertion, it was a complete rebirth.

After two months it was time for me to head back to the rain forest. I told Sophie I had to go to New York first, to finalize my divorce. This was a major departure for me. I wasn't actually getting a divorce. I would never do something so callous. I believe in commitment. But I'd never told a woman that I'd been married before. Sophie needed me to have a past, so I told her about Katerina, the rich, shallow American socialite I'd married when I was young and stupid. I made our upcoming (and totally fictitious divorce) sound like a political statement. This was perfect for Sophie. It made me complicated and not completely trustworthy. She didn't want to trust me completely, or rather she wanted to trust me reluctantly. There was surprising depth and complexity in the older man and mentor role.

Finalizing my divorce and a season in the rain forest to Sophie meant reconciliation for Katerina and me. Katerina was contrite and in the mood to smooth things over. She cried the moment she heard the operator announce the collect call. She gushed her apology. She'd been too harsh confining me to the Colorado ranch and she wanted to patch things up. An airline ticket to New York arrived the next day. Katerina was waiting for me in New York, in the same hotel suite we had first stolen away to. It was a great few months. I was the good cad again. We saw the town. We bought each other many presents with her money. It was like a second honeymoon, and I felt I was back on my game.

I sent letters to all my wives. My letter to Kym came from a Florida jail, telling her not to expect to see me for a few years. My letter to Steph was a pained scrawl of oblique self-censored sentences, as if most of the things that I wanted to say I would not be allowed to write. To Sophie, I wrote that my divorce was finalized and enclosed an old wedding ring I picked up in a pawnshop. I hadn't worn it for years. It only reminded me that cyanide-laced gold mine tailings had poisoned the water source of the little Peruvian village I loved. Sophie must have cherished this symbol of tainted love. She could only love things with conflicting double meanings. I imagined her wearing it on her thumb as a warning and a reminder to all the college boys that she was beyond them.

In New York, I soaked up Katerina's money, sent letters to Kym from the Florida jail house and Amnesty International updates to Steph, assuring her that I was still alive and that they were working towards my release. I read articles about the gold mining industry in Peru. The *New York Times* ran a big story about a Peruvian tribe trying to block the construction of a mining company dam. I had a fictitious New York NGO forward my letters to Sophie from the same village. I described how I was helping some Mormon missionaries build a new school, and organizing the villagers' protest. I invented very touching stories about the families there, about earnest fishermen, wise elders and precocious youngsters with pot bellies and bad teeth. Katerina saw me researching and writing all day and thought that her good-for-nothing husband had finally buckled down to doing some serious work. I did not disabuse her of this notion.

Sophie's letters were committed and passionate. She was burning to do something for the cause. I told her that she should spend her reading week with me in South America. She could stand with me in the path of the bulldozers in solidarity with the villagers. The village, I knew already, was no more. The bulldozers had already arrived to reroute the river, and the village had been abandoned. It never hit the North American papers, but the local papers described it all.

So my outrage was well rehearsed by the time Sophie and I discovered my beloved village empty. Sophie had to stop me from storming into the mining encampment. She thought I was going to burn down the mining office or sabotage the equipment. It was a thrill to see her eyes harden with determination, as she restrained me, tried to talk some sense into me. She reminded me of Manuel the fisherman and Pilar the dumpy little girl who laughed at my glasses. Manuel and Pilar, Sophie protested, would not want me to resort to violence. I finally let her drag me away. We hiked and took buses back to the capital, a trip of three days, during which I looked sullen and heartbroken.

In a Quito hotel room, Sophie did her best to make me see sense and hope. She told me the fight wasn't over. I told her I wasn't strong enough to fight alone any more. With clenched fists and ardently pursed lips, she vowed that I would never have to. She would be with me. And then I proposed. In the rush of excitement, she said yes, but in the days that followed I could tell that she was wavering. Sophie always wanted a past, but a husband was too much of a past. She kept it up until the morning we drove out to the dusty church. In the car outside, she told me that she couldn't do it. She was ready to commit the rest of her life to me; she would be my best friend and lover. We would fight side by side for what we believed in, but for that reason she couldn't marry me. Marriage wasn't something she could believe in. Our relationship wasn't based on white lies and doing what was always done. It was based on radical commitment to our beliefs. On those grounds she couldn't be my wife. This was the out she gave herself.

Yesterday Sophie and I flew back to New York together. This morning she flew on to Montreal. I'm to meet her again in Quito in the summer, once she's finished her finals, but I don't know if I can do it. This has been too big a setback. I don't know if I can carry on with this charade now she won't marry me. I'll stay here long enough to pick up some credit cards from Katherine and then I'll go home to Steph and the boys. I need some time to regroup and figure out my next steps. I have to figure out whether I've reached my limits as a bigamist, if this is as far as I can go, or whether I can take it to the next level. At the moment I don't feel up to it.

Mireia's desertion was the first blow. Sophie's balking at the church door might have just finished me off. I knew it was touch and go, that it wasn't a slam dunk with Sophie, but I had to try. I had to see if I could pull it off. The thing is that I don't know if I have it in me to try again. I worked hard for Sophie. She stretched me further than I've ever had to stretch myself before, and even that wasn't enough. It's not just my failure that sets me back. (And I've no doubt it is a failure. If Sophie was ever going to marry me it was down in Quito. That was my best chance. And for a bigamist, marriage is everything. Being her 'lifelong partner' doesn't cut it. Even I can't turn this loss into a partial victory.) But it's more than my failure. For the first time I feel that I was the plot point, someone else's challenge. Sophie saw me the way I see my wives, as a way of accessing another part of her own personality. She'll keep on doing this. She'll find a naive boyfriend, a money-obsessed yuppie, a disdainful Eurosnob. I don't know what else, but she'll choose each specifically to help her unlock some potential Sophies within her. Her refusal to marry me was not just a loss. It was a defeat, a victory for someone else.

THE PARLOUR GAME

Avery: Before the Curtain

She ought to be here. It is her sort of occasion, and the omens are encouraging– these new cufflinks, for instance, which arrived this morning with a scribbled poem and her initials, and there are Cecil's sly winks over drinks at lunch. These suggest to me that she is here in Florence and if in Florence then certainly at this party – or at worst, significantly avoiding it, premeditatedly absent, as a message to me, one message amongst many, and like all the others, a message of omission, present absence. These signs have ruled my daily existence since the evening we first did not meet, that first implausible failure to be introduced. Since then my life has been a sea awash with bobbing bottles – bottles stuffed with only partially decipherable notes, but meant for me nonetheless, and all sent by her.

I must have my wits about me if I'm to spot her tonight and still meanwhile do some semblance of my job. A pause here in the foyer as someone takes my overcoat. I straighten the sleeves of my dinner jacket and inhale athletically, composing myself, in the manner of an Olympian attending the pistol for his mile. And like any good miler I pace myself through the receiving line. Ah, here is the waiter with his well-balanced tray, but I need to pace myself here too. If the receiving line is the mile, then the drink tray will always be my marathon. I must save something for the finish.

Nod, shake or raise each hand to the lips, whatever seems appropriate, smile knowingly, winningly, humbly, whatever seems appropriate, but keep moving, carry momentum through the line and then launch oneself into the crowd of spectators at the finish. But God's teeth, what's this? Can an introduction to this bejewelled monster be averted? I wish I could forget *her* face, but it will likely haunt me till my deathbed.

The Boy Racer

– Clay Atlee. I race automobiles. Recuperating here in Italy between Le Mans and the Mille Miglia.

– Are you tired, Signora? No doubt you've kept yourself out late at too many parties this week.

– Well, it can be, especially on the longer runs. I think I dozed off for several miles of the Oslo–Constantinople, somewhere in the Balkans, I think.

– I suppose it is, a little, but I'm still alive.

– Not myself particularly, but I can't speak for the death wishes of all the other 'boy racers' as you call them. I compete for commercial reasons, primarily.

– No. There is no Cadillac dealership back in Pittsburgh. My car is quite special. I drive the Atlee Special Mark II, built by hand in the workshop of my own father and grandfather, master carpenters both.

– No joke at all, Signora. Built by my father and grandfather from the tree up, turned every piston and spoke, mitred and dovetailed every joint with their own hands.

– It can happen, if the combustion timing is off. That's how the Mark I went. But even metal cars catch fire. Our bigger worries are dry rot and such. During the twenty-four hours of Le Mans we had trouble with termites. I put it down to that old French barn we had to use as a garage.

– All the moving parts are made of hardwoods like Argentine quebracho and Brazilian wenge, but the secret weapon is Atlee's Special Oil, or Atlee's Essential Lubricative Fluid. We're not sure what to put on the label yet. Which sounds best to you, Signora?

– Special Oil does sound ordinary. I'll keep that in mind when I'm back home: the ladies of Europe prefer Essential Lubricative Fluid. I very much appreciate that opinion, Signora.

Beatrice: In time for the Prologue

Arriving late is a trite and unimaginative fashion. I refuse to follow it. One would never begin a book at the third chapter or drop into the opera after the first act. Why would you neglect a party's prologue, go without the admirable clues of the *dramatis personae* and the helpful moral points of the author's introduction? I always arrive at the time specified on the invitation. I consider myself above fashionable lateness.

I wonder if he is here yet. I rather doubt it. He is too much of a dandy to be punctual. He will be primping before a mirror, admiring his new cufflinks in various gestures, shaking hands, doffing his hat, taking and kissing a lady's hand. He will be here soon enough, and easy enough to spot. He cannot resist a receiving line. If I wished to see him I need only install myself there and attend those exquisite cufflinks.

But who is this now? To whom am I being introduced? I should really listen better.

The Dadaist Poetess

– No, you must have misheard, I am Bramante Lewis, the dadaist poetess.

– You don't believe me? Why would I joke with you, sir?

– Haven't I? There is more to dada than barking like a dog and signing your name on the hostess's prized Sustermans. Sometimes attending a party and conducting oneself as a girl of proper breeding is a dadaist act.

– You aren't outraged by such behaviour? Well, you are more hardened to the shock of the new than most men your age. I congratulate you.

– Or perhaps you believe novelty is no longer possible, that there is nothing new. Do you know Apollinaire's aphorism: 'The world is already exhaustive and exhausting'?

– Oh, I thought you might.

– To be absolutely honest I was ousted from the dadaists. It annoys them terribly that I use their name in vain. They are a sensitive lot. Just to goad them I still perpetrate my acts in their name. As we speak a dadaist inquisition is forming in Paris to consider my trespasses. They spend a great deal of energy denying and refuting me. They follow me everywhere I go, trying to dissuade me with bribes and threats.

– No, no. I quite understand. You would be remiss if you didn't pay your respects. I must go find my pot of red paint anyway.

Avery: Complications and Plots

An agreeable shifting of parts across the inseam, repeated and accented with each step up this broad staircase. I wonder if I am alone in enjoying the subtle erotic pleasure of climbing stairs. Is it common knowledge? Do women snicker at us and nod knowingly to each other as we indulge in this pleasure? Is this why she suggested we meet at the top of the campanile yesterday? Perhaps she has watched me climb so many flights of stairs that my enjoyment is too obvious. No doubt she is watching me now. Of course she did not keep our appointment on the campanile, nor at the top of the Boboli Gardens, nor in the San Lorenzo library upon Michelangelo's apparently famous steps. Missed appointments are the simplest of our courtship games. Silence and absence dominate, but on nights like these, when meeting is almost unavoidable, we lapse from romantic silence and resort to beautiful lies. Lies have become our love tokens. We prove our affection by the audacity and intricacy of the tales we weave for each other. It is a form of courtship or flirtation, making ourselves more mysterious for the benefit of the other.

And is there a mystery here at the top of these stairs. This could not be her, could it? This ageing trophy wife. But how aged? And what sort of trophy? The light couldn't be worse in here.

The Gigolo Polygamist

– Why, thank you. They were a gift, just today.

– Then you are a woman of great taste and your husband is a lucky man.

– Gigolo is an unkind word, Madame.

– I prefer man of leisure.

– Whose leisure? That's very good, Madame. You have wit to match your beauty.

– To be honest, Madame ... certainly I will call you Belle. It is a joy to say, not least because it is perfectly accurate. To be honest, Belle, I feel that I am not quite cut out to be a kept man.

– Something of a moral flaw I suspect.

– Quite the opposite really. I love them all possibly too much. It's that I cannot stop myself from proposing. I get so carried away being the devoted lover that I take it to its absurd extreme.

– It wouldn't be so bad if they didn't accept. I've been married four times now.

– I suppose they would be messy divorces, but I've yet to go through one. I couldn't bear to subject my darlings to such an ordeal.

– Yes, I suppose that is the word for it, but it sounds so sordid when spoken aloud.

– Quick thinking and avoidance. I'm avoiding one of my wives at this very moment. I am escorting my Canadian bride this evening, my first love actually. I'll introduce her when I get a chance, but I've just learned that my American wife is here too.

– She has a terrible temper, yes. It all comes of a life of privilege and always getting what you want.

– You're terribly understanding, Belle. Would you consider marrying me?

– Yes, I suppose it isn't wise. Thank you. I'll see you later, shall I?

Beatrice: This does not always require a book

I suppose there is something childish about this game with Avery. It is not so far removed from the play-acting of my girlhood. As a child I longed to transport myself into the pages of a book. I could play out the same imaginary plot all summer – invented characters coming and going in endless intrigues, all plot twists and subplots, never any real culmination. The carnival of Venice reminded me so much of this, all performance and no plot. I wish I could have lured Avery there. It was the perfect location for our futile little masquerade.

I call my game childish, but that's false modesty. To be honest it is the perfect solution. I came to the continent for excitement, for experience. I want a life of imagination, and it is thrilling to find that this does not always require a book. It is such a pleasure to find that novelty and play can be found in the wider world and that even here I can be both author and character. I hope it never ends.

I thought Avery attractive from the start. He was handsome and witty, but just a trifle oafish, charmingly oafish. Cecil told me that I had caught his eye, and that seemed quite enough. Why spoil it with the untidiness of an affair? I immediately began trying to forget what Avery looked like. It is an easy trick. As a child I used to be able to forget the meaning of a word by repeating it monotonously to myself. The same can be done with faces. I simply imagined each feature of Avery's face over and over again, until my imagination could not conceive of it as a whole. It wasn't difficult at all. Now I couldn't even begin to tell you what Avery looks like. I have managed to completely forget his face. I don't want to know him by sight. If I was conscious of his gaze, I'd act differently. This way I can imagine that every man I meet might be him. I can imagine that every man in every room is infatuated with me and dying to know me. Like this stiff young aesthete here now – he could be Avery, or an Avery.

The Cult of Isola Tenebris

– Why, thank you. I *have* been keeping very much out of the sun. I have just returned from the very northernmost regions.

– No, not Sweden or Lapland, though those are excellent spots.

– It is called Isola Tènebre, though you won't find it in any atlas I know of.

– An explorer, yes, but not of the ordinary sort. I am an explorer of darker continents than exist in the terrestrial sphere.

– That is something of a derogatory term. If you must have a name, I prefer supernaturalist.

– Of course, Madame Blavatsky is a great example for us. She taught us that there is a great deal beyond the senses and indeed our senses often mislead us.

– Not so outré as all that. Didn't Plato say as much? And what of sensible John Locke? Surely it is naïve to believe that the senses are reliable interpreters of all of reality. The senses don't see gravity, or electricity or intelligence, and yet we believe these things exist.

– That is very conciliatory of you. It is a pleasure to meet a man whose mind is open to possibilities beyond his eye's ken and his fingertips' reach.

– At Isola Tènebre? Well, this is really the culmination of many things. I have been a student of the esoteric for many years, and I've studied with all the great masters of Europe. I have discovered the most amazing things through automatic writing, active dreaming and symbolic reasoning. Through such methods I've learned to find the truth that the senses obscure. At Isola Tènebre we have gone so much further. There we have managed to rid the body once and for all of the despotism of the eye.

– Of course not. I'm not so foolish as to blind myself. You must think me quite mad. No, I founded, at the highest tolerable latitudes, on Isola Tènebre a retreat beyond the sun. During the arctic months at Isola Tènebre we are completely without light. Our imaginations, freed of the tyranny of the visual are able to search out and uncover higher realities.

– We have a community of some twenty girls there now.

– Yes, all girls. I have only left the isle myself to seek patrons. We have written some hundred volumes of our researches and we are seeking subscriptions. Would you yourself consider subscribing to our researches?

– That's very generous of you. I quite understand, not right away. If you give me your card, I can send you some of the examples of our discoveries.

Christ, I'd murder for something to eat, but the old matrons have formed a defensive ring around the buffet table, and there's precious little prize for breaking that thick red line, puny little discs with a veneer of pâté. I had thought there would be a meal.

I feel a bit of a fool at this some nights. Beatrice seems to be both umpire and bowler of this game. (Though I am not fool enough now to believe this is her real name.) She laid down the rules, after all. It was a few nights after I first saw her. Her note was waiting for me when I came home from a long party with too many drinks and too many introductions. How dare I, she wrote, be simply myself and withhold nothing from conversations with mere strangers, new enemies and even weary old companions who've presumed for so long to know me? Did I know to whom I was talking half the night? She had hoped I would preserve some mystery for her.

I had no idea that she had been at the party. I was distraught to realize I had forgotten her face so completely, because as I had already confided to Cecil, I was quite smitten by her. The particulars of her face may have escaped me but the impression she had made as a person was deep. Beatrice's letter complicated my dilemma further. For some reason she had disguised herself, and expected me to follow suit. It was some sort of game. Even if I had been able to overcome my shame to ask her, she wouldn't have told me what her disguise had been that evening.

I was left to wonder whether my beloved was the lady aviator, challenging me, as she did all the men, to arm-wrestling contests, the wife of the Montenegrin ambassador, who flashed me such a lascivious look over her shoulder as she left my company, the blushing San Francisco heiress, fighting her teeth to speak, or some other that I failed to notice. Cecil pretends not to know. He may even be telling the truth. He thinks it is extraordinarily funny that I have forgotten her face and that she toys with me by playing these masquerade games. Since that first night I've played along. What else can I do?

I wonder sometimes what it is she sees in me. I am past believing I am wiser or more sensitive than anyone else. Is it just that I am willing to play along with her parlour game? It is quite a game, involving and time-consuming. I only barely understand the rules, but it appears to be a treasure hunt with Beatrice herself as the prize. Each little note and cryptic hint inches me closer towards her hiding place. As long as I play along, she holds out the possibility of revealing herself eventually. But what then? Is the prize mine? Or does she go on to find another partner for this sport of assumed identities? I play this game as courtship, but it may be mere flirtation for her. Would she go to such lengths just to amuse herself? Surely this is also a test of some sort. At one of these parties I must show that I've played the game well enough, read the notes closely enough to recognize her despite her inventions and disguises. The treasure is hidden, but hidden in plain view, and I must merely recognize it for what it is.

Beatrice's perspective on this game is entirely different. She laid out this treasure hunt, drew the map and reveals the clues. She knows very well what I look like. She need only assume a new identity when she speaks to me. I have to pretend to be someone else whenever an attractive lady of her age is within earshot. She watches and listens, judging me all the time.

I wonder if she knows that I no longer recognize her. I dare not let her know that I cannot recall her face perfectly. It has been just a few months since I first saw her at the opera house, but then I stole just a few glimpses in the dark up towards her box. Her face was half hidden by her fan. Even later that night, as I lay in a bed alone, I was unable to recompose the features of her face. Beautiful yes, but beauty how construed? Cecil, her childhood friend, knows better, but he undermines every glimmer of recollection. Each time I nod my head sideways towards some new beauty, he scoffs as if to imply I must be mad – that that is not nearly the colour of Beatrice's hair, the shape of her face, the pitch of her laugh. I am a poor lover who cannot identify the object of his love.

Well, there is nothing for it. I must make a push for the buffet table or else this champagne will be the death of me.

Please, please, step aside from the pâté. It is a matter of life and death. God no, do not introduce yourself.

Archaeologist (Zeno's Tortoise)

– I think you'll find that most of those in my profession do not respond kindly to the term 'relic hunter'. It has a disreputable ring to it.

– No, in fact I'm off to Elea in the morning. The equipment has been sent ahead. We have a very specific goal in mind.

– Well, I suppose I could tell you, as you seem like a woman of uncommon seriousness and discretion.

– I have your word that you won't compromise the expedition?

– What I'm in search of is a priceless artefact, a foundation of western philosophical thought.

– You are familiar with the great philosopher Zeno, yes?

– No, that is Pythagoras, another fine gentleman. I intend to go in search of his protractor next year.

– Yes, his protractor, an instrument for measuring angles.

– No, not angels, angles. My English pronunciation is imperfect. But this year, the prize is Zeno's tortoise.

– Of course it will no longer be alive, but I am confident of finding its shell, the shell upon which Zeno built his great theory of time. I am very excited.

– Oh, many museums have contacted me and expressed interest, and of course many private individuals of considerable wealth.

– You wouldn't be interested in such an artefact yourself, would you?

– I have every confidence that it will be a quite magnificent specimen.

– Some scholars believe it might be plated with gold …

– Perhaps you'd like to take my card, in case you develop an interest in …

And good riddance to you then, you brittle, overstuffed bint.

Beatrice: I would say, if I were reading about myself in a novel

I would say, if I were reading about myself in a novel, that I am hopelessly repressed, that I invented this little masquerade to forever postpone authentic relations with a man. In fact, I do say this about myself, but I do not see it as a problem that requires resolution, as I might if I were to read about myself in a book. Whether I am right or wrong to be wary of men is neither relevant nor resolvable. It seems to me that the real point is whether I am happier fending them off with these games and diversions.

I ask myself this question frequently. I give it serious thought, because I do not want to carry on out of habit. My entire aim is to maintain control. If habit controls my actions, I have lost my self-determination, just as much as if I involved myself with a man. Every time I ask myself whether I might not be happier consummating the relationship in some way, such as perhaps engaging in an earnest conversation, I have determined that I am much more content to keep him at bay a little longer. I choose to keep playing, allowing myself to think that each man I meet might be him and pretending that I am a different person for each. I choose not to limit myself, yet.

I choose to say hello to this person, just now.

The Other Archaeologist

– Really? How extraordinary, two at one party? (The cad has been plagiarizing.)

– No, don't point him out. I will see if my professional skills are sharp enough to unearth him myself.

– I suppose he was after the usual Roman or Etruscan sites.

– Hmmm, yes. No, that is a little odd. Are you sure he was a professional archaeologist and not just a crank?

– You might be right there. There are all sorts of pretenders in this business. The trouble is that they make a terrible mess of the sites and spoil the place for legitimate scholars.

– He didn't try to sell you anything, did he?

– Well, I will certainly keep my eye out for the man.

Avery: Villains and Rivals – Cecil

Cecil and I are old friends, partners of course, but competitors too. There is a solid crust of trust at the base of our relationship, but a meringue of rivalry above that. Cecil and Beatrice are distant relations of some kind. I envy his familiarity. I hate that he attended the same picnics and weddings, watched her grow up intermittently at holidays and family celebrations. It riles me no end to imagine him pushing her on swings when she was four, trouncing her at croquet when she was eight. I cannot tolerate the thought of them wrinkling their noses in unison at the contemplation of a visit from a remote aunt, and yet I cannot avoid these jealous fantasies.

Cecil appears astounded to see that Beatrice has become such a beauty. He must regret that he was not kinder to his young cousin when she was just a girl. To console himself he mocks my imperfect love. I try to take it as lightly. I buy more than my share of the drinks. It is easier to have good grace when you are the favourite, when the notes are addressed to you and you are not merely the messenger asked to deliver them.

Cecil clearly obtains great amusement from the predicament Beatrice has put me in. In some situations my forced fictions are useful. They add an appropriate amount of ambiguity to our transactions. They are accepted with a wink. But there are those to whom misrepresenting myself could be disastrous. Cecil enjoys watching me squirm through such moments, watching me decide whether it is safe to drop the charade and conduct business normally, or whether it is best just to keep my mouth closed and let Cecil do the talking. So far we've done all right, but as we make our way through Europe, the same people keep appearing at these parties. This makes the game more difficult as I have to keep my stories straight or deny they have met me before. And though Cecil keeps telling me that with practice I'll develop more tolerance for the gallons of drink we seem obliged to consume at these things, I still have the head of a debutante at her first ball. It makes me do foolish things, like attempt accents I have no business imitating.

The Cornish Newton

– No, I'm sorry. The name's Ainsworth. Pleased to meet you.

– Well, it's one of those faces.

– Here in Italy? Well ... actually, doing a bit of private study.

– Italian explorers – Caboto, Columbus, Vespucci and that lot.

– Funny story actually. Inherited a book from my mother's father, a Newton – Newtons of Newquay. You may know the name, that part of the family has a bit of a business in bottled medicines. Thought you might. Well, this book, you see, was written by my mother's grandfather's grandfather or something of the sort. Anyway, it's all about his voyage to America with John Cabot – Giovanni Caboto, you know.

– Of course we English didn't completely trust this Italian chap we hired to go and discover some colonies for us, so we sent along a few spies. This ancestor of mine was one of them.

– Not so much cloak-and-dagger as Red Indian headdress-and-warclub.

– Seems that old Newton got lost on one of their shore sorties and got himself captured by savages.

– Funny thing is that Newton says these savages spoke a dialect of Welsh, and being not far off Cornish, he understood them well enough.

– When they cottoned on that he understood the lingo, they made him tell stories in exchange for not murdering him. Seems they were short of entertainment. He spent three years of his life telling them old fairy tales and the like.

– Well, that's what everyone's always thought, but since I'm here in Italy, doing my poor man's grand tour, I thought I'd have a look at some of the old captain's logs and maps, see if there's any truth in the old book.

– Library of the Doges in Venice, Medicis here in Florence, the Vatican in Rome next. Trouble is, though I've been at it for three weeks now, I've yet to get the knack of this Italian. It's a devil of a language, you know.

– Yes, well, thank you. I'll keep hammering away at it. Arrivederci to you too.

Beatrice: Supporting Characters – Cecil

And here is Cecil, with a wink and a wineglass. What a dear. He's a something of mystery himself, cousin Cecil is. I know what I'm about with this masquerade with Avery. I'm not as naïve as I usually like to pretend to myself. Who does not enjoy being pursued? Cecil's business in all this is unclear. Perhaps he feels he is saving me from Avery by abetting my little theatre. Perhaps he imagines he is saving Avery from me. It might be nothing more than the pleasure in seeing his more handsome friend made a fool of, but he goes to such lengths. He has composed half the notes himself, though his spelling and penmanship is atrocious and I'm forced to rewrite them all. Very likely there is some other purpose to his meddling, something to do with this business of theirs. I can't say that I care very much. Cecil can play whatever game he likes with his friend, because in a way by playing along he is pursuing me too, recognizing that I am an object to be desired, putting me at the centre of his intrigue.

And what a frivolous and wonderful intrigue it is. What preposterous thing shall I say to this stuffy old prelate? I wonder how quickly I can put him off.

The Anarchist Bomber

– Well, I haven't actually been to the Uffizi as yet. Of course I mean to, but I have been so very busy with my work.

– I'm *trying* to assemble a bomb, but you've no idea how difficult it is to find the right materials in Italy.

– It is no joke at all. I never joke about bombs.

– I don't give a damn who hears it.

– Because it suits my purposes.

– Perhaps it serves the same end. The purpose of an anarchist's bomb isn't so much to blow things up as to make people aware that there are such things as anarchist bombers. I can achieve very much the same ends by telling any busybody at a party.

– Aren't you going to ask where I learned to construct explosive devices?

– Oh, don't be like that. Stay. Let's talk. Surely you've wanted to blow up something at some point.

Beatrice: Dramatic Exits

It is getting late and I am tired. That is the second time tonight I have resorted to the story of the anarchist bomber. I shall get myself arrested one of these nights. I should be going now, anyway. I never turn up at the theatre late, but I have no qualms about leaving before the final curtain, or excusing myself from parties before they peter out. I have the good sense to know when all that remains is denouement. If I were to stay any longer, I would become melancholy. The end of a party is so sad, the room slowly emptying to reveal how dishevelled it has become over these few hours. It is much better to make my exit now while the entertainment is at its height, when people can still in an hour or so wonder where I have disappeared to. There is some theatre in this for me too, like Cinderella leaving before midnight, or Juliet poisoning herself and lying there on stage allowing the secondary actors to lament and summarize the tedious business of the last scene.

I say my goodbyes now and take home the tingle of excitement and success. I've read that actors and actresses cannot sleep after opening night. The excitement lingers after they have left the stage and they huddle in dressing rooms or cafés reliving their success. Like them, I shall lie awake all night telling myself the stories of this evening, imagining the faces I have worn and the faces I have seen. All the many possible Averys who have taken my hand, offered me a glass of wine or their card or some other silliness. Yes, it is time to leave now while the evening is unsullied. I am off home to write my own reviews.

But who is this handsome fool now. Surely I know his face. He pretends he knows mine at least. Perhaps he can be of some help with the coat, an escort through the crowd to the door perhaps, an aid to a dramatic exit.

Stage Right

– And what is it you said you do?

– Coffee? I suppose that is awfully boring.

– So it is more than bean counting. Really, as far as Sumatra?

– Cannibals. How awful. How long were you held captive?

– Two years. How terrible! You must have been in constant fear for you life.

– Really, by telling stories? How peculiar. But what sort of stories?

– And their favourite really was 'Three Blind Mice'? I wonder what they saw in it. Perhaps it has something to do with their own mythology. Did they like other mice stories?

– You should certainly write down your adventures. It would make a fascinating book.

– No, no, quite the opposite. I'm just tired. I really should be heading home. His handsome new cufflinks emerge coyly as he checks his wristwatch.

– It's perfectly safe. It's not far.

– I think I know the way by now. How long have *you* been here in the city?

– You are a very adaptable man. I see how you survived amongst the cannibals. In the course of thirty seconds you go from offering to show me the way home to requesting that I be your tour guide. I suppose I could show you some of the sights along the lungarno on the way home. The Ponte alle Grazie is really quite pretty with the moonlight on it.

I have been enjoying the frequent warm touch of his hand on my shoulder for half an hour now. His playful little stories have kept me here long past my intention. His dark eyes are intent on me and I am suddenly very tired, weary. It is exhausting being pursued, being the rabbit before the greyhounds. It is easier to let him place my wrap about me and take his arm down the stone steps. Somewhere in the Piazza Signoria my waist finds the support of his arm. At occasional spots along the lungarno I find we have stopped and I am being kissed. Avery has outdone himself tonight and invented a much finer version of himself than I could have imagined. He is strong, confident, calmly ardent, clever almost – which I had almost thought beyond him. He follows me silently up the stair to my rooms.

Later I am a little sorry that I relented, that I yielded for one night, but it is only one night. The poor man has earned the one and he was quite lovely.

Avery: Denouement

Towards the end of a night like this, I can't help but be cynical and think that there is something else to Beatrice's game of hide and seek. Standing here in the shadows (I am exhausted by this test, the constant re-invention of myself), I submit to the suspicion that this elaborate masquerade is the culmination of our affair rather than the prologue. Could it be that a normal relationship is impossible? Surely it is something like that after all. We can never be together. Her situation does not allow it. Or she is intended by fate and family obligations for another. Could I safely kill the bastard I wonder? She could already be married for all I know and I am a mere diversion to illuminate a long season of parties. It is something of this gloomy order. I will have one last drink and call this evening done. But who is this creature interposed between me and the bar? Those eyes, twinkling and active, so engaged. They could so easily be Beatrice's eyes. If only my memory and my desire could agree. Beatrice withholds herself too long and prolongs this game long past it being amusing. It is exhausting and immensely, immensely frustrating. Despite all this I persist. I cannot resist the possibility that one day she will let the mask fall. And here, those eyes have caught mine. I will introduce myself one last time.

Stage Left

– Bernadette – what a lovely name.

– May I have the pleasure of this dance?

– But why? The night is young.

– Where are you staying?

– Ah well then, it's no problem at all. My friend and I will be driving back to our place in the hills later this evening.

– Of course not. Let your companion go ahead. We will get you home safely to Fiesole.

– Or I'll have Cecil tell her.

– Cecil, will you let this young lady's travelling companion know that we will give her friend here a lift home in an hour or so. She may go ahead. We will see Bernadette safely home.

Cecil reaches protectively for the car keys in his pocket. His look is of a man woken from several years' slumber.

– Snap out of it, man, and let's have the keys while you're at it. I want to ensure this young lady arrives home safely.

He's like an automaton handing over the keys. Staring alternately at me then her, clearly amazed, dismayed even, that I have finally caught the elusive Beatrice. But he does finally wander off to inform her nonexistent companion that I will escort her friend home, on the way to my own nonexistent villa.

– Excellent chap, but a bit dim.

It is less than an hour later, and I have guided the big car, less expertly than I hoped, to the crest of a hill on the winding road to Fiesole. Here I stop to show her a famous view. Later that night I conduct her safely home to the borrowed villa. She has surpassed all my expectations, so meek and compliant after leading me on such a chase, but this too must be another disguise. Too artful by half, she pretends to wonder why I laugh when she asks if we can meet again tomorrow. I know full well that I shall be left waiting atop some staircase somewhere.

SOME CLIPPINGS FOR MY ARTICLE ON MACHINE LITERATURE

The Spirit in The Machine:
Alcohol, Combinatorics and the Heretic Inheritors of Raymond Lull
– *The Journal of Medieval Science and Technology*

In the thirteenth century, Raymond Lull (Ramón Lull) pioneered the science of combinatorics with his so-called thinking machine. Lull described a simple machine of two rotating discs, inscribed at regular intervals with words that described attributes of God. The wheels could be spun to create combinations of words from each disc. These combinations, Lull proclaimed, described further refined attributes of God. If the inner circle contained such attributes as *great, just,* and *singular* and the outer such attributes as *omniscient, powerful* and *creative,* the machine would come up with such combinations as *justly powerful, singularly omniscient,* et cetera. Today we can easily dismiss Lull's assertion that his machine could think, but we can imagine that the random action of these two wheels inspired a sort of spiritual awe at the hidden design of the universe.

For the longest time it appeared that Lull's designs were a solitary medieval excursion into the land of combinatorics, but a series of manuscripts has emerged lately that shows that others took up Lull's thread, and twisted it much further. A little-known sect called the Erigenians is just one of hundreds on the heretic rolls of the medieval Church. It was always assumed that their heresy was a form of diluted pantheism that evolved from the writing of John Scotus Erigena. But their manuscripts, lately unearthed in the Outer Hebrides suggest an altogether more intriguing reason for their expulsion.

The Erigenians took the idea of the thinking machine and combined it with another technological innovation praised by Lull. When Lull described distilled spirits as *ultime consolatio corporus humani* – the ultimate comfort for the human body, he was only giving voice to the best wisdom of the day, which commonly referred to distilled alcohol as *aqua vitae* or the water of life. The science of distillation was the closely guarded secret of many abbeys, and the Erigenians were the local experts. Their distillations were sold as cure-alls throughout the British Isles and Northern Europe, and made the abbey wealthy and influential. Erigenian spirits were apparently also much enjoyed within the abbey walls. Neighbouring monastic communities wrote to Rome complaining that the Erigenians were giving them a bad reputation. If you read between the lines you can see that they envied the Erigenians ability to attract new initiates and wealthy alms-givers. In the popular mind the Erigenians ran the medieval equivalent of our contemporary party schools.

The Erigenians believed that Lull's original thinking machine was simply too mechanical. A dull machine could not adequately describe divine nature, and without partaking of life it could not create. Now, with the introduction of a little *aqua vitae* perhaps ...

The Erigenians built a vast thinking machine of Lull's design, but rather than two discs, it had twelve. The smallest disc alone held a hundred words; the outer disc contained ten thousand. But the machine could not be operated by just anyone. Only a monk who was deeply inspired by *aqua vitae* could be entrusted to infuse the machine with the right amount of creative living energy. These monks and these monks alone were permitted to spin the wheels and record its combinations. It's an amusing scene to imagine, a room full of drunken monks madly spinning these huge discs, squinting to read and make sense of the new combination and huffing to the scriptorium to commit them to paper. It would possibly be enough to make the old scholar Lull recant all he had written on thinking machines and the powers of distilled spirits.

It is impossible to know how readable these texts were. If they still exist, they are buried somewhere in the Hebridean silt or the restricted rooms of the Vatican library. Only a partial catalogue exists. It includes such peculiarities as the Gospel of St Daedalus, the Martyrdom of St Molloy and the Vision of St Susan the Templar. Bishop De Selby eventually took alarm at the steady stream of new apocrypha the Erigenians were turning out and ultimately the Pope stepped in to have the order disbanded. And that would be it if rumours of its continued clandestine existence didn't persist. Its symbols – the twelve concentric discs and the fire-filled bottle – have been used by several secret societies through the centuries. A late eighteenth-century text, whose author claims to be the Grand Abbot Manqué of the Erigenian Order, proclaims that the continued mission of the sect is to correct the texts of ordinary human authorship using the Erigenian discs. The Grand Abbot proclaims that they will not rest until all the libraries of the earth are filled with the true spirit. It is difficult to imagine that enough Erigenians have ever existed to fulfill this mandate, but it is intriguing to think what Lull's renegade inheritors might do today in an age of electronic computers and twenty-four-hour drive-through liquor stores – one shudders at the thought.

The Golem Raconteur

– *Some Memorable Monsters*, Bogey Press, 1986

The Golem is the manmade monster of European Jewish folklore. It is brought to life by uttering magical incantations hidden in the Hebrew sacred book, the Torah. In most tales of the Golem, the Golem is the life work of a dedicated scholar, who dreams of imitating creation, but like the spells of the sorcerer's apprentice, it is a dream that usually becomes a nightmare.

Not long ago in the city of Krakow, there lived an ancient teacher known to all the city as the wisest of men. He had read more books than most people had heard of and he could recite the Torah with his eyes closed. The people of Krakow came to this teacher for advice on their problems or help in settling disputes. There was not a single controversy that he could not resolve with a wise quotation of scripture. Nobody could remember the teacher's real name, because for years people had known him as Old Solomon.

Old Solomon lived alone with his ancient wife and his books. As he grew older his eyes failed and he could not read his beloved books, so his wife had to read to him. When his wife became ill and died, Solomon lost two lifelong companions, his wife and his books. Though his neighbours brought him food and cleaned the house for him, they were poor, illiterate people. They could not read to Old Solomon. Without his books he grew sombre and sullen. He yearned for a helpmate who could read to him.

Old Solomon did know one way to obtain such a helpmate, but it was a dangerous thought and he was not sure that he had the skill to accomplish it. For one long winter after his wife's death Solomon lived without books and tried to forget the dangerous solution. One dark morning Old Solomon woke up and proclaimed that he would prefer death to this silence and resolved to make a golem for himself. Out of candle wax the blind old man fashioned the figure of a man. The figure was rudely made, as the old man could only feel and not see what he was doing. Then for five days and five nights the old man stayed by the mannikin's side and muttered spells of the kabbalah, the ancient magic hidden, like a secret code, in the words of the Torah. He was not sure of his incantations. This was sorcery reserved for the wisest of men and even he had never before dared to utter these spells. These magical incantations rearranged the letters of scripture. For most blind men this would be impossible, but for Old Solomon, this does not always require a book. Knowing the scriptures by heart, he had only to strain his memory and rearrange the words like mosaic tiles as he spoke. Finally after five days and five nights the old man fell exhausted to the floor and slept.

When Old Solomon woke he groped around in front of him for the figure he had made, but found only the bare boards of the table. He listened carefully and thought he heard the sounds of low hissing breathing.

'Is that you, Golem?' he asked, in a quavering voice.

'It is, master,' a voice not unlike his own answered.

'Will you read to me, Golem?' the old man asked, shaking with fear and disbelief.

'I will,' answered the Golem. 'What shall I read, master?'

The old man asked the Golem to open the Torah and read the story of creation. Old Solomon heard the Golem shuffling to the bookshelf and take down the book. Then he heard the pages of his beloved old book being turned, and his heart rose within him. But when the Golem began to read, he knew that something was wrong. The words the Golem read were words of the scripture, but the Golem read them as if they had been rearranged to create another story.

'Golem,' Old Solomon asked, 'are you reading the words of the book as you truly see them?'

'I am, master,' replied the Golem.

And though he thought the Golem's distortion of the old stories strange and sinister, after so long without anyone to read to him, the old man was eager to hear any new story.

'Continue then, Golem,' he said. And the Golem continued.

The Golem read to Old Solomon every night after this, and whatever the Golem read he transformed into a new story, some terrible, some marvellous, but always new. If the old man asked him reread the book he had just finished, the Golem would find yet a different story in it. At first this troubled Old Solomon, but he quickly overcame his anxiety. Soon he forgot his worries and merely enjoyed the stories that the Golem brought to him.

And then one night a neighbour came to Old Solomon's house. Because the old man did not want the people of the town to know he had been dabbling in magic, he hid the Golem in the cellar whenever visitors came knocking. Old Solomon was sitting alone in the dark when the neighbour entered. The neighbour sounded worried, and had difficulty saying what he had to say, but the old man calmed him down and persuaded him to say his piece.

'Someone has been bringing strange books to the booksellers of Krakow,' the neighbour began. 'I am not a wise man, but my betters tell me that these books are full of blasphemies and untruths.'

The old man shuddered with guilt, because the Golem's stories were often strange and impious, and though Solomon tutted and outwardly disapproved, he never stopped the Golem from telling them.

'What's more,' said the neighbour, sounding more worried than even before, 'these books are signed with your name.'

The old man gasped when he heard this, but the neighbour could not stop now without telling the whole story.

'The people who know you say that you could not write these books because you are blind, and even when you could see you would never have written such books, but strangers are beginning to accuse you of using magic to see and write these terrible books.' Once the neighbour had finished saying his piece he sat there in silence. The old man thanked him gravely for this news, and the neighbour left relieved that he had completed his heavy duty.

The old man stayed awake all night considering what to do. He did not ask the Golem to read to him that evening, for he had guessed what had happened. The Golem had written down his blasphemous stories and sold them to the bookshops in his master's name. Old Solomon knew that there was only one thing he could do. He must destroy the Golem and his false books, even if it meant that he too would die and his own library be destroyed. With the Golem was still in the cellar, Solomon his placed his chair upon the trapdoor. Carefully he lit an oil lamp and sat upon the chair. Without another thought he threw the lamp on the floor setting fire to his books, but remained in his seat over the cellar, resolved to die with his creation.

When the neighbours saw flames rising from Old Solomon's house, they rushed to put the fire out and to save their old friend, but the flames rose so high and burned so hot that no man could get into the house to carry the blind man to safety. While they stood silently with mournful faces watching the house burn, a figure burst from the flames. They could not know it, but it was the Golem, his rough waxen features disfigured even more by the heat. He shrank from their terrified cries, and fled beyond the city, and though they formed parties of brave men armed with pikes and old swords, they did not see the creature again.

From time to time after this, people heard stories from villages ever further north, of a hideous creature that crept into the town at night to steal books. In the years that followed the monster was chased so far north that it fled across the sea ice. Whaling crews that became trapped in the ice often thought they saw his awful shape moving about their ice-bound hulls, and occasionally a book or a message thrust in a bottle would appear on deck with a story so terrible and sinister that the sailors knew the Golem had written it, and the only safe thing to do was to cast it back into the ocean.

A Hallucinating Hal: Swiss Scientists Simulate Sensory Deprivation

– Popular Mechanics Online

In Geneva, Swiss scientists have managed to make a computer hallucinate. Computer scientists and cognitive psychologists have been working for years to simulate the activity of a human mind when deprived of sensory input. Their hope is to gain insight into how the mind creates something from nothing, and can develop machines that can not only use logic to solve problems, but also the more human skill of intuition and creativity.

Their ten-year effort is finally bearing fruit. The Swiss computer uses a combination of fuzzy logic and genetic algorithms to analyze text, creating indexes and abstracts of online information. The computer has also been programmed to think it is human. For the last decade scientists have been feeding the computer more and more information. Last year, they suddenly stopped providing input, but left the analytic algorithms running.

For months the computer's CPU buzzed with activity, but no output was generated. Last month, though, the computer began outputting apparently random descriptions. These eventually became more articulate, as the computer tried to explain to itself why it lacked input. 'The computer thinks it is human, and it is accustomed to continuous input,' lead engineer Jorg Muller explains. 'It has searched its stored archives for a plausible explanation for the lack of input. It seems to think that it is stranded in the Arctic.' Since it has concocted this explanation for itself, the computer's output has become more and more psychedelic and the scientists are now left with a new dilemma: How do they bring their hallucinating computer back to reality?

The Merry Prankster

– *Prevailing Currents: A Life of Jack Hughes, Godfather of Oceanography* (Chapter 34)

One of Hughes' neighbours in Ireland was the author Jonathan Swift and their acquaintance occasioned one of Hughes' more memorable practical jokes. The two met occasionally at dinners hosted by their common acquaintance Dr John Lyon, but their conversation was not extensive and the rapport only slight. The jovial Hughes found Swift dour and ill-natured. He had tried several times to persuade Swift to dine with him at his own home, but Swift always put him off with excuses of busy schedules and prior engagements. One night after dinner at Lyon's, Swift was expounding on a text by the medieval scholar Raymond Lull that proposed a sort of thinking machine. Swift held Lull's machine up for mockery, calling it a sophist's toy and declaring that a machine could never imitate the workings of the human mind. 'Only a monstrous vanity or ignorance makes it seem possible,' the writer declared.

Hughes listened patiently while Swift lectured and the collective heads of the listeners nodded in agreement. Only when it seemed that Swift's pronouncement was unassailable and unquestioned did the oceanographer wade in, saying that though he agreed Lull's machine was primitive and ineffectual, its principle had been refined by modern scientists and that today a thinking machine was much more viable. Swift of course scoffed, saying that this was mere vanity again, whereupon Hughes recalled a friend at the Royal Society who had delivered a paper on this same subject and if all present were willing to attend, he would gladly arrange a demonstration at his own home. This is how Hughes finally persuaded Swift to dine with him.

Several weeks later the company dined at the oceanographer's home. Before dinner Hughes introduced a Mr Burnside, an engineer and member of the Royal Society. Mr Burnside led them all to the parlour where a large mechanism about the size of a grand piano was installed.

The surface of this mechanism was a dark mahogany square with five hundred small bowl-like indentations. Each of these indentations held what appeared to be dice. Mr Burnside removed one of these dice and passed it around to the gathered company. The dice were actually twelve-sided polygons. On each of the twelve sides a single word was inscribed in dark blue ink. These dice, Mr Burnside explained to the crowd of guests, contained the variables from which his 'random narrative dynamo' constructed its texts. Burnside then bid them observe the indentation from which he had removed the die, pointing out the small hole at the bottom of the indentation and a tiny brass rod that emerged from this opening. This, Burnside explained, was the randomizing rod, which moved the dice to change the words that faced upwards.

He went on to demonstrate the inner workings of the machine explaining how the randomizing rods rolled the dice continually, making very many, usually nonsensical combinations of words, until a parsing system beneath the rods found a valid combination. It would then leave these intelligible fragments, stopping the randomizing rods beneath them, but continuing to agitate and seek out intelligible fragments in the rest of the frame. When several fragments had been found the machine attempted to string them together. The machine usually found that a fragment, though intelligible by itself, did not fit together with other fragments and had to be discarded. The most terrible thing, Burnside said, was to see a text that emerged beautifully from the frame, but to which the parser was unable to find an appropriate conclusion. Perhaps only the last five or six polyhedra remained unresolved, but the machine had to retreat back, row after row, to find a story it could terminate properly.

Throughout this explanation, the company, with the exception of Swift himself, whose skepticism remained undinted, grew more curious and asked more questions. As Burnside answered these questions Hughes looked on with the intense interest of a scholar hearing an explanation for perhaps the second or third time, but only now beginning to grasp its intricacies.

Burnside explained that the machine could work entirely randomly or it could be seeded with any number of fixed words, which it would not attempt to change. He now removed a die for each of the guests and asked them to place it back on the frame with the word they selected foremost. When each of the company had done so, Burnside shifted a huge brass lever at the side of the machine, which caused all the dice to begin vibrating in their receptacles.

The company then retired to the elaborate dinner laid on by Hughes. After each of the seven courses the guests returned to the parlour where they saw that sentences had begun to emerge amongst the dice. Each time they returned the text was more sensible. When they had finished their meal the guests gathered around the machine to see that, sure enough, an intelligible text had been made from the words. They congratulated Dr Burnside on his invention and speculated on the nature of the fabulous parsing engine beneath the machine. Though Swift saw the machine for the hoax it was, he knew he would seem a poor sport if he tried to debunk a display so clearly enjoyed by everyone present. He reportedly shook Mr Burnside's hand, congratulated him on his performance and left in good spirits. Perhaps he already had his counterattack in mind.

Hughes' love of jest carried through to his own work, and provided Swift with the means of revenging himself upon the oceanographer. Hughes used bottles to track the speed and direction of currents of the Atlantic, depositing the bottles at regular co-ordinates out at sea and noting the date and place they were later found. To help with the recovery of his bottles Hughes distinguished each of them with a small note. Rather than a simple letter to the finders asking them to return the bottles to him for a reward, he filled the messages with outlandish pleas for help: claims of being held captive by Amazons, of being afloat on ice drifts, marooned on ancient Atlantis or upon a volcano whose crater led to the centre of the earth. He then put out the word along the coastal settlements of Ireland and Scotland that he was a great collector of messages in bottles and that he would pay half a crown for any brought to him.

Swift took advantage of this practice to return the favour of a good practical joke. He began composing his own messages, enclosing them in bottles and tossing them out to sea each day. They soon washed up not far from where they had been launched and fishermen and truant boys alike delighted in the excellent crop of bottles that could be redeemed for one of Hughes' half-crowns. Though Hughes knew very well they were not his own bottles and told him nothing about the currents, he was obliged to pay lest he lose his reliable network of bottle collectors. It became clear soon enough who was behind these impostor notes. Swift could not temper his ironic pen, and Hughes saw himself lampooned accurately enough in some of them to be quite certain of the author. Hughes was not a bitter or vengeful man, and did not think a joke at his own expense was unfair. Far from being outraged at the expense he had been put to, he took great pleasure in having drawn the Dean into a battle of wits, even if it was a battle he was bound to lose.

Hughes invited the previous company to dine with him yet again, whereupon he demonstrated to them that the famous parsing mechanism of the machine was Hughes' own secretary, who emerged from beneath the machine with a cramped sort of bow. Mr Burnside, it was revealed, was an actor friend of the oceanographer. After dinner Hughes gave Swift full credit for seeing through the hoax and entertained the guests with the story of the author's revenge and a full reading of the collected messages in bottles. Swift apparently was not appeased by this good-natured display and continued his grudge against Hughes in the Laputian section of *Gulliver's Travels.*

The Romantic Difference Engine

– Australian Journal of Women's Studies

Charles Babbage's granddaughter Boedicia is less famous than Pascal's niece Ada, and perhaps undeservedly so as she too was a woman of unique gifts, who made significant improvements to her illustrious ancestor's invention. The direction of Boedicia Babbage's studies, as much as her own secrecy and reclusiveness, goes a long way to explaining her current obscurity. Miss Babbage's genius was of a peculiar kind, broad ranging and intuitive, but impatient and mercurial and her domains of study reflected this. Besides the differential calculus, combinatorics and a theory of time startlingly prescient of Einstein and Heisenberg, Miss Babbage also aspired to paint in oils and compose novels. For such a woman, imaginative and inventive, but unfocused and antisocial, fame, that feeble immortality, is unrealistic. Brief notoriety within highly specialized circles is now, however, within her reach. Babbage's literary output, though never published in her own lifetime, has garnered some interest in the last decade, not due to any intrinsic literary quality, but because of its method of composition. All of Miss Babbage's works, and there are two hundred and fifty-six known volumes, were composed by her version of the difference engine.

Miss Babbage's machine is unique in the history of story-telling automata. Unlike any of the devices that preceded it, which used concepts or words as their primary variables, Miss Babbage begins with a higher order concept, using characters as the seed variables for her combinatory machine. That she chose characters as her starting point provides an interesting and exciting insight into Babbage's theory of literature. It is also a reflection of Babbage's Romantic humanism. Her underlying premise is that stories are constructed not of abstract concepts or lexical units, but by the interactions of diverse human beings. Accordingly Babbage stocked her narrative difference engine with a cast of extremely diverse characters, from knights-errant and heretic nuns to flawed kings and drunken poets. The cast of characters exposes the inventor's own literary tastes. There is pronounced favouritism towards the outlandish, the dark, and a certain romantic medievalism, as if what she had in mind was a monstrous Gothic novel. But if Miss Babbage favoured the past and paid only slight attention to the present, she compensated by dabbling in the future.

Had she ever attempted to write anything herself, we might have considered Boedicia Babbage the mother of modern science fiction. A number of her characters would not be out of place in a novel by H.G. Wells or Jules Verne. We have space travellers and builders of supplementary mechanical moons, mesmerists with psychokinetic ability, men who discover the ancient passages through the hollow earth to America and other paradises.

As with all science fiction there is the usual random prophetic accuracy. So many of Babbage's characters, improbable as they might have seemed to her contemporaries, do resemble roles and characters that would eventually appear: the anarchist bomber, the racer of motorcars, the professor of comparative literature. All of these characters exist as variables of Babbage's narrative difference engine. These fortuitous accurate predictions reveal as much about the principle of random combinatorics as they do about Babbage's intuition. By continuous random creation of possible future characters, she was bound to develop at least a few characters that would eventually come true. This almost vindicates the principle behind all story-telling machines.

What of the stories produced by Miss Babbage's machine then? Do they vindicate the principle of building stories by the random combination of a fixed set of characters? Sadly, it appears not totally. The primary failing of Miss Babbage's stories is an almost total lack of plot. There is so much hinted at. The characters contain the germ of a premise, but this seed never grows. The characters lack the proper settings and events to act according to their unique traits. It is as if they have been pulled out of their natural environments and invited to a huge party. The characters meet; they chat, but little else happens. Many of her volumes are simply records of conversations between the randomly associated characters. The possible conflicts or agreements between these characters hang there, but never materialize.

A minority of scholars have seen this effect as design rather than accident, that the inertia of Babbage's stories is the point. The feminists amongst this group, drawing parallels to the fiction of Virginia Woolf, see this lack of motion as a reflection of and a commentary on the powerlessness of women in Victorian society. Though clearly a genius and one of the few people in history to actually construct a difference engine along the lines her grandfather only envisioned, Boedicia could never attend a university or become a member of the Royal Society. The best she could expect is to be allowed to continue in obscurity, a creature of potential and promise never actualized, just like the characters who populate her stories.

An even smaller group of scholars (I count one article that argues this so far) sees in Babbage's novels an early innovator of some modern and post-modern forms, notably the plays of Beckett that use the indefinite postponement of action to reflect a spiritual or emotional morass, usually associated with what we call the 'modern condition'. Both these approaches draw on evidence that Babbage suffered from agoraphobia and social anxiety. Until late in life Babbage was very reluctant to leave her own home and preferred to communicate in writing rather than meet people.

The actual machine has never been found and is thought to have been destroyed. To the surprise of her family and friends, after years of productive if reclusive spinsterhood, Boedicia married a very religious man and erstwhile Luddite named Cedric Aviston. Mrs Aviston was a very different woman from Miss Babbage. She became more zealous than even her husband, eventually converting to Roman Catholicism. Mr Aviston's Luddism was seemingly as contagious as his religiousness; in her later years the former Boedicia Babbage developed a disdain for and deep hatred of machines of all sorts. When her inheritors came to itemize her estate the machine and her experimental notebooks were nowhere to be found. The novels, composed decades earlier by the machine, were discovered in a disused room of the Babbage's country home several years after her death.

The Electronic Plot Device

– Northwestern Institute of Technology Journal of Computer History

In 1940 a German U-boat made a startling and rarely reported raid on the U.S. naval base in Burnt Armpit, Newfoundland. The pattern of destruction was meant to look random, but U.S. intelligence always believed that the goal of the mission had been to capture the electronic computer housed in the base's communication building. This suspicion was confirmed when the computer was recovered along with other American computing technology that had found its way into Nazi hands in the rocket complex at Penemunde. The Americans had used the computer to develop search patterns for antisubmarine operations in the North Atlantic. The Germans adapted it to calculate rocket flight trajectories and ballistic charts, but the Germans apparently found additional capabilities built into the computer, previously unknown to the American military.

The developers of the original software had included alternate programming, which they either intended to exploit later or designed as a surprise amusement for its eventual users. If so, it would be the first known implementation of what we now know as an Easter egg. And what a strange egg it was. The subroutines have been investigated by dozens of researchers at various times and the only conclusion they can come to was that the software was used to develop plots for novels or perhaps movies. Using the same search routines developed for the U.S. Navy it generated plot graphs or paths of events. The events or plot points on these paths remained generic, such as a reversal, climax, disclosure, complication. They were numbered to show their order and given a magnitude. These template plots could thus be applied to different characters and specific events. When the Germans added their trajectory programming to the computer, the plot graph generator was able to access these too, so that it could construct plots out of a combination of trajectory and path search algorithms.

Eventually the Penemunde scientists discovered the concealed software and fathomed its purpose. They were anything but amused by this apparent Easter egg. In fact they were quite alarmed. Their paranoid interpretation was that in addition to technological and military superiority, the Americans hoped to use computers to achieve cultural superiority. The Ministry of Propaganda and Public Enlightenment was already concerned that Hollywood had surpassed the German film industry in output and popularity. What if Hollywood and those New York publishers were to use the plot-generating device to accelerate their production and innovate far beyond what German cultural industries were capable of? Clearly Germany must keep pace. They too must use the plot-generating device. The orders came down from on high that the cultural scientists were entitled to a share of the computers' cycles and so for one quarter of the day the trajectory calculations of Penemunde were suspended while the cultural engineers generated their plots.

The catalogue of plot graphs is immense. It includes hundreds of variations on plots that describe perfect hyperbolas like the arc of an arrow and a similar number of subtypes of the plot that turns this arc upside down, ascending at first only slightly until gradually increasing its angle like the inside edge of a bowl. The catalogue describes plots that ascend at a constant rate and upon approaching their targets plummet directly down upon them; plots that move in low, just above the ground, following the contours of the terrain; plots that ascend in stages, like steps to higher altitudes; and plots that shoot up at acute angles beyond the atmosphere towards an aerial target.

On the horizontal plane the computer produced plots that proceed undistracted and determined towards their objective; plots that circle their targets, spiralling ever closer in towards them; plots with no apparent motive that spiral out in widening sweeps; plots that meander like old rivers towards their outlet; plots that zig and zag like prey evading a speedier pursuer; plots that never approach the subject directly, that move tangentially like a sailboat tacking into the wind; plots that have to pretend their target is elsewhere only turning on it at the last moment as if to surprise it; and plots that cover half the distance to their target every second, but never reach it.

There are plots that seem inspired by wave forms on an oscilloscope: plots that proceed elegantly and unnaturally like pure sine waves through their stages; plots that proceed abruptly and formally like square waves. Plots with rapid ascents and descents like saw-tooths; plots whose oscillations increase until they break up into static and white noise.

There are over ten thousand variations in the official compendium of the computer's output, but there is no proof that a single one was put to use. The disgruntled rocket scientists always objected to the hijacking of their computer. Stories aren't going to win the war, they argued. Computing power shouldn't be wasted on fiction. It's more than it deserves. If it was not for trajectory and flight path calculations, they wanted the computer for fuel requirement, aerodynamics, and thrust calculations. From the reams of printed output that have been preserved, their outrage seems justified.

It is impossible to know how much the distractions of plot graph research impeded German rocketry, but it could not have been insignificant. A device valuable enough to risk a daring raid on the coast of North America for was too valuable to be tied up calculating endless variations on rising action and denouement. It is easy to imagine a less happy ending to this story if the Germans had ignored this little subroutine and carried on along their intended path.

Nolan's New Plunge

– *SPAM Magazine,* June 2001

Reader beware, accompanying this articles are pictures of a dangerously pink Nolan Plunge sitting beside his pool, in the Umbrian hills, clad in horrendously orange swim trunks and D&G sunglasses. Of the glasses and swim trunks Plunge immediately quips, 'I like to think I wear them with a certain ironic integrity.' But of the alarming skin tone he appears dismayed, 'I thought the years in front of a CRT would have made me immune to this.'

Immunity seems to otherwise cling to Plunge. He is living the good life here in Italy, rescued from the high tech downturn by the timely sale of his company ThinkThirst to the consumer electronics giant Milliard. He's apparently immune also to the regrets and creative doldrums that strike so many entrepreneurs who've sold their start-ups. The same Plunge who once trod the conference circuit touting his brainchild Impetus has a new enthusiasm, and it is, he says, the software he wanted to write all along.

'I always loved the idea of computer-generated literature. As a kid I couldn't get new books fast enough. I used to consume those pulpy fantasy novels by the handful. I'd have to buy two or three at a time, but I still used to find myself without books. I used to think how cool it would be to just have your PC churn out a new book every time you needed one. Even as a kid, I knew that books were formulaic. I thought it would be so simple to program the formula and have the computer generate new variants.'

It proved harder than he ever imagined. Through high school and college he wrote a dozen variants of the software he now calls Amanuensis. None of them satisfied the imagination or his voracious appetite for books. Finally Plunge rented an apartment over a used bookstore and turned his programming talents to what seemed the more solvable problem of corporate decision support. His company ThinkThirst grew out of that apartment into several adjoining units, until it owned and occupied almost the entire building. The only tenant ThinkThirst did not evict was that used bookstore.

'I think all along I knew I would get back to the problem of computer-generated literature, that Amanuensis would some day rise from the dead. All the while I was at ThinkThirst I kept jotting down new ideas, new ways of tackling the problem. During the last six months at ThinkThirst, I was bored with Impetus and eager to get back to Amanuensis. I wouldn't have sold the company, if I didn't have things I wanted to do more.'

And so the sale of ThinkThirst and the lifestyle transplant to sunny central Italy. Neither Milliard nor Plunge seems inclined to disclose the value of the sale.

'It was enough so that I can hole up at this little house for a year and build the basic elements of Amanuensis,' says Plunge, 'but not enough to buy the title I wanted. I really wanted to be Duke.'

It's hard to know how seriously to take Plunge's aristocratic ambitions, but his continued susceptibility to the Italian sun would indicate that neither the scenery nor his newfound affluence have distracted him from his stated goal of software-generated fiction. Most days find him holed up inside his shuttered house with his computer and what he claims is the largest whiteboard in central Italy. 'I had it imported myself,' he says wryly, as if commenting on a fine wine.

He hauls the whiteboard poolside to help illustrate his new concepts. Pointing at the tangle of geometric shapes he explains that this is the key to his new software.

'Earlier software never understood the deep geometry of most fiction, that fiction is more than the line of the plot. It has complex relations that can be represented by various polygons, arcs and various-sized circles. The first person to try this method was Boedicia Babbage,' he says, dropping a name he may have just made up. 'Very few people seem to realize that her fiction computer-based everything on the triangle. Everything was constructed around three points, A, B, C. That was the most complex geometry she could encode. It was primitive, but a very powerful idea. I've used the same principles, but I generate stories with more complex geometries, and embedded many more of them in each fiction.'

He goes on to describe a novel based on the geometry of the dodecahedron. 'Each of the twelve faces represents a different narrative. The thirty edges represent the relationships between these stories. The twenty vertices ...' Plunge's girlfriend of five years, who has been coaxed outside to help hold the whiteboard, raises her eyebrows ever higher as he goes on.

'It's a bit much,' she says when I ask about her boyfriend's latest concept. But Plunge is undaunted by her skepticism.

As she heads back indoors to her forensic detective novel, Plunge's eyes follow her. 'She refuses to marry me,' he confides, as if proud of her good judgment.

Plunge is, after all, a man who has done well by irony. His corporate support software Impetus is now embedded in millions of toys worldwide. Plunge sees this as poetic justice.

'Impetus was bought by people who were looking for a sort of artificial intelligence tool, but it was always really a combination mood ring and magic eightball, so it's returned to its rightful market niche.'

Considering the diverse applications of his last software effort, Plunge's opinions on the Amanuensis market niche are interesting. 'I see two major applications. The first is my original motivation, the huge demand for mass-market consumable fiction. That's a big market. That's where the money is. The other area is at the edge of serious literature, and for this I think we'd market the results rather than the software, because the results seem to be hit and miss with these higher-order geometries.'

So does that mean Plunge sees himself becoming an author? 'Probably not,' he says with a strange emphasis on the probably. 'I can see creating a stable of pseudo-authors for this sort of work. Remember it's not likely to be commercially successful stuff, but it will be groundbreaking, a sort of experimental laboratory for literature, there just to generate ideas, some of which may be exploited by authors down the line.'

You hate to dint Plunge's enthusiasm, but given the past failures in this field, his own and others', you have to question the viability of Plunge's new project.

He rattles off a dozen ways he has tried and failed to create a novel from a software algorithm. 'Despite this I persist, because I know it's doable, and now I think I have something.'

How far along is it now? How much is still theoretical?

'It could write your article for you,' Plunge says, with an eager grin.

But I have spent the fee already. I don't want to give my publisher any reason to demand it back.

THE LAST STORY

That Genies Are Stories

I'm into my final phase now. A decadent period, like all final ones, a period of excess: I'm no longer careful and I talk too much. But then I know it's just a matter of time. My days are numbered. It's been a good run, but the writing is on the wall. All the others are gone, caught, itemized, ratted out, elaborated, told. I can't say I've been wiser than the rest, just luckier and less of a target. The best went first a long time ago, the prize specimens, who made spectacles of themselves or just couldn't help being noticed, and were carried off as trophies. A few escaped those early, energetic roundups, but once you've been in their grasp once, you're so much easier to track down. A few of us lesser examples hung on, retreating to ever-decreasing territories, lying low, remembering that we're always being hunted and smarter ones than us have been nabbed. We've been endangered for longer than the word danger existed. For decades now we've been extinct in the wild and never successfully bred in captivity.

It's strange to admit that I'm the last of my kind, the last untamed spirit, the sole remaining unbottled genie, the only untold story – whatever – I'm more ancient than any language. None of these names feels comfortable. Each is a sort of constraint, and that's the problem, isn't it? This naming thing that people do. It's the subtle poison with which all human traps are baited. We can be debunked. We can be defined. We can be anthologized, anatomized, taxonified. We can be bottled and extorted to grant wishes. It's terrible what people can get away with. But Amnesty International doesn't care and no animal rights group recognizes us.

Anyway the torture and forced labour of genies is largely a thing of the past. The usual way it's done these days, the most secure and the most inescapable, is to put them into words, to capture their spirit as a story.

Words aren't the only way to get caught, but they're by far the most pernicious of perils. It's a terrible trap. Words are so seductive. I love them myself. It's easy to see how so many were lured to their doom.

Just listen to me prattling away, talking about myself, flirting with danger. Words come so naturally, unbidden, to try to express what we are – spirits, inspiration, genies, genius, genes. Such lovely names. There's a dark attraction to all of them, that I resist only half-heartedly now. Sooner, rather than later, I will be caught too.

It used to be easier to keep out of sight, to elude capture. Before languages, when everything was grunts and pointing, we used to think people were silly. We toyed with them. We used to scare them a little bit. People don't like the unexpected and are easily spooked. You make such easy targets. These last few millennia have been the history of human revenge on us, though I doubt that you would have been kinder, if we'd resisted that first urge to tease and taunt.

There is a part of every genie that always wants to know – what you'd look like, what you'd sound like if put down in words, if your story were finally – told. I've no idea what I'm about. How can you know what you are about? How can you say that about yourself? I like to speculate and fantasize that I am some as yet unimagined epic, the last great untold story, but it's stupid to think this way. I know very well that the great ones were all told long ago. The ones that held on were the small fry. The unremarkable stories, the tedious, the forgettable and frankly boring minor plots escaped notice the longest. It stands to reason that the last story is also the least worth telling.

I still dream of hidden greatness, though only vaguely. We can never dream concretely of what we might be about. I can never come up with the story myself. The only stories we can think of are the ones that have been told already. We are not really, when it comes down to it, very creative. We are the imagined, not the imaginers. How can we believe that anything we have to say has not been said before? If I ever suppose that I've come up with something new, something that might be my story, I need only wait a while for it to appear elsewhere and remind me that it existed long before.

Delusions of grandeur though they might be, I still dream of being that last truly great story. I try to imagine my discovery, the shock and joy of the new, the wonder that there still remains a story such as this to tell. It's futile, really. Stories don't live to witness their acclaim. These dreams are like the fantasies of a lonely suicide who visualizes the great uproar of blame and terrific mourning that will greet his death.

Genies in Bottles

There is something very like a death wish in the psyche of the genie. Surely you have wondered about this curious custom of putting messages in bottles? I know I have. Do people really have such a meagre understanding of the laws of probability to believe that a message enclosed in a bottle and entrusted to the currents of the sea will reach a helpful audience in time – one who speaks the same language, one who has the inclination and capacity to send aid? They are deluded by the natural magic of these things. Stories want to be in bottles. It's a basic, if only metaphysical, law of attraction, like poets being attracted to death and rich old men to shallow, greedy young women. It's not a happy attraction. So many of us have been undone by the bottle. Everyone from the wisest genie to the stupidest boy knows that genies can be trapped in bottles. We know it. All of us do, and yet we fall for it over and over again. It is a fatal attraction. We love our doom, though none of us understands why.

Every genie I have known has tried to deny his attraction to the bottle, but denial and avoidance don't help you resist the temptation. They merely turn it into a fetish. I have known so many of these genies who flirt with the bottle, taking a dark thrill in their enclosure, almost daring fate to put the stopper in. They say they know where to draw the line. They insist that they always leave the bottle before they are in any real danger, but they push their luck, and sooner or later the cork is in. All this because they refused to acknowledge their problem.

Unlike my departed colleagues, I have tried to understand the logic, the complex psychological flaw of the genie that attracts us to the bottle and to words. The bottle and the word, I have come to believe, are merely two different manifestations of the same urge, our search for self-knowledge. Yes, please allow us these simple, self-indulgent desires. We are not entirely different from you people. You have no monopoly on the self. We too wonder what we are all about. In fact it may be worse for us. Because we are by nature formless, nebulous, unbounded by physics and physicality, we find it more difficult to provide definitions for ourselves. Self-expression and self-exploration are feeble excuses, but they are our excuses nevertheless for our terrible weakness for words and bottles.

The bottle (and I speak from my own experience here, I am not immune to these temptations) is curiously comforting. A person would say that it was womblike or cavelike, evoking some prenatal or primitive security, but no genie ever deigned to live in a cave or to gestate in such a thing as a womb. For a genie, the cosy enclosure of the bottle is not a recollection of a consoling memory. It is the attainment of something we have never had, a sort of limiting that is not natural to us. And words are merely metaphysical bottles, containers of a lovely shape that we cannot resist pouring ourselves into, knowing even as we do so that it transforms us, performs a metamorphosis by which we gain self-knowledge, but which instantly snatches away our freedom to appreciate it. We have a glimpse of what we are and then lose ourselves.

Genies are cursed and blessed with freedom. We are like your idea of the superman, unburdened by morality or corporeal vulnerability. (Where do you suppose this idea of the superman came from in the first place?) And yet this freedom, this formlessness is exhausting. It is exhilarating to be able to be whatever we desire, but the constant manufacture of novelty and of new desires takes its toll. It is occasionally pleasant to seek confinement and the restriction of the bottle or the pretty scribblings of man. None of us would relish a prolonged stay in such a prison, but on occasion, periodically, every now and then, it's a nice break. Too often though, the stay is permanent.

Genies and People

There seems to be this idea that genies don't like people. In general this is not at all true. I suppose this notion that genies are misanthropic creatures comes from the long, sordid history of putting them in bottles and making them grant wishes. This is not a situation in which a genie can be expected to handle himself with grace. I doubt though that the rage of these genies is actually meant for their captors. Genies don't really blame people for putting them in bottles. Genies know they do this to themselves. The genie is really only angry with himself for putting himself in the situation. Some genies maintain a gruff, antagonistic front when they are around people as a sort of protection. We are afraid of our own desires, our own terrible proclivities and the trouble they will get us into around people. We try to toughen ourselves up to keep temptation away.

If we were to blame anything but ourselves, it wouldn't be people. It would be the vessel, be it the bottle or the language. Why do they have to be so seductively attractive? Why do they seem made for us? Surely they can stop it. Surely they can tone it down, make themselves not quite so desirable. It seems to some genies that language willingly entraps us, that it gets some pleasure out of enclosing and defining us. This is infuriating. We try to help ourselves, but we could use some help on the other side and it is not forthcoming. Language seems to treat it as merely a game. It takes the telling of stories so lightly. I suppose it loses nothing in the bargain, so why should it care.

Genies don't really blame people for telling stories either. We see that language uses people as much as it uses us, that it is almost irresistibly attractive. Most genies are indifferent about people. I myself quite like them. I find you so curious and energetic. It's so very charming. Though it's always a risk being in the company of people, I rarely resist. In fact I invariably fall in with the wrong crowd entirely. I hang around writers continually, good or bad – I can't tell the difference. I frequent bookstores and places of learning. I once managed to get myself onto the faculty of a large state university, where I taught a summer course called 'The Psychology of Genies'. It was considered a bird course and was taken by engineering students who needed an arts or social science credit and by jocks who needed to maintain a certain grade average. I took the course very seriously though and was without exception disappointed with my students. They seemed to think they were taking a course in creative writing rather than serious psychological study. I gave them all failing grades, but the university overturned the marks before they dismissed me from the faculty.

Genies I Have Known

Sometimes I seek the company of people simply because I am bored. It is lonely being the last genie. People must substitute for all my departed comrades. In the company of people I can hear the old stories I once knew. It doesn't exactly cheer me up, but it fills me with a nostalgic yearning for the old days. I grow maudlin and think of the fine stories I have known. I don't think that genies in their natural state are capable of anything like happiness. Our freedom and self-ignorance gnaws at us. The closest we ever come to happiness is when we are first bottled or first told as a story, but it is such a fleeting and doomed pleasure. Genies are by nature melancholy, and when they see that they are caught, a terrific despair consumes them.

I have known only one genie who derived any sustained pleasure from being told. He managed to persist in a sort of half state for centuries, half told, half free. He was the happiest genie I have ever known. He was written down and told hundreds of times in different versions, but did not submit completely at the first telling. Too wily to give himself up completely, he kept versions of himself in reserve. He never let any version become authoritative. This genie was the story of the undiscovered or concealed country. He had about as many names as there are versions of his tale. He was Atlantis, America and the lost cities of Cibola. He has been Brobdignagia, El Dorado, Shangri-la and Nestoria, but none of these really qualifies as a name. Genies and stories don't really have names, not ones that stick or that they respond to. When their story is told in its definitive form, you could say that then they are named conclusively.

I haven't seen my old friend for a century or so. I assume that he's perfected, patented, bottled and shipped. But for a while there he kept ahead of them. As long as there was the possibility of an undiscovered country still existing, he was free to mutate and change with every retelling. He was alive. Once he became merely fiction, a mere formula, that was it. His long run was over.

I said before that the genie of the undiscovered country was the happiest genie I knew. It had something to do with the self-knowledge that all we genies crave. He had a general outline of himself, and this gave him an enormous sense of relief, a sense of, shall we say, actualization, but he wasn't yet imprisoned. He wasn't bound to a single version of himself. He could still elaborate, be creative. He had a lot of fun with Renaissance Europe, and he had a great affection for flat-earth theorists, and for the Mormons, who gave life to the story of the lost country when it seemed to be on its last legs. Sadly, I think this story has been told to death now. I doubt there are any more possible variations. I know people talk of life on other planets and other such nonsense, but I suspect it isn't the same story. I have not seen my friend for some time now, and I believe he is what passes as dead for us genies.

I myself have had many close scrapes. I have flirted with pen and paper as much as the next genie, if not a little more. I'm destined to go the way of all my old friends. Friends is a funny word for the relationship between stories, but I am waxing nostalgic in my old age. This nostalgia colours all the memories of the various stories I have known, and I have known a great many of them. Most are my betters. My glory was I had such friends, blah, blah, blah.

Let me see. Whom have I outlasted? I knew the grand story of the perpetual car chase when he was but a gleam in the eye of that mad Italian, Zeno. He always was a popular one, a lad's lad, a bit of a braggart, but at worst a loveable blowhard. Who else? The son avenging a wronged father – a good yarn, bound to rouse the blood, if a bit, well, a bit too easy, such a blatant appeal to the basest emotions. The unfortunate wish –

there was a good one, a story worthy of folklore, the ubiquitous three wishes, King Midas and all that, a bit moralistic in its irony, perhaps not as fun to be around as, say, the story of the mistaken death. There's a genie I miss, the story of the mistaken death, that good one from Romeo and Juliet. He thinks she's dead and so kills himself; she wakes up and sees he's dead so she kills herself. Good stuff. The best. There's none like that these days. But these are just a few. I worked with the story of the message in a bottle, not well liked naturally, but a fine one just the same. I had business with the story of stories within stories – a surprisingly tedious fellow. I can't say I miss him.

I could go on. My list could be exhaustive, but to what purpose? As a tribute to my exhausted comrades, the fallen stories, the ones told out? I don't have it in me. I am not after all an anthologist. It is humbling, though, to think of all the stories that used to be, when they were at their best – before they *were* stories, when they were something previous, something infinitely more wonderful, brimming with potential, potent and inspired, and how they are diminished in the telling. That thing we imagine is out there cannot be captured on paper. The story is always something less than it was supposed to be, something less than when first glimpsed by the imagination. What's there is just a semblance, a faded cipher of what was intended or envisioned. I think writers know this. I have seen the guilty looks on their faces when they are alone, and they understand what they have done. I don't blame them. How could they know? But I think they blame themselves. I think they feel like traitors. I wish I could cheer them up somehow, but I suspect that all this, these words here, will do only the opposite. Sorry for that.

Why I Am the Last Genie

I am, after all this, left to wonder exactly why I am the last story. It is an ambiguous distinction. I would decline the honour if I could. It is not that I have been extremely clever or secretive. If I have ever hidden, it has been that old ploy of hiding in plain view. I frequently tell myself that it is nothing to do with me, that I have just been lucky. At the beginning I always kept the company of other, better genies, and it was they who were more obvious targets. I stood by and watched while the story of the captive who keeps herself alive by telling stories was told, while the story of the message in the bottle was spilled. These were gaudy genies of bright literary plumage. I, it seems, am dull coloured and well camouflaged.

Later, when the herd of genies had been culled to the point of near extinction, I made no special effort to stay hidden. In fact I loitered in libraries and schools, these cemeteries of told stories. At all these places I found people were more interested in my fallen brethren, the fine dead specimens they had collected, than in me. And who can blame them?

Though I seek out the company of authors of all sorts, I usually find them during their periods of creative morass. I seem to have an affinity for writers suffering from writer's block, those who are delaying their great enterprise, are suffering some blockage or crisis of motivation.

Maybe it's something about me. There is something in my story that resists telling. Perhaps people just don't want to hear it. I find this very unlikely. I have known many unpleasant stories in my time and they all seem to find their authors and their audiences. No matter how horrible the story, there would always be some segment of humanity ready to put it into words.

There are several short lapses in my memory, which is peculiar. Genies don't lose consciousness. We don't sleep, nor do we dream, but I have this vague intimation that I might have been written down once or twice, just briefly, then somehow lost, destroyed or erased. Maybe this is just another one of my fantasies. If this happened I have no recollection of the circumstances or, more importantly, just what I turned out to be. I can never know if it happened. I'm probably deluding myself, adding adventure and romance to my dull existence.

Ultimately, I have to conclude that dullness has been my saving grace. Obviously I am not a very good story. After all, what story out there remains to be told? None of any real consequence, surely. My inevitable conclusion is that I am simply not worth telling. This conclusion should bother me ... and it might, but it is so difficult to know how one really feels. Ah, the woeful strains of that broken record, self-doubt, I hear them once again, my operatic theme. I cannot know, until it is too late, what I am really about. I can merely speculate. It could turn out that I am the story that explains that stories are genies, something as simple as that. I might only be the story of the last story. It's possible that the only story left to tell is that all the stories have been told. But I wouldn't count on any of this.

PLAGIARISM

I had been alone in the lounge an hour when the other passengers arrived. Each had heard partial explanations for our delay that differed on significant points, but agreed unanimously on the end result. The honeymooning couple returning from the very exclusive and very remote resort had heard that their plane for the next leg had mechanical problems. The four very varied individuals on their way to see the solar eclipse were booked on the same flight, but they'd been told that it had been quarantined at its last port of call (speculative variations on this premise ranged from Ebola to bubonic plague.) The two Chilean engineers going in the opposite direction had overheard, amidst the incomprehensible local dialect spoken by the men in overalls on the tarmac, the awful word 'hijack'. Two missionaries heading off to the interior had been told that their pilot was ill and a relief pilot was two islands away. The relief pilot himself, however, declared himself present, lamenting that he had been summoned from the warm bed of a female friend. In beautifully Spanish-tinged tones he wearily assured us that it was something as simple as a *coup d'état* or civil war on one or two of the neighbouring islands.

I suggested that we amuse ourselves by telling stories. I had a premonition that our delay was only beginning and a suspicion that whatever crossword puzzles and airport novels we had each brought to help pass the time had been exhausted long ago. I can be jovial and appealingly eccentric when the situation requires. I can assume the sort of personality that people want to indulge. 'Why don't we take turns telling stories?' I said, as if this were a well-planned dinner party and they had been led to expect party games. 'We are all strangers here, never likely to see each other again. We don't even know each other's names. We could tell each other anything, the most outrageous lies, the stories we've been told but don't believe ...' I leaned in closer towards the centre of the room, and realized I'd adopted the false English accent I fall into when I am trying to be anything I'm not. 'We could even confess our darkest secrets without fear of consequences.'

Their reluctance was palpable. The younger eclipse pilgrims regarded me with a mix of disbelief and embarrassment, like bored adolescents whose parents had just suggested a game of Monopoly. Their elderly companion smiled kindly and claimed he was too tired to tell stories. The bride looked worriedly about, as if this was a pop quiz she was ill prepared for. A lovely girl, clear-skinned and wide-eyed, she protested that she didn't know any good stories, and had never really liked public speaking. Her husband, though, was big, hale and talkative. His eyes flashed with the canine alertness of a man who's made a long career of being the life of the party. It was no surprise that he was the first to take up my invitation.

The Groom's Tale

'I've got a story,' he said, shifting his big jaw as if chewing gum. I was sure he would. He looked like the type who saved a few good tales for the clubhouse or the poker table, a man who enjoyed life.

'This is an absolutely true story,' he began. 'It happened in college. I played this joke on a friend of mine. This guy called Andy, a frat brother.' The story must have happened almost a decade ago, but as he told the story the groom slipped more and more into his old college-boy vernacular.

'Andy was a real quiet guy. He was a good guy, but he was quiet. Not exactly a lady's man, you know what I mean? He wasn't ugly or anything. He just had no moves. I used to say, just watch me, pick up my moves. I'd always go in and be his wingman, you know, breaking the ice with chicks, saying something stupid, making myself look like an idiot but getting us in there and giving Andy the chance to look good. He always wasted it. Anyway, one morning after a party Andy found a piece of paper in his pocket that was all smudged by spilled drinks. He asked me if I knew what it was and I said, "Hey, don't you remember, you got Brittany's phone number last night?" He got all worried like he'd done something wrong, but I told him he was a perfect gentleman and that he and Brittany really seemed to get along. Andy couldn't remember who Brittany was. I said, "Sure you do, dude, she was the total honey you were with all night." He was all impressed with himself and kept asking me if I knew how to get hold of her. I told him no, but I knew some of the girls she hung out with and if we threw a party, they'd probably bring her. He was all over that.

'Anyway, before the party I tell Andy that Brittany's all pissed that he hasn't called her, and that she and her friends want to give him a test. They think that Andy was so drunk he's forgotten what she looks like, so he has to try to prove he remembers her. If he really likes her, he has to tell her some crazy story about himself when he meets her, like he's an astronaut in training or he was raised by swans or something. Andy is all freaked out by this, but I keep pumping him up on what a babe Brittany is and how totally into him she was and after a few beers he seems to buy it. Anyway he spends the whole night telling chicks these weird-ass stories. He tells them he's some super spy, or he's already been married twice and hasn't the guts to divorce either of his wives. Most of the girls think he's a superfreak or just messed up, but some of them figure this is Andy's move and play along. All the time, Andy's trying to figure out which one is this hottie Brittany. But get this – there never was a Brittany. I totally made her up. I guess it would be pretty sad, Andy making an ass of himself looking for some chick who doesn't exist.'

The groom paused to gather in the various looks of disapproval or feigned disinterest. 'But the joke was on me I guess. At the end of the night Andy actually hooks up with some girl. I guess he thought she was this Brittany chick. They got together that night and started dating after that. He must've figured out her real name sooner or later, 'cause I heard he married her.'

The groom smiled as he finished his story and nodded with his whole body as he delivered the punch line. 'I wish he'd invited me to the wedding. I could have told an awesome story about how they met.'

A few of us managed a smile at the gift-wrapped ending.

The First Missionary's Tale

That might have been it. The groom might have been the only one of the twelve to take up the invitation. Sometimes that's the way it goes. You get one person interested, but his enthusiasm isn't contagious; everyone else remains bound by the awkwardness of the situation. This time, I was sure that someone would pick up where the groom left off, but I was surprised to hear one of the missionaries speak. I had watched him surreptitiously while the groom told his story. He kept his eyes on the floor for the most part, but glanced up occasionally and regarded the groom with a look that might have meant anything from disdain to envy.

He was a big fellow. He had grown tall as a kid and was expanding laterally as he headed towards middle age. His hair was cropped close, a little ragged and he wore tiny wire rims that only just covered his big grey eyes. His face had a superficial layer of fat that made him look fat and piglike, but if you imagined away this layer of fat and gave him a decent haircut you could imagine the handsome version of himself in his story.

'Providence – or fate – arranges such things.' I doubt I was the only one surprised to hear this sentimental commentary to the groom's story from the sour-faced priest. 'Some people are meant for each other.' The missionary nodded towards the groom. 'You were the instrument of fate for your friend.

'You needn't all look so shocked,' he said, amused perhaps by our surprise. 'We have lives too before we dedicate them to God.' The other priest studied his partner intently, as if a great secret was about to be revealed. The big priest warned him off with a sharp glance, and his companion quickly averted his eyes.

'I used to be like you,' he said, nodding towards the younger eclipse seekers. 'I used to travel, between college courses. This was in the early seventies when you couldn't do places like Asia and South America on a package. You had to figure things out yourself.' He'd begun almost harshly as if resentful of the new generation who got their exotic locales so easily, but he didn't maintain this edge. He softened as he continued. 'I suppose it's all the same though. *Finding yourself* was the expression we used to use, but you got to hate that when you heard it often enough. I guess it was about finding something different, making sure the world still had surprises in it and making sure you weren't settling for something, before you'd seen the other options.

'One day I found myself in this little city down in Latin America. It had been something one day, when some mountain nearby still had gold to plunder, but it was a forgotten place when I arrived. The newest buildings were a century old. I had been by myself for a week and I was considering my next step, whether to head to the coast or further south. Half of me was thinking about going home. There was a girl back there, a sweet American princess type, who said she loved me, but who I took for granted. I wasn't a man of impeccable morals in those days. I took advantage of her trust and abandoned her for the road too frequently. All the while I was confident that we would end up together one day. I was missing her more than a little.

'As I walked around this South American city, I stumbled on a small museum. I stood there for a while, trying to figure out if it was open, until a guard came out and pretty much dragged me in. It seemed like he was opening the place just for me. He escorted me around, described the paintings and the exhibits. He was a bit of a windbag, but I had nothing better to do and it was a break from the sun outside.

'I don't know, it could have been the weariness or the residue of the various hallucinogens in my body. I did some foolish stuff as a kid, chemicals, mushrooms, peyote. I'd even tried toad licking.' The missionary shook his head in apparent disbelief in his own debauchery, then shot the younger eclipse chasers a 'don't try this at home, kids' look.

'Whatever it was, the whole museum started to be about me and my girlfriend back home. There were old Inca gold statues that somehow stood for all the money I'd borrowed from her. A hall of elaborate Colonial Spanish mourning garments represented every time I cheated on her. Maps and battle dioramas seemed to expose the tactics of every fight we'd ever had. The mannequins in various military costumes from the last few centuries stood for every time I went away and left her.'

It occurred to no one in the waiting room to tell the priest this was indeed a very bad trip. The missionary looked far too solemn and deeply contrite for any such joke.

'The museum guard kept telling me that the museum was looking for a curator. He seemed to be offering me the job. My head was very muddled and I had no idea what he meant by this. At first I thought that it meant that I should hurry back home to my girlfriend. I was ashamed enough by that point to know I ought to. I was making up my mind to go right back to her when I came to a portrait that explained it all to me. It was a painting of a colonial lady, some governor or viceroy's daughter, a beautifully luminescent face that I recognized immediately as my girlfriend's. I don't know how long I stood there mesmerized, trying to read the look on her face, so content and optimistic, so unworried by anything. I had not seen that look on her face in a long time.' The older priest's grey eyes clouded, as he paused and adjusted his glasses.

'When I finally realized what the portrait meant, I almost took the curator's job. It meant there was nothing to return to. I knew somehow, by the look on her face in that portrait that she had met someone else. She was meant for me, but I had only ever made her suffer. Now she had found someone who would not throw away her gift and she was happy.'

The priest removed his glasses now and rubbed them on his shirt before continuing.

'I didn't become the curator of that museum, but I didn't return home either. I took refuge in a Franciscan monastery for eighteen months. I took inventory of my life and found it to be a catalogue of vanities. I am slowly abandoning them all. I thought I deserved that girl, merely by being who I was, witty, charming, sensitive. I never thought about losing her. I am not yet the man I must be, but I am past believing I am wiser or more sensitive than anyone else, and I think these missions back to the wilderness suit me. I may yet save my own soul.'

His confession done, the priest looked a few of us in the eye, not challenging, interrogative perhaps. There was a long silence in which I considered his parable and unspoken question to us all. As he told it, I almost believed his story. Now he was done I didn't believe a word, but I heard its message anyway. I wonder how many others in that room considered what would be on display in the museums of their own souls.

The First Pilgrim's Tale

One of the eclipse chasers finally broke the uncomfortable silence. A few tense shoulders dropped when she spoke up. She was a thin little thing, with strong, plastic-framed glasses. I would have guessed she was in her late twenties. She seemed nervous as if wary of saying the wrong thing.

'I worked on the Church of San Francesco in Assisi,' she said quickly. She glanced at the missionary as if asking for permission to continue, but his face was impassive.

'The church was damaged during an earthquake about ten years ago. Parts of the roof collapsed along the nave. There was a lot of structural damage, but also the frescos and tempera decorations of the great Giotto and Cimabue were destroyed.' She spoke in spurts, as if she had to think of what she would say before speaking, and her accent was German or northern European.

'I'm a restorer,' she said, apparently embarrassed at having claimed a title or some area of expertise. 'I'm not an art historian. I am only a technician. I know how things were made, the plaster and the paints used. I had special training to do these things, so I was one of many who went to work there after the earthquakes.'

A few of us nodded, encouragingly, reassuring her perhaps that we believed she was qualified and deserved the job.

'Before I arrived, many other technicians had sorted through the rubble for fragments of the roof decorations. They found more than three hundred thousand pieces. They were sorted by colour, size, location and, if pieces were big enough, by visual elements. I did well on my first project putting together a small bird decoration, so I was asked to work on a section of a gable painted by Giotto, the figure of St Jerome.' Again, she glanced towards the big missionary and added, 'St Jerome who translated the Bible into Latin.'

The missionary nodded this time and smiled gently. Like a nervous student given approval by her teacher, the young restorer blushed and rushed on.

'The restoration is like putting together a jigsaw, except the pieces are not flat. They have broken off at different depths and are curved like the ceiling, so we work in little sandboxes to provide a foundation for our puzzles. We all work on our allotted parts of the roof. As a guide each of us has a picture of our segment. Some of the fragments are large enough to be identified clearly, but we argue over the smaller pieces. Every technician believes that every piece is part of his own puzzle. Some complain that it is a tiresome process, but I like it. It gives you great joy when you find two pieces that fit together.

'My restoration of St Jerome went well at first. I found that a colleague had been trying to fit Jerome's eyes into St Augustine for days. After I restored Jerome's sight, I worked outward from the eyes towards the hair, which was also there in large pieces. I fitted perhaps a dozen small fragments in between these, but after that I was stuck. I tried segments that had been identified as part of his robes, but I found that whenever the fragments fit together physically they did not match to the picture of Jerome, and whenever I put together pieces according to the picture, the fragments did not fit together properly. It was very frustrating. We were not many people at the laboratory there. There was more work than people. Our rule was that if a segment did not proceed quickly enough, we would set it aside for something that was more fruitful. I was afraid that they would soon take Jerome away from me.

'When they told me that I would be moving on to another section, I asked for permission to stay late. My idea was to spend one more night on St Jerome and perhaps, if I made some progress, they would let me keep him. For the first few hours I got no further, but near midnight when I was tired and frustrated I tried something new. I decided to ignore the picture and fit together all the pieces that matched physically. I put together more than twenty stones in my workbox in this way, but they made no picture. In the next few hours I had added fifty more pieces from the bins to my puzzle. In the morning I had a complete fresco.

'Even in our best work there were gaps where the fragments were lost or ground to powder. My reassembled fresco had not a single gap or chip. It was perfect but ...' For a third time she looked at the big priest before continuing, 'but my fresco did not show St Jerome. It showed the figure of a large lion.'

The restorer stopped there. We did not immediately realize that this was the end of her story. We pressed her for details. Where in the ceiling did this lion belong? Did they find other pieces of it? She looked uncomfortable continuing, adding only a little to her story.

'But that was it. There was no lion of that size in the frescos of the church. It was a mistake. We dismantled it. I moved on. I couldn't concentrate after that. The lion worried me. I felt I had committed a small sacrilege. Instead of taking another work term, I decided to travel a little. My boyfriend persuaded me to come see the eclipse with him.' Glances flicked between her travelling companions, clearly none of them was this boyfriend. It was another awkward moment before the big missionary spoke.

'Did none of the art historians tell you that the lion was one of St Jerome's symbols?' he asked quietly. The look of surprise, the small silent 'o' her lips formed told us that no one had. This caused a great discussion amongst us. A few of her fellow pilgrims told her she had a supernatural gift. The second missionary suggested it was a miracle. She seemed more disturbed by this than anything.

The First Engineer's Tale

The delicacy of the Chilean engineer surprised me. Seeing that the restorer was nervous about all this talk of miracles, he turned the conversation to more technical matters. He asked how the roof of the church was strengthened, how the reassembled frescos were mounted. He shook his head when he heard that much damage was caused by the weight of stone reinforcements added fifty years before the earthquake. 'We always think we are so clever, we engineers,' he said. 'We always say, There are better methods these days. Here is how we will improve things.'

It fascinated him that after the earthquake the roof of the ancient church was rebuilt with the honeycomb aluminium used in aeroplane hulls. A relieved look descended on the restorer as attention drifted away from her and the engineer began talking about the ingenuity of the Renaissance architects who had built these great cathedrals and his admiration for these men who five hundred years ago managed to be artists and engineers at the same time.

'At university I had a professor of civil engineering who wanted to be another Galileo or da Vinci. This professor was the chairman of the department of engineering. The government consulted him on important projects. He'd worked abroad and supervised a spectacular dam in Argentina and an undersea tunnel in Indonesia. He was admired and feared a little by everyone, but he felt inadequate because he did not measure up to Leonardo da Vinci. He wanted to write poems and paint pictures as well as build bridges.' The engineer laughed softly and shook his head.

'There was a great deal of gossip at our university about the professor and his wife. The wife was very beautiful, and a little ...' the engineer searched for a word, 'difficult, perhaps? Maybe she thought she had married a footballer or a politician, not a professor of engineering. She was in love with melodrama. There were rumours of fights and of her affairs.' He shrugged as if to excuse his participation in gossip.

'One story about the professor and his wife outlasted all the rest. The professor had concluded that his problem was that of the bicameral mind. According to this theory the brain's left hemisphere governs the right hand, the right eye and the analytic faculties, while the right hemisphere governs the left side of the body and the synchronic, imaginative faculties. The professor decided that to rise to da Vinci's level, he needed to stimulate the right hemisphere of his brain. Da Vinci had a way of writing with his left hand, backwards across the page. Our famous professor thought that if he practised writing like this, his great right hemisphere would rise to the level of his fabulous left and he would be able to create poetry.'

The engineer halted now, apparently unsure how to proceed.

'This is of course all a rumour. It was a small department. We had so little else to amuse us, but the story I heard was that the professor did actually start writing poetry of a kind, but he didn't understand a word of it. It was very ...' he searched for a word again, 'surreal, I think, and perhaps a little macabre. Talk of secret lusts and a love of death, is what I heard. Also the professor began to have periods of lost time. While he was writing he would lose track of time and not recall what he had written. It caused many arguments with his wife because he was gone for hours at night and could only say that he had been in his office at the university. She began to suspect he was having an affair. The professor took to writing at home, locked in his study, but when his wife heard him muttering urgently to himself she thought he was whispering to his mistress on the phone.

'One day there was a sign on the door of the lecture hall cancelling the professor's classes. A lot of us students stood around, speculating on what had happened. One of the graduate students told us that the professor had gone to the department offices that morning in a deranged state. His eyes were bloodshot as if he had not slept in days and he was going from office to office begging his colleagues to save him. He believed that his right brain was trying to kill him. He claimed that he had suppressed the right half of his brain for so long that he had alienated it. It despised him and wanted to destroy him. None of us students really believed this story, but it is easy to gossip about the powerful.

'I still do not know if that part of the story is true. All I know is that a few days later the professor's wife killed him. There had been a fight over some letters she found. She confronted him with them, daring him to deny that they were from his lover. She did not believe whatever story he told her. He was shot three times in the head and the chest. If the rumour is true, that these letters she found were the poems he had been writing in his lost time, I suppose you could say that the right hemisphere of his brain did kill him after all.'

With that startling conclusion he looked around at us and shrugged again, as if to disassociate himself from the story and left it to us to judge its truth and portent.

The Second Missionary's Tale

The engineer's story was met with various expressions of disbelief. Some of us scoffed or laughed. Others complimented him on his ingenuity. One of the eclipse seekers tried to say something through the chatter. He was a very tall, very thin and pale fellow, with a bit of a stutter. He started to speak, then swallowed hard, trying to dislodge the words from his throat, and the second missionary seized this opportunity.

'Your story reminds me,' he told the engineer. 'I had a friend once who thought his own body was plotting against him, a man who studied with me at the seminary. It wasn't a particular part of his body that he feared, but the whole thing. He was a bit of a zealot, very devout and very puritanical. The idea of original sin tortured him. He felt that his body was unclean and corrupt because of it. He was always fasting and taking long penitential walks through dangerous neighbourhoods.

'We have to take anthropology courses before we take up our missions and during one of these classes he heard about mitochondrial DNA, how it was different from the rest of the DNA in our bodies, and that it was probably a bacteria or other organism that had been taken on by single-celled organisms at the beginning of animal evolution. My friend mixed up this idea with original sin. He had this theory that they were the same, or one an allegory for the other. Each cell is an Eden. Mitochondria are the snake in the garden, the corruption of man. Long ago our evolutionary Adam's cells were tempted. They could have rejected this other organism, but they took it in and nurtured it. They became impure because they gave in to that temptation.

'I didn't think that this theory of his was any more harmful than any of his other ideas. I agreed that it sounded plausible. Like any person of faith, I'm reassured when the allegorical truth of scripture is confirmed by science. I didn't think that it did any harm, but after a while it became a sort of obsession with him. "Do you ever notice," he used to say, "how you get these urges to sin?" I'd nod warily. You have to be careful with this kind of talk. "Or urges to harm yourself?" he would ask. I would let him keep going without agreeing with him. "Like when you're up high on a building. It's like you feel you have to stop yourself from jumping." I had to admit that vertigo had that effect, to make you distrust yourself. "Yes," he would agree enthusiastically, "you distrust yourself. You should, you know. You know why? That's your mitochondria talking. It's still tempting us now. It's made our bodies impure and untrustworthy." I tried to argue that this wasn't an inevitable conclusion, but he barely listened to me. "Mitochondria is hissing like an evil serpent in each of our cells, urging us to our destruction, inciting us to complete our fall from grace."

'Naturally I had to discuss my friend's ideas with one of the fathers. My friend was asked to take counselling and he was taken out of some of our classes. He stopped talking to me, as if he no longer trusted me, but I always tried to be kind and considerate. I knew he was troubled. He eventually left the seminary. When I saw him a year later, he had joined some cult or something. I had a long conversation with him, trying to persuade him back to the right path, but his ears were deaf to my words. All he could talk about was his evil mitochondria.'

'I heard some time after that he killed himself.' The missionary spoke his conclusion solemnly. He said a quick prayer for his old friend's soul and crossed himself.

The Second Pilgrim's Tale

The pilgrim that the missionary had cut off was quicker this time. No one else felt like talking after this sad tale of madness and suicide. I think we all would have preferred a few minutes of silence, but the eclipse seeker seemed indifferent to the tragedy, as if he had heard nothing else since the Chilean mentioned that he was an engineer. 'I'm an engineer too,' he said, 'or I am at least studying to be one.' He spoke quickly, as if trying to get it over with.

'Have you heard of Müller, the Swiss inventor?' he asked, looking only at the engineers. When they shook their heads, he looked disappointed but he continued, fighting his stutter bravely. 'He made a huge fortune during and after the First World War, probably on war profits primarily,' he added bashfully. 'He did *some* work for the Nazis until he figured out what they were really about. The Nazis rejected his plans for Nuremberg because his vision was too much for them. He wanted to build the ideal city, to tear down anything that didn't belong, to engineer everything from the ground up. Muller disappeared after the rejection of Nuremberg. A lot of people think he tried to build his perfect city somewhere else. It's one of the reasons I came here. I mean I wanted to see the eclipse and everything, but I had this idea that he might have tried to build his city on one of these little Pacific atolls. There's this book called *The Perfect City* ...' He rummaged through his knapsack, looked panicked, when he didn't find it. 'I must have packed it in my other luggage,' he said, as if to reassure himself.

'Anyway this book describes how Müller built an oil refinery for the Japanese, and they paid for it by giving him a whole island.' As the traveller became more absorbed by his story his stutter faded, but he spoke so quickly he had to stop to gulp air occasionally in mid-thought. 'These guys who wrote the book went through Müller's finances and there are these huge withdrawals from his bank accounts through the forties and fifties. They figure that Müller was financing his perfect city.

This book has pictures from Müller's notebooks on what the city would look like, its layout and buildings, what the street plan would look like, the sewage system, the electrical and water utilities and public transportation. There were hundred-metre-high waterfalls and cable cars between the high-rises and electrical generators that used the tides. It was really all fantastic.'

Some of us looked around the room at each other as the boy spoke. It had little to do with the stories that preceded it, but it was a relief not to hear another demented suicide tale. He told his story so excitedly though, that we all worried he might choke or hyperventilate before he finished.

'There are two mysteries about the city,' he said licking his lips. 'The first is what happened in the late fifties. Why did the withdrawals stop? Was the city finished? Was it self-sufficient by then? Did Müller die? The other mystery is who lived there. The guys who wrote *The Perfect City* think that the people were the problem. As soon as people started to move in, they interfered with Müller's vision or maybe they made Müller realize that his city wasn't perfect after all and that he'd made mistakes. Any way, they figure Müller walked away from his city and sold the whole island to the Americans to use as a nuclear bomb test site.' He looked at us all now as if he expected us to be outraged.

'I don't believe for a minute Müller would destroy his city. I think it's still there. Can you imagine it, a whole abandoned city, like a lost civilization, but less than a century old? It would be awesome. Imagine what you could do there, if you started where Müller left off.'

He sat there breathless, his eyes gleaming with excitement at the idea of this perfect city. None of us knew what to say, and the boy seemed to realize that his passion had got the better of him. He buried his head in his knapsack and resumed his search for the book. 'I wish I'd packed it in my carry-on,' he said. 'Anyway that's my story, I guess.'

The Bride's Tale

The bride, who had been sitting nervously in the corner seemingly uninterested in the storytelling game, suddenly spoke for the first time, shocking more people than myself I think.

'I'm not so sure there's such a thing as a perfect city,' she began quietly. We all leaned towards her to hear her better. 'Everybody's so different. I think that different places suit different people. Maybe there's a perfect place for all of us. A couple of years ago I visited my sister in Italy. Her husband's a professor and has summers off, so they always rent this same villa in Italy, some place called Umbria. I stayed there for a couple of weeks after I graduated. It was nice, but we were kinda out in the country. The closest town was this tiny tiny village. There wasn't much to do there except sit around in the little square drinking coffee and eating gelato at one of the little bars, and even they closed down for most of the afternoon. I know that lots of people think that Italy's really beautiful, but there's lots of ugly old buildings. There are no supermarkets or anything to buy groceries and the water pressure's bad, so you can't take a real shower and there's all these creepy Italian guys checking you out. I went shopping in Rome one day and that was cool, but after a few weeks I was pretty bored.

'Anyway at my sister's villa there was this old woman who did the washing, cleaned and cooked the meals. She looked about eighty, but she did all the work. She was this typical old Italian mama, cooking the food, spoiling my sister's kids and doing all the chores in whatever slow, old-fashioned way she could find. When I went into town I sometimes saw her there talking with her cronies or doing her shopping at the market.

'I guess I really didn't like this old woman very much – she was called Maria. Sometimes she'd touch my hair 'cos it's blond, and they like that, and she'd say *Bella*, and smile like I was a doll or a little girl or whatever. It kinda creeped me out. Anyway I guess I said one day to my sister that if they got some modern appliances like a washer and dryer and dishwasher they wouldn't have to have Maria poking around the house all day. My sister just kinda gasped and looked at me like I'd said something horrible. I didn't know what I'd done.

'My sister pulled me aside and whispered to me. She said she guessed there was no way of me knowing this, but Maria was her husband's mother. I didn't understand. I'd met my sister's mother-in-law Mary at the wedding. She was this skinny little British thing with a hat and a twittery voice. "Yes, that's her," my sister said. "That's Maria."

'My sister's husband brought his mother to stay with them in Italy after his dad died. She started doing all the cleaning and cooking and stuff. My sister didn't mind. She thought it was just Mary's way of dealing with her husband's death, you know, keeping busy, keeping her mind off it. My sister used to drive to the village to buy vegetables and bread, but Mary began walking into town early each morning, and my sister was always surprised at the fresh vegetables and stuff she was able to get. She cooked these awesome Italian dishes every night and took her siesta just like a real Italian.

'One day my sister went into town to send a fax or something and she saw her mother-in-law in the piazza talking with these other old ladies. Mary was moving her hands around, so my sister guessed she was trying to use signs and stuff the way we sometimes did in the stores, but when she moved closer she heard that Mary was speaking Italian and everyone seemed to understand her. Everyone was really impressed that she'd picked up Italian so quickly. By the end of a month Mary spoke Italian perfectly. By the end of the summer though, she would only speak Italian. If you spoke to her in English she'd scrunch up her face and look really hard at you, like she didn't understand. When everyone was ready to go back home, Mary told my brother-in-law that she was staying. She'd look after the house while he was gone and keep house when they came back in the summer.

'I guess he tried to talk her out of it. Tried to get her to see a doctor, but she used all her Italian mama excuses on him and said he should be a good boy and leave his mama alone. Anyway, she stayed. She's been there for four or five years now, a perfect little Italian mama, makes homemade pasta and truffle sauce, drinks red wine like it's water and walks five kilometres in and out of town to shop each day. I guess that's her perfect home, where she was always supposed to be.'

The Relief Pilot's Tale

The pilot hadn't paid particular attention to our story telling so far, preferring to look down his long nose at the wine magazine he was reading, but he became more interested as the bride told her story. He slowly closed his magazine as she spoke. She was an attractive girl in the American way. Her eyes, if they weren't contacts, were a startling colour of blue, and the islands had given her a fine sand-coloured tan. The pilot appreciated such things. He clearly took great care with his own appearance. His uniform was immaculate, and while my shoes were covered with dust from the walk across the runway, his were as shiny and black as the eyes with which he gave the young American a casual once-over. He came by his deep tan naturally, as his thick black hair and glossy black eyes attested. I took him for a Spaniard or Argentinian, and when he spoke his

English was tinged with a suave Spanish turn of the mouth.

He congratulated the couple on their marriage. 'You are a very lucky man, Señor. I congratulate you,' he said. His eyes were fixed on the groom when he said this except for the last half syllable, when he glanced momentarily towards the bride and flicked a quick unsubtle smile. Oblivious to this last gesture and the nervous stirring of his new wife beside him, the groom laughed and agreed heartily with the pilot.

'If I have one piece of advice for you, Señor, it is to never dine without fine wine.' The pilot lifted the food and wine magazine slightly as it was evidence in the case. 'A glass of wine should always precede the marital bed. A fine wine improves the flavour of sexual congress, just as it improves good food. Perhaps this is the real reason your friend's mother stayed in Italy, no? The wine spoke to her?' He raised one thick eyebrow and fixed a casual eye on the now blushing bride.

The groom was not yet sure whether to be offended. He made some half joke about not needing to get women drunk to get them into bed any more.

'Oh, I am not talking about inebriation, Señor, nothing so boorish,' the pilot replied. He spoke English with that languid Spanish luxury, as if he was swirling caramel around his tongue, 'just a glass of wine with a meal to bring out the flavours of your companionship. Permit me to tell you a little story of a man I once knew. His wife was a gourmet chef. They married young. He was as yet without a career. His chief pleasure was the love of his new wife, and I do not blame him, she was a lovely creature. His wife, the chef, always served the most sumptuous meals and his only task was to choose the wine. He chose without much thought. He knew nothing of what wines best accompanied which foods, but he was learning. His greatest discovery though was this – that the wines they drank at dinner affected the nature of their sexual pleasure.'

The big priest fixed a disapproving glare upon the pilot. Some of the eclipse pilgrims stifled giggles, but the pilot continued at his own leisurely pace. 'The spirit of the wine flavoured their lovemaking, whether it was a light and flirtatious Gewürztraminer, an urgent and euphoric champagne, a sophisticated Barolo to be savoured and prolonged or a strong, earthy Brunello full of dark flavours and musk. I am not such a connoisseur as my old friend, but I know a little.' He glanced playfully at the bride again and told her, 'The wines of your sister's region that I know are the whites of Orvieto – sweet and fresh, a wine of no regrets, and the

Sagrantino of Montefalco, a voluptuous clear red, to be shared between true lovers deep into the night.'

If the groom was going to protest, it would have been now, but the pilot's calm, unconcerned air allowed no objection. 'Discovering the sexual flavours of each wine became my friend's great passion. He made himself an expert in the subtle differences between each variety and vintage. He once told me he could taste the evening's pleasure with a single sip, sometimes merely by the slightest scent of a wine's bouquet. I never heard a word of complaint from his beautiful wife either. It will come as no surprise to any of you that my friend became a great expert in wine. He chose wines for very rich men and was paid very well. He judged competitions throughout the world.'

This might have been the end of the story, but judging from the slim smile growing across the pilot's lips, it was nothing of the sort. He rubbed his smooth chin slowly and said, 'Alas, it all ended in disaster. The keen sense of a wine's sexual properties, which had made him such a master of his profession, eventually destroyed him. The associations became so strong that he was unable to control his own reactions. Tasting a good vintage of a wine he loved would make him weak at the knees and disoriented. The connection between the taste of the wine and his own sexual pleasure became so powerful that merely sticking his nose into a glass of fine Bordeaux brought him to sexual climax. Naturally he could not work in such conditions. He had to give it all up.' He paused and regarded us all as if cautioning us. We had been warned.

'I understand now that he must strictly ration his consumption of wine and his wife retains the key to their wine cellar.'

If it was a punch line, he betrayed no humour. He shook his head as if it was a true tragedy. I doubt I was alone though in suppressing a smile.

The Third Pilgrim's Tale

The groom, who had been teetering on the edge of insult the whole time the pilot spoke, finally decided to take the whole story as a joke. He laughed his excellent, deep frat-boy laugh and a few of us joined in. The rest of us smiled vaguely. Only the missionaries remained tight-lipped. The oldest of the eclipse seekers laughed theatrically with his hand on his belly as if the convulsions pained him, but no noise came out of his mouth. He had seemed a peculiar fellow the whole time. His mimed laugh only emphasized his strangeness. His clothes, his manner of speech, and his slow exaggerated gestures were jarring. He wore a white linen suit and fedora, like a character from a Victorian novel, finishing his Grand Tour in Egypt or the Levant. He carried a cane, which he waved in vague circles, but he seemed able enough to walk without it, and he spoke slowly and dramatically, with an affected accent like an American actor reading Shakespeare. If he had been acting from a stage a hundred feet away, his appearance and demeanour might have been more appropriate.

'I enjoyed your story very much, Señor,' he said, gesturing grandly with his cane towards the pilot. 'It demonstrates a principle, which I myself have often been heard to expound, that the concept of expertise in most areas of human endeavour is a sham. Who here today, for example, can even tell the difference between a five-dollar screwtop red and the so-called fine wines gushed over by the self-proclaimed experts?'

The relief pilot protested that the dandy had misinterpreted his story, but the linen-suited pilgrim went on undaunted, and the pilot was too suave to engage in anything like an argument.

'It's not that I blame these *experts*.' He put a nasty emphasis on the word regardless. 'I would do the same if I could. Our friend's story demonstrates the flimsy grounds upon which a judgment of taste or value might be based, and you must admire the self-belief of these people, who on the whim of their own tastes foist themselves upon the world as the arbiters of the right and the true in their chosen field. It is only that, you know, self-belief – "balls", I believe, is the colloquial expression.'

He was settling nicely into his theme now. 'In fact I have a little confession of my own to make. You did invite confessions, did you not?' He waved his cane in my direction. 'And only the padre has obliged.' The missionary's slim smile was waning towards a condescending sneer.

'I am myself an expert in many areas, self-declared, of course, as all experts are. I require no authorization or legitimization for my opinions. I sanction them myself, though I know they are lies.' He put his cane in front of him, leaned upon it, and spoke in a loud stage whisper. 'In fact, I did attend an institute of higher learning at one point in my storied past. In my youth I believed that authority and wisdom abided in such places, but it became apparent that our ivory towers are governed by self-important fools ordaining their merest opinions as unequivocal facts. The process of my disillusionment was not short. Nor was it painless. It ended with the rejection of my brilliant thesis on the lost tribes of the

Israelites. The cowards just couldn't accept real scholarship that didn't regurgitate what they themselves spouted in the lecture hall.'

I felt myself wincing as he went on. The man's syntax was as awkward as his accent.

'I have seen justice done though. I've exposed them as the purveyors of snake oil that they are. Though I have no degree from any of their petty institutions, I regularly publish my articles in their so-called scholarly journals. A few false initials after my name and a few thousand words of pseudo-academic prose are usually sufficient. I can't tell you the tripe that I have passed off as scholarship. I have here three articles published in the last few months alone on the subject of thinking machines. I have fabricated a lady novelist, a medieval scholast and a heretic Jew to whom I attribute the invention of the modern computer. They are all lies, all pure fabulation, and if scholarship and authority were anything but puffed-up opinion, they would never have been published. And yet they have, and they are neither the first nor the last. I have authored authoritative opinions for literary journals, for art magazines, for philosophical magazines. Did you know I am the father of a philosophical movement called phenomenology of all things? You wouldn't believe the lies you can foist off on people.'

His eyes trolled the room, looking for outrage or argument, but found none.

'You may ask why I do it. What benefit do I gain?' No one had asked anything of the sort. If we were to ask anything of the old fraud it would have been to hurry up and finish. 'I suppose I once thought of exposing them. Making a great show of debunking trumped up "expertise" in front of the world, but fame, that feeble immortality, is unrealistic. The world would rather not know that it is built on bravado and false premises. The few times I have tried to tell my tale, when I have told the truth, I have been met with rejection. While I lie and concoct, I am a great success. So I lie for the pleasure of lying now, for the joy of mocking their folly and the flimsiness of any authority to myself, as I am the only audience fit to comprehend it.'

He had been rising to a crescendo throughout this last part of his speech. As he finished he was on his feet flourishing his cane as if he expected applause.

The last pilgrim had sat by himself away from his travelling companions while we told stories, looking mildly terrified by the circumstances and proceedings. He looked increasingly grim as the fraudulent historian told his story. By the time the tale was done the pilgrim looked positively vengeful.

'So, you're a fake?' he said disbelievingly, and a little disgusted. 'And proud of it.'

'Very much so!' the charlatan academic replied and took his seat, as if no further justification was required.

The last pilgrim gazed at him in a leaden, unfocused way, as if he was seeing something else entirely. At first glance I'd taken him to be in his early twenties, a college student or a recent graduate, like most of the other eclipse seekers. The baseball hat, jeans and shy eyes had fooled me, for when he spoke, the frown lines around his mouth and across his forehead exposed another ten years of worry.

'Well, I'm a fake too I guess, but I'm not so proud of it.' He spoke haltingly, his voice strained.

'This is the first time I ever left Canada. I'm thirty years old and I've never travelled further than the next province.' This hardly seemed worth the confession and the penance. Fear of flying, if that was what it was, is hardly a crime. We let him continue anyway.

'When I was a kid I had big dreams. My mom always said I'd do something great one day and I guess I believed her. I always thought I'd be something – a hockey star, or an actor or an inventor or something. I had delusions of grandeur. It's easy to think like that when you live in a small town in Northern Ontario, when you're the captain of all the school teams and the only one in your graduating class to go to university. I was a big shot until I got to university in Montreal and I realized how little I knew and how little I counted. I flunked all my courses in first year. I could have passed, if I'd worked harder, if I'd cared about it, but I was scared and unhappy, so I guess I made a choice to go back home and live the rest of my life there, where people knew me and thought I was something.

'I went home, married my high-school sweetheart, and prepared for a lifetime of work for the Ministry of Forests, but even then I didn't have the guts to tell people how much I'd screwed up. I didn't tell Stephanie –

that's my wife's name. I didn't tell her that I'd dropped out of school. I went back to Montreal in the fall and waited on tables. I did this for three years, coming back every summer to work for the Ministry of Forests. They used to hire students to sit in towers out in the bush and watch for forest fires. When I was supposed to have graduated, I took a permanent fire-watcher job. It wasn't the sort of job that a big shot college guy would take, so I told everybody that I was working for some government department they'd never heard of. Stephanie convinced the whole town that I was a spy or something, and that when I went away I was on some secret mission overseas. Instead I was just sitting in my fire tower dreaming, imagining what I might have been.

'Every few years I'd get sick of myself and bug out for a while, holing up in some cabin, hiding from the world. When I came back I'd cook up some John le Carré kinda story for Stephanie. She always believed me. I started to hate her for it, almost as much as I hated myself.

'One day I just snapped. I saw I was a thirty-year-old guy doing a brainless job meant to keep eighteen-year-olds out of trouble. I'd done nothing with my life and I was nothing. I wanted to go home and tell Stephanie, but it sounded so stupid, so pathetic. Right?'

He looked up as if he expected us to affirm this. We kept our silence, but each of us, I expect, agreed. It seemed to me that he'd shrunk as he told his story. Seeing him slumped and drawn up in his chair I could not help but recall the expression 'sad little man'. I only knew the half of it.

'I wasn't a big shot. I wasn't even a huge villain. Even the bad things I'd done were cowardly and weak. I wanted something worse to confess, something that would make Stephanie hate me, not just think I was pathetic. I took a coward's way out again. I left a note for her, just more lies. I wanted to write something to make her hate me and wish I was gone. I made her kick me out instead of just leaving. I wrote that I'd had three other wives all around the continent and that my spy missions were excuses to go see them.'

I was not the only one who failed to stop my jaw from dropping. The self-proclaimed pathological liar and polygamist impersonator seemed to register our disbelief.

'I know it sounds crazy, but not half as crazy as some of the stuff I'd told her before. She believed me this time too. She kicked me out. I expect she'll divorce me. The first thing I did was book this trip to almost exactly the other side of the earth. I figured I should start doing things.'

He finished with that. He looked no happier for either his adventure or his confession. I wonder if he wished he was in his fire tower right now instead of here.

A long silence followed his story. No one seemed to know exactly what to say. Most of us, I dare say, were stunned and a little appalled by the gall of the man. The missionary who had told us the unbelievable tale of his own disillusionment seemed poised to speak, but closed his mouth quickly, thinking perhaps a quiet word alone might be better. We were left with that awkward silence.

The Second Engineer's Tale

The second of the two engineers had sat quietly as everyone told their stories. In the silence after the last pilgrim's tale he continued staring at the man with a mix of disgust and disbelief. It seemed to come as a surprise to him that only he and I had yet to tell a story. We exchanged glances and he seemed to understand that since I had suggested this game, the privilege and obligation of the last story was mine.

'To be honest,' he said slowly, 'I'm not much of a story teller. I used to think so, but ...'

He paused. He seemed to be deciding what or how much to say.

'But I think I understand the power of childhood illusions,' he said with a reluctant nod to the last storyteller. 'My father was an artist, and something of a poet. He made woodcuts, printed posters, and small illustrated books of poetry. He was quite famous in my country, and I think a little famous abroad too. He was invited to Paris in the last years of his life and to Texas for retrospectives of his work.'

'As a boy I was very proud of him. Strangers were always coming to consult him and buy his work. They always praised him highly, and I thought he was one of the greatest artists in the world. His fame influenced me to become a writer. My father was a great artist – so naturally I expected to become one too.

'I wrote a few poems when I was very young, nine, I think, and my father made woodcuts for a small book of them. He printed perhaps a dozen copies, enough for Christmas gifts for all my family. I was immensely proud of them, and encouraged to write more, and though I wrote hundreds more poems like this in the years afterwards, my father was never as impressed and could not be persuaded to print them. At the age of fifteen, I wrote a novel of some two hundred thousand words, a story full of kidnappings, mistaken identities, messages in code and elaborate revenge. My father was impressed with the labour, but not, I believe, overwhelmed with the results. He told me it bore the distinct influence of Stevenson and Dumas.

'It is difficult to write long works with the reward of brief praise, so as I grew to adulthood I wrote shorter and shorter stories. They were perhaps what you call prose poems, a little surreal perhaps. I had begun to feel that I did not understand what was valued in literature, so to create something of value I wrote things even I didn't understand. I was entering university when these works were printed in a small magazine published by some older friends. I was ashamed of them by the time they appeared. It had been a year since I wrote them, and I had had time to think the better of it. I did not enter the faculty of arts, as I had always planned. I studied to become an engineer. It has made me much happier. I have found that art is not necessary for my existence. I do not buy pictures for my walls. I don't read novels. I do not miss them. I am only glad that my father died before I realized how unnecessary art is. I would not have liked to have hurt his feelings.'

The Author's Tale

I do not think anyone judged the young man. He seemed to care very much for his father and had no intention of insulting him. I dare say a few of us indulged in a little amateur psychology as we considered the story of this man who had renounced stories.

'You are too hard on yourself,' I said. 'We can't all be Rimbaud or Keats, stumbling into genius before our beards have grown in. I understand that you resented the influences that your father observed, but we place too much stock in originality these days. Originality is a phantom, given credence by ignorance. Read enough and originality disappears.' I had, I suppose, begun my own story.

'Every author I know cringes when some new acquaintance asks if he or she will turn up as a character in the author's next novel. It's not so much that each of these bland humans believes they are fascinating enough to demand immortalization in words. It is the assumption that the author's reserves of imagination are so meagre that he must troll every coffee shop and cocktail party for material. If exceptions indeed prove the rule (and this is a precept I have never understood), then I am that exception, for every single character and every plot I have employed in each of my novels has been purloined from reality. I would never admit it to anyone who knew me, but I feel safe telling you all in these circumstances.' I scanned the faces of my fellow travellers to gauge the effect of my declaration. They seemed untroubled, accepting my confession as they would any fiction.

'It is not just laziness, though I confess to a gargantuan excess of that virtue – I will never consider it anything else but a virtue, since all invention rises out of avoidance of unnecessary labour. I resent the assumption that such borrowing exposes a lack of creativity on my part. On the contrary, in fact, it requires no ingenuity to unfold a tale that is entirely fiction. There are no facts to constrain you. Anything can be trimmed, removed or altered to fit. Working with characters and stories that I steal from life, I feel obliged to use them whole. Not to trim or shape them, but turn them in every direction, placing them with other found narrative objects, observing every angle for a fit. It is not unlike your work on the frescos of St Francis,' I told the young restorer. 'Have no doubt about it. You too are an artist. Do not let old Cimabue and Giotto intimidate you.' The restorer smiled weakly at my compliment.

'No one understands my technique. They cannot see the difficulty I make for myself by working with these constraints. It is more than a little futile. Despite this I persist. It is almost a pleasure to be misunderstood.' I do not know why I added this. It is not part of my usual patter. I did not want to end on a melancholy note. And so I brightened and told them the good news.

'And so I must tell you that there is no strike by the baggage handlers, no civil war raging on the next island, no new tropical disease that required our quarantine. I confess that I arranged this little conference. A small bribe to the air traffic controllers is all it usually takes. The novel I'm working on is a little thin at the moment. It needed to be populated a little more. I thank you all for your fine stories. I trust that I will not require signed waivers from any of you?'

Some of my travelling companions laughed. None appeared to believe a word I told them. They took the appearance of an airport official telling us our flights were boarding as a mere coincidence.

AUTHOR'S AFTERWORD

When I began to write *The Dodecahedron, or A Frame for Frames,* I was thinking very much about the geometry of short story collections. Many modern short story collections have a larger structure that provides continuity and makes them read like novels. They are conceived as whole books and have a unity beyond a simple miscellany of tales. Characters or ideas progress through each subsequent story until the final story provides a resolution, or at very least a point of perspective from which to look back and re-evaluate the previous stories. Frequently these collections have a cyclical geometry, where ideas introduced in early stories are resolved or recast in the final story.

I wanted to produce something that shared many of these qualities. Each chapter was to be as self-contained and whole as any short story. As in a story cycle, each story would cast a new light on the ones that preceded it, and promote a novel-like unity of themes. What I did not want to write was a cyclical book, in which the final story is the final word, a story with more authority than all others, one that casts a sort of judgment on the rest. I was aiming for something more ambiguous than that. From the start, my intention was to write a book on the subject of perspective, a book in which any one of the stories could be taken as the starting point or the endpoint of the collection, in which each was capable of exerting that conclusive judgment usually the sole prerogative of the final chapter. I wrote a book based not on the geometry of the circle, but on the geometry of the dodecahedron. I'll get back to that, but first a word from the French.

This book is constructed on mildly Oulipian principles, that is on the principles of the Ouvroir de la Littérature *Potentielle* (OuLiPo). OuLiPo is a group of mostly French authors who create literature based on highly arbitrary constraints of their own making. Amongst the most famous of these are Georges Perec's *La Disparition,* a novel written entirely without the letter E and Raymond Queneau's *Exercices de Style* in which the same object is described over and over in different rhetorical styles. The most obvious model for *A Frame for Frames* is another Oulipien text – Italo Calvino's *Se Una Notte d'Inverno un Viaggiatore,* a novel composed of a conspiracy frame story and ten first chapters of hypothetical books.

The arbitrary constraints I put on myself while writing *A Frame for*

Frames emerge from the geometry of a dodecahedron. I envisioned a book in which each of the twelve chapters or stories represented a face of the dodecahedron. A dodecahedron's faces are pentagonal, each a five-sided polygon. In *A Frame for Frames* these sides represent a relationship to an adjacent story. This was the first constraint. Each story must refer to or be referred to by each of the five stories adjacent to it. These references to and from adjacent stories provide the shifting perspectives of this book. Any face of the dodecahedron may be taken as a starting point from which to evaluate the adjacent sides.

A dodecahedron has twenty vertices, points where three sides meet. In *A Frame for Frames* these vertices are represented by certain repetitions and recurrences in each of the three stories that meet in these points. If the elements that represent the vertices were extracted and placed in the order of their first appearance, they would form another text of sorts, which might provide another perspective for evaluating the whole.

The order in which the stories unfold is somewhat arbitrary. Any one could have been the first story, but once that choice was made their sequence was governed by a predetermined pattern. I considered only two patterns. The most obvious was the 'orange peel' sequence, using the pattern by which you can remove the peel of an orange in a single strip, by proceeding around it in a spiral. This would have produced a spiralling away from the themes and subjects of the first story to the point where the last story had no edges or vertices in common with it. Instead I followed two strips around the top and bottom hemispheres (or perhaps more properly hemihedrons), but left the top and bottom pentagons until the end. This saved one reference to, or from, each of the first five stories until the eleventh story, a goal that was supported by no other constraint than the author's desire for another kind of unity.

TRACY GLENNON

Paul Glennon is the author of *How Did You Sleep?* He lives in Ottawa where he works in the software industry.

The title story of *How Did You Sleep?* won the Writers' Union of Canada Short Fiction Award. *How Did You Sleep?* itself was shortlisted for the Ottawa Book Award and the ReLit Awards.